And Vanessa, draped in a white sheet and lying on the table itself, her head directly at Reddick's waist. She was conscious, and her face was contorted in a mélange of rage and terror.

As Linc watched, unable to move, Reddick accepted the poker from his henchman and gripped it by its brass hilt, raised it until his arms were almost straight over his head.

Then he looked up, straight into Lincoln's eyes.

"Ah, Blackthorne," he said. "I'm afraid you're too late."

And plunged the white-hot tip toward Vanessa's heart.

THE KING OF SATAN'S EYES

A LINCOLN BLACKTHORNE ADVENTURE

THE KING OF SATANS EYES

GEOFFREY MARSH

TOR

A TOM DOHERTY ASSOCIATES BOOK

THE KING OF SATAN'S EYES

Copyright © 1984 by Geoffrey Marsh

Reprinted by arrangement with Doubleday and Company, Inc.

First Tor printing: February 1987

A TOR Book

Published by Tom Doherty Associates, Inc.
49 West 24 Street
New York, N.Y. 10010

ISBN: 0-812-50650-2
CAN. ED.: 0-812-50651-0

Library of Congress Catalog Card Number: 84-7995

Printed in the United States of America

0 9 8 7 6 5 4 3 2 1

This is for Carmen,
who stuck with me when
the roses weren't blooming

ONE

THE TAILOR shop was nearly as obscure as the country town it was in.

Inverness was hidden for no discernible reason in the middle of New Jersey's northwestern corner, surrounded by wooded hills, dairy farms, and breeders of horses; it was also totally ignored by county and state highways on their way to the lakes and state forests that beckoned the tourists. It was on a low hill itself, the largest homes atop, the open-sided white steeple of the First Presbyterian Church visible for miles if you bothered to look. It had a town square and a Revolutionary War monument, shops and four-story office buildings as new as a decade and as old as two centuries; it had little to offer to keep its young after high school, not much more to offer professionals and blue collars beyond practices already existing, a family-owned tannery, a venetian blind factory, and an old quarry that specialized in gravel and sand.

But it thrived nevertheless.

It was quiet, and the Victorians and Federals, Colonials and occasional Capes were pridefully well kept, more solid than anything a developer could muster. It lured young couples (and often lured back its young) because of its safety, because of its schools, because it gave them all a chance to breathe clean air for a change.

And after the world had had its licks on psyche and body, it was refreshing to be able to sit on the benches in the square for gossip or just looking when spring had finally bloomed; to walk from a front porch to the movie theater in five minutes or take the car to the drive-in for a triple horror feature and homemade popcorn. For some it was unsettling that the shopkeepers were so friendly, that word of their arrival went through town like Kansas brushfire; but for others it was comforting, like the heavy beams in the cellar or the sound of nesting birds in the chimney, and the way the town didn't advertise for industry or plazas. They were there, of course, well outside town on the highways where it seemed the right place for all that plastic, but more often than not it didn't seem to make a difference.

Inverness grew as it always had, by pure word of mouth from inhabitants to friends, though never in its history did it hold more than six thousand.

The local businesses were concentrated in a three-block section of Creek Road, downtown, with brick sidewalks and curbside trees and passage so narrow that parking was permitted on only one side.

The tailor shop was in the middle, and newcomers seldom saw it until they had been there a month or so. On its right was the aluminum-sided

and garishly red-lettered druggist, with more sham-
poo than the A & P and more paperbacks than the
bookstore; on its left was Ginny's Olde Time Tavern
& Restaurant, fronted in brown cedar shakes and
neon Miller signs. Behind it, down a sharp slope
that ended at the next street, was a parking lot
used by those heading for the bank, or the corner
theater, or Howard's Department Store. It was, in
fact, the only establishment that didn't have a
back sign announcing the building's occupant.

The front was narrow, scarcely wider than a
blink. A single somewhat dusty display window
with two mannequins on an unevenly round shelf
—a man in a dark blue pinstripe three-piece, and a
woman in a flowery white summer dress—and at
the end of a short indentation a door whose shade
was always pulled down. In front was a green iron
bench provided for shoppers who wanted a brief
respite, or for men engaged in girl-watching, or
oldsters in nostalgia, or on Friday night for serious
drinkers getting relief from the band that blasted
eardrums in Ginny's.

Or for Lincoln Bartholomew Blackthorne.

It was two in the afternoon, a dry and scorching
July, deep blue sky and smoke-puff clouds drifting
on a breeze that nobody felt. Creek Road was virtually empty despite the high crowns and rich
foliage of the maples and oak that lined it. The
tailor shop bench was in comfortable shade from
the maple that rose as high as the building, and
two men and a woman, all well past their fifties
and wearing light sweaters, wide-brimmed hats,
with shopping bags resting on the brick between

their feet, waited for the sun to sweep behind them before they moved again, to Ginny's.

"Hot," Macon Crowley said, nodding as he scratched his white beard furiously with one hand, idly dusting the sharp crease of his white trousers with the other.

"Yeah," said his brother Palmer, clean-shaven, twice as broad, red-faced, and double-chinned.

"Soft. You're soft," Old Alice said peevishly from the other end of the bench, and adjusted her mauve sweater with plucks and impatient brushes of a chicken-claw hand. "The old days was hotter."

"There weren't any old days," Macon said sternly, with a white-toothed grin. "There was yesterday, and there's today. The old days are on the TV."

"Yeah," Palmer said.

Old Alice shrugged; it was too hot to argue when Macon was being pompous. She reached up to be sure her straw skimmer was still in place, the clutch of plastic cherries and pears at the band not melting from the heat.

They watched the traffic, and the few pedestrians out at the shops, and shortly after three saw a long black hearse park at the curb, a few doors down on their left, on the wrong side of the street. It had managed to find the only spot on the block not protected by the shade. No one got out. The windshield was blinded by the glare of the white sun.

"Gonna get a ticket," Old Alice said. Then she reached into her red-spangled purse and pulled out a pack of cigarettes—long, thin, tan-filtered, and pink. She lit one with a wooden match, igniting the head by scratching it with a thumbnail. She wore baggy designer jeans and Greek leather sandals.

"Yeah," Palmer said.

"Nope," Macon said, lifting his head to peer out from under his green Tyrolean hat. "Funeral."

"No cars," Old Alice told him. "Ain't from the parlor, either. If somebody died, I would've known it."

"Hippies," Macon judged then. "They got the back carpeted with a bunch of pillows and water beds and they drink and screw all day."

Old Alice sighed.

Palmer fell asleep.

Five minutes passed, and the hearse didn't move and no one got out.

"Suppose we oughta tell Blackie?" Macon asked.

"Why? Is he dead?" And Old Alice laughed, slapped her knees, and dropped her cigarette. She lit another, and pursed her lips. "Maybe we should."

Macon considered the problem for several more minutes, while a clutch of high school girls in halter tops and cutoffs passed the bench and smiled at him, smiled at Alice, stared at the closed shop door and started to giggle nervously. When they were gone, he put his hands on his knees and pushed himself to his feet, smoothed his sweater over his chest, and walked stiffly to the door. He knocked—once, twice, once—turned around and sat down.

"You tell him?"

"If he's in there, he heard."

Alice leaned over and looked to her right, down where the street ended at the square's western edge; then she stared at the stores opposite, blinking at the sparkling glare that flared off the windows, looked to her left at the hearse at the curb.

"Air conditioned," she said, leaning back, puffing, blowing smoke rings at a blue jay in the maple's lowest branch.

"Have t'be."

"Motor's off. Can't work without having the motor on, right? Right. They're gonna fry their little brains sittin' there like that. Fry their little brains."

"Maybe they're eccentric."

"Maybe they're dead." And she cackled.

Macon blew his nose on a starched handkerchief. "You sure you did it right?"

Macon puffed his chest. "I do not make mistakes."

Palmer snored.

The door opened loudly, and Old Alice straightened her hat.

Lincoln Blackthorne wasn't tall, wasn't broadshouldered, didn't have a massive chest. He was average and slender, and the handsomest man Old Alice had ever seen. His thick brown hair was just barely combed, his eyes were so dark they saw through the soul; when he smiled his eyes squinted, and when he laughed they disappeared. He was in rolled-up shirtsleeves and faded jeans, black boots scuffed and needing a polish. Over one shoulder was a tape measure, in one hand a pair of trousers. He leaned against the corner of the window and didn't bother to cover a yawn.

"Hearse," Macon said without looking behind him.

"Air conditioned," Old Alice added. Then, "Hippies," with a snort.

Lincoln pulled a straight pin from his mouth

and frowned, the frown vanishing when the high
school girls passed the shop again. This time they
didn't look, but their backs were straighter, their
midriffs barer. He grinned when one turned to
him and winked, her hand briefly touching the
curve of her breast.

"Jail bait," Macon warned him.

"San Quentin quail," Old Alice added.

Palmer stirred, snored, crossed his legs at the
ankles.

"How long has it been there?" Lincoln asked,
still watching the girls as they passed by the hearse.

"Fifteen minutes."

"Ten," Old Alice corrected, with a sharp nail
stabbing at the Cartier on her wrist.

"Give or take," Macon compromised.

"He's going to fry in there, whoever he is," Lincoln said. "Damn, it's hot."

Directly across the street, the door to the Inverness Record and Tape Shop opened, and a woman
stepped out.

"Oh . . . hell," Lincoln said.

"Too late," Old Alice giggled.

"Only for some of us, my dear," Macon said
with a sigh.

The woman waved and started across the street,
broke into a brief trot when a painted van almost
clipped her.

"Alice," she greeted brightly, "Macon. Tell Palmer
I said hi when he wakes up."

Carmel Estanza was a head shorter than Lincoln, her hair long and raven-black to match the
dark of her eyes; her skin was tan-deep, her lips
red, her figure noticeable but slight. She wore a
red plaid shirt, and jeans so snug Macon could see

the outline of her panties. She looked straight at Lincoln with her hands on her hips.

"You haven't forgotten about tonight, Linc?"

He shook his head. "How could I?"

"You could," she said, pouting playfully. "You've done it twice this week already."

He lifted the hand with the trousers. "I've been busy."

"Momma says she'll cry if you don't make it for supper again. She's wicked when she cries, Linc. Her mascara runs and she looks like a corpse."

"I'll be there," he told her, just short of angry.

"Poppa says you should marry me and make an honest woman of me."

He frowned, less at the not-quite-mock threat than at the fact he knew she enjoyed his discomfort. He shifted, glanced at the waiting hearse again, and looked back to her boldly. "You really want to marry a tailor and live in this town for the rest of your life?"

"I didn't say that, Poppa did." She grinned.

Her family lived in a vast, two-story apartment over the store—mother, father, a sister, and an aunt who had posters of Fernando Lamas covering the walls of her bedroom. They were fourth-generation Spanish, but the adults managed to sound as if they'd just come off the boat.

"But now that you mention it—"

"I didn't, you did," he said hastily, scowling at Old Alice laughing so hard she couldn't light her match.

"Listen, Poppa is taking everyone to the drive-in tonight, so we can make out on the sofa when they're gone, okay?"

The hearse pulled away from the curb.

Lincoln nodded absently, and moved slightly back into the entrance, into the shadows.

"Macon, for god's sake tell him he's not a monk."

"If he is, I'm not," Macon said, tipping his hat.

"You're sweet, but I'm not into mature this year."

Old Alice choked when Macon's face went red.

Lincoln watched the hearse slip by the store, speed up and round the square and head out of town.

Carmel suddenly strode to his side, grabbed his chin, and kissed him hard. Then she stepped back and examined him, shook her head and ran back across the street.

"Jesus," Alice said, poking at the flat between her breasts, "her shirt was open to *here!*"

"I know," Macon said. "God, how I know."

Lincoln hadn't noticed, nor had he felt the kiss. He was wondering why the hearse's license plates had been painted over in black.

TWO

THE INSIDE of the small shop was air conditioned and dark. In the front room a center aisle was created by two long display counters of ties and custom shirts, the walls hidden by shelves and pigeonholes holding bolts of cloth and hats, a wooden counter by the door that supported a cash register Lum and Abner would have loved. At the back was an open space centered with a low platform, the platform facing an array of mirrors arranged so a customer could see himself front, top, and back with only a slight turn of his head. A door in the back wall, covered by a faded green curtain.

There were no racks of jackets, or suits, or trousers; there were no cardboard cutouts touting manufacturers' top lines or specials; everything that came out of here came out handmade.

As soon as the door closed and the tiny bell overhead stopped ringing, Linc forgot the hearse and headed for the black, foot-pedal sewing machine off to one side in the back, a machine decorated with hand-painted sprays of daisies and violets twice as old as he was. He shook his head as he sat on his stool, set the trousers into position, and started working again. The hearse was a curious thing indeed, but he'd seen stranger; right now he was wondering what to do about Carmel.

He squirmed then, feeling oddly guilty, more than a little discomfited. She was a lovely woman, no question about it, and were he inclined to get married she would easily be his first choice. Unfortunately, aside from her obvious attributes both physical and idiosyncratic, Carmel also had ideas. She wanted him to stock Brooks Brothers, Bill Blass, St. Laurent, and all the rest, open an exclusive branch in the county seat to get all the lawyers, and one not so exclusive but just as expensive at the huge mall twenty miles east to get all the commuters; she wanted a house up on the Knob, she wanted two kids—one of each—and she wanted more than anything to quit teaching school and get away from her parents and her domineering aunt.

Linc didn't blame her, but he wasn't about to help.

The ideas she had would only make him more visible. But that's the whole *point*, she would tell him in exasperation, and he wouldn't be able to explain why that whole *point* could get him killed.

Carmel, he thought sadly, why don't you meet a nice boy and settle down.

Then he worked on the trousers until the door opened, the bell rang, and he looked up from his worktable, knowing he was hidden by the shadows in the back.

He waited until the door closed again.

It was only Old Alice.

He grinned and rose, smoothing the trousers and dusting his hands.

"Palmer's still asleep," she said, with a nod toward the window.

"He's tired."

"He's always tired, the old fart."

She set her shopping bag on the counter and peered down at the ties. "Men really wear these things?"

"Some. Not much anymore."

"You sell enough to make a living?"

He walked behind the counter and leaned his elbows on the glass top. Old Alice, despite her age, had the softest, pinkest skin this side of a nursery. She took off her skimmer to scratch her wiry grey-black hair.

"Had no license plates."

"So I saw."

She pulled her wallet from the shopping bag, opened it, and pulled out five one-hundred-dollar bills. "For Macon's winter coat. Cashmere, tan, I don't care if it ain't the fashion, I want it long enough to cover his knees. Skinniest legs I ever saw on a man."

He took the bills, folded them, slipped them in his pocket. "He'll need a session."

She frowned. "It's supposed to be a surprise."

"Now, Alice, how can I make a coat for the man if I don't have his measurements?"

"In the movies they just look at you."

"In the movies I'm Cary Grant."

She looked up at him without raising her head. "You really make this stuff, huh?"

He nodded. "That's what the sign in the window says."

"You don't hire out or nothing?"

"Nope."

"I see."

"I'll bet."

"I just wondered."

"Then stop."

She grabbed the shopping-bag handles and swung it to her side. "I'll get him drunk at Ginny's and bring him after."

"You do that, love."

"Don't think I won't."

When she left he barely had time to take a step toward the back before Macon came in, sweeping off his hat and breathing deeply the cool air. He nodded to Linc and began a slow examination of the cloth on display, grunting, stroking his beard, finally spinning around and slapping his alligator wallet decisively on the counter.

"The old fool needs a new coat for winter, Blackie." With a single deft hand he extracted five hundred dollars and laid it on the glass. "I don't care what color, long as it isn't black. God, she looks ghastly in black. Like my mother when she died back in '41. Jesus."

Linc folded his arms across his chest. "Macon, why don't you just marry her and be done with it?"

"What?" Macon stepped back, his eyes wide, one hand over his heart. "What?"

"Marry her."

"That's what I thought you said."

"So what's wrong?"

"So if I married her, my boy, then she'd be my wife."

He nodded. "Yes, that's the way it usually works in this country."

"And if she were my wife, I'd have to give up all my other women."

"Oh."

"I'm too old, Blackie, to give up all my other women."

"I see."

Macon jabbed at the bills with a manicured hand. "Anything but black."

"I'll need her measurements."

"I'll get them. It's supposed to be a surprise."

"No," he said, grinning. "I have to do it. Remember who's the tailor here."

With the brim gripped front and back, Macon replaced his hat. "All right. I'll think of something."

"I'm betting on it."

Macon stopped with his hand on the doorknob. "No license plates, Blackie."

"I saw."

"Two men in back."

Linc's eyebrows rose.

"Or a man and a woman."

The door opened.

"Or two women."

He stepped over the threshold.

"My eyes are better'n Alice's. The old fart won't wear her glasses."

The door closed and the telephone rang. He watched Macon take his seat on the bench, then hurried to the worktable and snatched up the receiver. Palmer stirred, and Macon laid a hand on his shoulder until he settled again. Old Alice offered him a cigarette and Macon batted the hand away.

"I love you."

He looked to the ceiling. "Hello, Carmel."

"You still picking me up tonight?"

"Yes, Carmel."

"You don't sound happy about it. I could always stay home and knit, or go to the drive-in with Momma and Poppa."

"I'll be there, Carmel."

"If you get me drunk, I'll take off my clothes."

"Carmel, for god's sake."

"Maybe I'll take them off anyway."

"Jesus, Carmel, your mother—"

She laughed. "I'm upstairs, stupid. Want to bet I'm naked?"

"I'll see you tonight, Carmel."

"Chicken."

He grinned. "Yep."

"I'll bet you're a virgin, too. Thirty years old, and you're still a virgin. Don't ever go to Mexico, Linc. They sacrifice virgins down there."

"That's virgin women, Carmel."

"Women, men, what's the difference if you've never been laid?"

He hung up, frowning as he felt the warmth crawling across his cheeks. Blushing, for god's sake, he thought as he sat again; goddamn woman's got me blushing, for god's sake.

Two hours later he was finished with the trousers, had them creased on the presser and hanging next to the suit jacket he'd completed the week before. He rubbed his eyes and stretched, looked out to the street and saw the shadows climbing the walls across the way, like wide black shades being drawn up from the bottom. He yawned. The air conditioner over the door clanked and spat. He pushed aside the green curtain and stepped into the back room.

It was small, just large enough for a chipped and dusty round table, two sagging armchairs, and a half-sized refrigerator; the back door had been bricked over long before he'd taken possession and he'd never wondered what was on the other side; there was faded rose wallpaper, and a few crooked movie poster prints he'd never bothered to remove. The thin carpeting had once been floral-patterned, but the flowers and their stems had been worn to near extinction, and the fringe around the edges had been worn to the nubs. A green-shaded bulb hung from the low ceiling. There were magazines in awkward piles on the floor, a cot in the far corner, and a faint scent of must the round floor fan couldn't dispel.

Gotta clean up one of these days, he thought, shaking his head and knowing he didn't mean it; I also have to tell those three to stop calling me Blackie.

He hated being called Blackie. It made him think of private detectives in trench coats, and sheep dogs on the moors with freckle-faced kids making them fetch sticks, not to mention cartoon villains being chased by stupid mice wearing huge yellow shoes.

His stomach growled, and he looked at the refrigerator with a start, suddenly remembering he hadn't bothered to eat lunch.

Way to go, pal; starve yourself into the grave.

There was a sportsman's calendar on the wall by the door frame, and he stared at it, at the tiny

printing in each day's space, then took a pencil
from his shirt pocket and crossed off the third. The
fourth was blank, on the fifth a notation to start
Poppa Estanza's sport jacket Carmel had ordered;
there was also the mayor's tuxedo, the mayor's
son's tuxedo, and three suits for Farren Upshire, a
breeder of Arabian horses just south of town.

He sighed and dropped into the nearest chair,
stared without seeing the faded rose-petal wallpaper on the back wall. What he needed was a dis-
gustingly long vacation; what he really needed
was the chance to stay in Inverness long enough
not to have to work like a fool demon just to fill
his orders. In spite of the fact that he was very
expensive, and selective, it seemed that he was
never able to turn down a request, especially from
someone who could barely afford it. Soft heart,
soft head, he told himself with a wry smile; charity begins at home, and you'll never make a good
Scrooge.

And he didn't realize he had fallen asleep until
he woke up and the room was dark, didn't realize
until he stood with a silent groan that he wasn't
alone.

The air was different.

As if summer had died during his nap and had
been replaced by a dry and frigid December.

As he stood there in the dark he could feel the
tension build around him like subtle electricity,
and he immediately bent over in a half crouch and
cautiously put his hand out to the curtain. Listening, not thinking, until he pulled the cloth slowly
to one side, just enough for him to see into the
front room.

The hearse was parked in front of the shop. The glow of the streetlamps was caught by the windows and the high gloss of the vehicle's polish.

He could see the car because the shop door was open.

The shop door was open because he'd forgotten again to make sure it was locked.

The bench was deserted—the Palmer brothers and Old Alice long gone into Ginny's.

And then he saw the shadows.

There were three of them, moving stealthily along the aisle between the display cases. Their size was distorted by the backlighting, but they were big, and he definitely didn't care for the odds they gave him. One of them stumbled into the edge of the platform and swore softly, another harshly jabbing him silent with an elbow.

And in that movement he could see the weapons they carried. They were all the same—old but undoubtedly efficient Thompson submachine guns, primed and ready to fire.

His eyes narrowed and perspiration trickled down the back of his neck. He looked from side to side but could see nothing he might use against them. His right hand was braced against the doorframe, and he could feel the pounding of the band playing next door at Ginny's. It figures, he thought; loud band, clanking air conditioner—they could hold World War Three in here and no one would hear a thing.

The telephone rang, and the shadows froze.

Linc cursed silently. That was probably Carmel wondering where the hell he was. And if he didn't answer, and she couldn't get him at home, she'd be over. She'd look out the window, see the hearse, and she'd come over to see what excuse he was giving her this time.

He cursed again, and the hand holding the curtain shook before he could stop it, the brass loops holding the cloth to its rod rattling like tin.

The shadows turned toward him.

"Good evening, Mr. Blackthorne."

And the submachine guns opened fire, filling the room with strobic blue light, tearing the curtain to shreds in less than five seconds.

THREE

THERE WAS little time to think, and less time to act. The moment Linc heard his name he flung himself across the room. The curtain snapped at him as it was shredded, gouts and chunks of wounded plaster showering like hail over his back as he grabbed the refrigerator's sides and pulled it effortlessly away from the wall. His ears rang from the detonations, and he could barely hear his own curses as he dove through the exposed gap and pulled the appliance back, snapped a thick brace across to lock it in place, and slumped against the narrow tunnel's wall.

His eyebrows rose and his cheeks puffed, and he ran a hand down over his chest to calm his lungs, settle the acid boiling in his stomach.

Good lord, he thought, that was a pip.

Then he heard footsteps, muffled and cautious, and he pulled himself upright with a stifled grunt and reached through the dark to a thin metal shield he slid noiselessly to one side. He was looking through James Stewart's eye on the *Glenn Miller Story* poster, but all he could see were dark ungainly shapes moving gingerly through the room's debris. The overhead light had been shattered, however, and he scowled at not being able to see a recognizable face.

A match flared, and he blinked, but the flame was doused before he had a chance to adjust.

The table was kicked viciously aside, his chair slammed to the wall; magazines and plaster shards were swept contemptuously aside. But they were still no more than shadows, and he was about ready to leave when he saw one of them pass in front of the refrigerator, pause, and reach out. He held his breath. The door opened, and a wash of pale light spilled into the room. The man was standing upright, shadows from his chin and outthrust gun hollowing his long, cadaverous face. He stared without expression until a companion spoke.

"He ain't in here."

"I can see that," the lean man said, slamming shut the door and obliterating the light.

"Maybe there's another door."

"Do you see one, Cashim?"

"No."

"Then he wasn't here, was he."

"But the curtain—"

"A breeze, nothing more. It moved, and we reacted. Hazards of the trade."

Cashim muttered something Linc couldn't hear, and the lean man whirled around almost too fast to follow, a broad open palm catching his cheek with a rifle's retort. The third man, who had stayed by the curtain, ducked out of Linc's sight.

"Let's go," the lean man ordered in disgust.

"You didn't have to do that, Reddick," Cashim whined. "I just wanted to know how he did it, that's all."

Reddick stood in the doorway and scanned the room, his expression hidden, his voice filled with hate. "You had better learn now, my friend, that he is Blackthorne. It makes no difference who you've hunted before—this one is Blackthorne."

The tunnel that led away from the shop was just three feet wide and barely high enough for Lincoln to move without stooping. It was dark, dank, and sloped gently downward, but he had no need for a light to guide him; he had traveled this route a hundred times while awake, a thousand more in his dreams. The brick walls originally raised during the Revolution were cold against his fingertips as he guided himself around a sudden sharp corner; water dripped loudly in the distance; the air was damp and lightly touched with the stench of rotting garbage. But he felt nothing, heard nothing, smelled nothing. He only moved on as quickly as he dared.

Reddick.

The name made him wince, made his eyes narrow, bunched his left hand into a fist that struck his thigh every ten paces.

Reddick.

It was just over five years since he'd last heard that name, just over five years since he'd last seen that gaunt face with the stabbing black eyes, the hawk's nose, the cleft chin with the scar that formed a cross at the tip.

Five years; he should have known he'd not be

able to live the rest of his life without running into him again.

He cursed futilely and almost stumbled to his knees when the tunnel leveled and he was able to break into a sprint, his keen eyes picking out the obstacles in his path—bits and chunks of stone and brick that had crumbled with age from the walls and ceiling, unnameable things he just as soon couldn't see. At one point he thought he heard faint squeals from a nesting of rats, but when he paused to listen he heard nothing at all but the angry pounding of his heart.

Ten minutes later the tunnel branched, and he immediately took the righthand path, slowing as the floor angled upward sharply, slipping in the invisible slime that coated it. He grunted when his shoulder banged against an outcropping of brick, stumbled when he reached the steps before he realized where he was.

He stopped and caught his breath.

His left hand grabbed a moist iron railing flaking with rust, and he hauled himself up, a step at a time, thinking perhaps he ought to quit smoking and give himself more wind. There'd been a time when he could take this route without losing so much as a single drop of sweat; now it coated his face and chilled his chest and back, and by the time he reached the top he was puffing so hard he had to lean against the wall.

Ahead of him was a thick wooden door elaborately banded in iron, its tapered oaken bar securely in place. When he was able to breathe again without wheezing he reached into his jacket and pulled out a key ring, hurried through it until he found what he wanted—a silver skull. He inserted it in the lock, jiggled it a few times, and turned over the bolt. The resulting *clang* was loud and he winced; his grunting as he lifted the bar was deafening and seemed to echo down the dark staircase behind him. But within moments he was through the door and had it closed and relocked with only a minimum of effort.

A second door—ten yards farther on and without a bar, though equally as solid—yielded to the death's-head key.

A third five yards after that resisted until he kicked the rusted lower hinge.

The fourth was greystone, with only the barest of fingergrips at the opening edge to give him purchase. He pressed his ear against it for a moment, straining and listening until he was sure there was no one on the other side. Then, slowly, a fraction of an inch at a time, he pulled it soundlessly to him, suddenly flung it back and darted through, yanking it closed and sitting on the ground, legs up, hands clasped casually about his knees.

A deep breath of relief, a grin, and he blinked his eyes to adjust to the starlight.

He was far above the main body of the town, directly at the top of the Knob in an exclusive high-walled and well-guarded cemetery whose occupants dated back to the War of 1812. He'd just come from the wide marble base of a fifteen-foot St. George, whose time-blunted sword was aimed directly at his back. There had once been a dragon curled at the knight's feet, but vandals had long since removed most of the head, one of the flared wings, and the marble maiden clutched in its marble claws.

He gave himself precisely a minute to rest before he rose to his feet, brushed himself off as well as he could, and took the nearest winding tarmac path toward the rear entrance. The moon was bright, and the shadows snapped out to snare him as he walked, snapped back as if realizing who it was they were challenging. He smiled to himself at the fancy, and shook his head slowly.

And he hadn't gone fifty yards before he heard the crunch of dead leaves behind him.

God, he thought as he quickened his pace, if it isn't one thing, it's another.

He took an abrupt smooth turn around a green marble mausoleum in the shape of an ark, allowing himself only a quick searching glance over his shoulder. He saw nothing out of the ordinary, but he refused to slow down. His suddenly alert senses told him it wasn't just a squirrel out for a late frolic. There was someone back there, someone determined not to be seen until he wanted to be seen.

Linc hated that.

Another ten yards and another quick turn, and the narrow pathway's tarmac yielded now to hard-trodden, leaf-covered dirt as he reached the cemetery's oldest and least tended section. The squared headstones here were made of dark stone much like clay, the simple poetic inscriptions almost totally erased by two centuries of harsh winters. Some were still straight over the graves they marked, more had been canted forward or back; and as his gaze drifted over them, one of them moved.

He stopped.

The headstone moved again, and he tensed,

quickly looking left and right for someplace to hide, cursing himself for not bringing a weapon, and not being able in the darkness to find one to use.

Then the headstone resolved itself into a man wearing a deep black motorcycle jacket with gold epaulets at the shoulders and festooned with silver zippers, and thick black boots winking with silver and red studs arranged in the outline of a coiled king cobra; he was just five and a half feet tall, stocky and redheaded, and charging toward him with bolelike arms spread to engulf him. He made no noise, and Linc did not run. Instead, he braced himself, and when the attacker finally reached him he leapt to one side and stuck out his foot.

The short man yelped and skidded across the path on his stomach, the two dozen flapping zippers sounding like Marley's ghostly chains caught in a spin dryer.

Linc was hard on his back before the man had stopped moving, had a forearm around his throat, his free hand dug fiercely into a thicket of curly hair.

"I can't *breathe*," the man gasped, his head pulled back and his large watering eyes bulging in the moonlight.

"No kidding," Linc said. He yanked once more to give the truth to his words. "Now what the bloody hell do you want, Unicov?"

Basil Unicov gagged and tried to ease the pressure of the arm across his throat. When he pointed at his mouth, however, Linc refused to give him release. He gagged again and said, "How . . . did you know . . . it was me?"

"I don't give away my secrets," Linc said harshly.

He yanked again to warn the man not to reach for one of his jacket pockets, then loosened his grip, though his hand remained firmly clawed in the red hair. "What do you want?"

Unicov shook his head.

Linc tightened the forearm.

Unicov coughed, and his eyes rolled.

"C'mon, Uni, let's not play games."

Unicov glared.

Linc sighed and pulled his hair sharply. "Reddick sent you, right? *Right?*"

Unicov denied it with a choking, and a gagging.

For some reason, Linc's instincts told him to believe it. The forearm loosened a second time. "What, Unicov? Come on, I haven't got all night."

"Eyes," the man gasped, his hands pawing weakly at the arm.

Linc leaned back and frowned. "Eyes? What eyes?"

"You . . . know."

"Uni, I'm getting impatient."

He was about to retighten his grip when he heard footsteps on the pathway and two voices in low conversation. A man, a woman, and she was giggling: lovers on their way for a tryst among the dead.

He scowled, glared down at the struggling man, and finally, with a sigh, released his hold on the hair and jabbed Unicov expertly behind his left ear. Unicov stiffened for a split second before his eyes closed and he fell limply to the ground. Linc grabbed him under the arms then and dragged him behind a tombstone before darting across the grassy graves to the iron-barred exit. He was sure he'd not been heard, but he couldn't take any more chances. He estimated the wall's height and stepped back five paces, broke into a sudden run and vaulted to the top, peered down at the sidewalk and jumped.

He landed silently and ran across the street, keeping to the shadows, avoiding the fall of white from the streetlamps along the way.

The houses here were huge and old—gabled and porched, most of the garages for three and four cars, most of their land sweeping out to the back. He reached one that lurked behind a tall untrimmed hedge and darted up the driveway, skirting the side until he reached the back. He waited, listening for sounds of guests from the lighted dining room above him. When he was satisfied whatever noise he made wouldn't be overheard, he moved slowly to the canted cellar doors, opened one and slipped into the dark.

At the bottom he pressed an indented button on the stone wall and waited again until he heard the unmistakable sound of a door opening in the far wall. There was no light, but he made his way unerringly across the uneven floor and through the portal. Once inside, the door closed, and locked.

Then a light was switched on, and he was temporarily blinded. When his vision returned seconds later he was looking at a man seated behind an ornate teak-and-brass desk. The man was smiling, and aiming a cocked gun straight at his heart.

"Good evening, Mr. Blackthorne," he said, winked, and squeezed the trigger.

FOUR

THE DERRINGER'S silver hammer slammed forward and George Vilcroft brought the muzzle's steady flame to his thirty-dollar Havana. He puffed a few times to be sure the cigar was burning, then released the trigger to snuff out the fire. A contented sigh as he studied the glowing tip for several seconds before tossing the lighter onto the desk. A glance to the star-shaped chandelier, and he visibly relaxed in a high-backed chair with diamond filigree at the top, gold-leaf representations of Chinese emperors around the sides, and ruby-encrusted lions' paws at the armrests. He smiled again and gestured.

Lincoln immediately slumped into a brass-studded, red leather wing chair and crossed his legs at the ankles, his hands folded over his stomach. He returned the smile, but only vaguely, and figured that Vilcroft, under the circumstances, would forgive him for not bowing.

The man he faced across the four-foot-wide desk was almost seven feet tall, massive in girth, yet oddly unimposing. He wore a muted and narrow-lapeled off-white suit flocked with silver threads; his silken button-down shirt was pale blue, his Windsor-knotted tie black and threaded through with gold. On each hand he wore a blank, gold signet ring, and around his left wrist a finely linked silver bracelet. His blue eyes were frozen in a perpetual squint, his nose was bent to one side, and above his thick upper lip was a caterpillar mustache blazing preternaturally red—it was, in fact, the only hair on his head.

Linc had never asked him if he shaved or suffered a condition.

"You're a mess, Lincoln," Vilcroft said with a fleeting moue of distaste behind a cloud of blue smoke rings. "And if you don't mind me saying so, you smell like a swamp."

"I've had an evening, George."

"So I gather." His voice was profoundly and disturbingly deep, with a resonance that made Lincoln think of thunderstorms in caverns, or stampeding mustangs across a vast uncharted prairie. "Ah, you've been through that damned tunnel again."

He shrugged. "I had no choice."

"Pests, eh?"

"Pesky."

"I see. Anyone I know?"

He hesitated before answering.

"Reddick."

Vilcroft's hairless left eyebrow rose in mild surprise. "My word, really? Lincoln, I thought you took care of him in Pretoria five years ago. Or was it our sister city in the Highlands?"

"So did I."

A pause before Vilcroft leaned forward and picked up a tiny silver bell, rang it twice, and sat back again. Within moments a striking barefoot brunette in a snug, green silk dress that scarcely wrinkled when she walked, appeared quietly at his side. He smiled lovingly and tapped her once on the wrist.

"Wine for our guest, Clarise. He's had a rather trying time of it this evening, poor fellow."

She nodded without a smile or a hint of commiseration, and as she turned to the Regency sideboard behind the throne, Vilcroft reached over the desk blotter and punched a button on a small control panel tangled with wires. Seconds later, Mouret's "Rondeau" fanfare trumpeted into the room.

Lincoln didn't react. Instead, he allowed his breathing to slow and his perspiration to dry amid the Norman tapestries on the walls, the oriental and Persian carpeting beneath his feet, the erotic Etruscan carvings and jade Burmese statues Vilcroft had been collecting for over fifty years. There was barely room to walk, and it took Clarise a full minute to negotiate a path from the sideboard to his chair, pewter tray in hand, crystal goblet aboard. He took it and grinned at her; she nodded once, without smiling, and returned to serve Vilcroft. By the time she was gone, through an exit Lincoln was unable to locate, Vilcroft was staring at him impatiently.

"Well?"

"Well what?" Lincoln said, sipping at the brandy and wishing he knew whether it was good or not.

"Well, what are you doing here? I have guests, you know."

"I didn't hear anything."

"We were meditating, my boy. We were discovering the inner self that makes us what we are."

"All right."

Vilcroft frowned. "You don't believe in meditation?"

"I sleep a lot."

"I see," the man said with stern disapproval. "Lincoln, you will never get along in this world until you learn to get in touch with yourself. You have to know where, as they say, your head is at. You have a moral, perhaps even divine obligation to learn to commune and communicate with all that is the essence of you so that you may successfully and forthrightly commune and communicate with others."

"All right."

Vilcroft gestured impatiently. "You're impossible."

"I've been shot at. That tends to make me impossible."

Vilcroft placed his glass carefully on the desk. "Shot?"

"At."

"By Reddick?"

"By Reddick, Cashim, and a third man whose name I didn't catch."

"I see." A blunted finger touched Vilcroft's squared chin. "Machine guns?"

Lincoln nodded, shuddering at the memory, suddenly hoping that Carmel had minded her own business.

"Yes," Vilcroft said, drawing the word into a hiss. "Yes. And there were three men, you say?"

"Three inside the shop. I don't think there was anyone else outside in the hearse."

"The hearse? Well! Well, well. Reddick and Cashim. Well, well. I would say then that the third one was Arnold Krawn. I gather from your expression that you don't know him. No matter, my boy. He is a man of little consequence in the scheme of things. He's not in touch with himself."

"He was in touch with me about an hour ago," Linc complained. "And he wasn't the only one."

A short laugh rumbled in Vilcroft's chest. "Carmel's father, no doubt."

"No, Basil Unicov."

"Oh dear."

Linc finished his drink in a swallow and ignored the pained expression on the big man's face. Instead, he placed the goblet on the floor beside his chair and shifted to the edge of the cushion. "George, are you trying to tell me something?"

"What?" Vilcroft almost rose. "Are you saying I sent those men after you?"

"Well, maybe not Reddick."

"Certainly not Reddick."

"Uni?"

"That toad? He rides around on that oversized motorized bicycle wearing those ridiculous clothes and still thinks to call himself a human being. I would not think to have him in the house. Clarise thinks he's full of shit."

"Clarise doesn't like anybody. She doesn't even like me."

Vilcroft said nothing. He stared for a long moment at the emerald crystals in the star-shaped chandelier, then reached into his jacket pocket and pulled out a key ring, selected one, and unlocked the desk's center drawer; there was a hesitation and a glance at Linc before he extracted a thin wooden box that seemed ready to splinter the moment he breathed on it. A flourish, and the box was on the blotter, open, its lid to one side. Lincoln could not see what was inside, but he knew he was going to find out. He also knew he wasn't going to like it.

"Reddick, Cashim, Krawn, and Unicov," the big man said quietly, pushing the box from side to side with his index finger. "A veritable quartet of incompetence."

"They weren't so incompetent tonight," Lincoln said sourly.

"You're alive, so they're incompetent."

Lincoln shrugged. He really didn't much care now, as long as he knew why he was being hunted.

Vilcroft's hand moved again, this time to extinguish the overhead light, turn off the music, and switch on the Tiffany lamp on the desk. His face instantly fell into deep shadow, a shadow as deep as the roll of his voice. The silver threads in his white suit glittered; the gold threads in his black tie winked.

"Lincoln, you're in trouble."

"Me?" He stood and strode to the desk, one hand out to guide him through the artifact maze. "Me? For god's sake, George, what the hell did I do?"

"Nothing," said Vilcroft sadly. "It's terrible, isn't it, but for a change you haven't done a thing."

Lincoln gripped the edge of the desk and glared. "I know that, George, and apparently you know that. But what about those other idiots? Why don't they know that?"

"Because I haven't told them."

He nodded as if he understood, sniffed once and made his way back to his chair. He sat stiffly this time, hands gripping the armrests, wishing the man would turn up the heat—he was beginning to sweat, and a chill walked his spine. The box still lay in the center of the blotter, and all he could see of Vilcroft was his chest, and his hands.

"You will explain," he said at last. It wasn't a question, and Vilcroft shifted slightly.

The room remained silent.

"George."

"Give me a moment."

"You don't have a moment. You have now."

Vilcroft inhaled deeply. "I collect things, Lincoln," he said at last, sounding less authoritative, more apologetic. "My house is a veritable museum of antiquity and contemporary superb taste. You know this because you have been instrumental in several of my acquisitions—this very desk for example."

Lincoln remembered, especially the time he had had trying to get it through customs. Eventually, he'd been forced to create a diversion, one that had effectively closed the airport for a week and a half. It was one of the hazards of playing with exposed sheep dip.

"Well, I'm on to something else."

Lincoln waited. Patience was hard to come by, but he forced himself to wait.

Vilcroft took the wooden box gently in one hand and tipped it over. Lincoln stared; stacked now on the blotter were what looked to him to be thick, old playing cards. Without asking permission he rose and returned to the desk, leaned over, and examined them more closely as Vilcroft fanned them, with a practiced brush of his hand.

Playing cards, but obviously custom-designed and hand-painted on slices of wood. And as far as he could tell, each of them was studded according to its rank with tiny gleaming gems. With a careful finger he poked out a face card, a Queen, and realized with a start that he recognized none of the suits. The Queen was a woman in regal attire sitting sidesaddle on a massive buck, each stone in her tiara real, each point of the buck's antlers topped with a gemstone.

"How old?" he asked softly.

"Five hundred years."

"I only see three suits."

"There are four."

"There's only three here."

Vilcroft nodded, though Lincoln only sensed it. "Stags, Hounds, and Abbé."

Lincoln looked up; Vilcroft drew a deep breath.

"The fourth is Satan's Eyes."

"Never heard of it."

"I know, Lincoln. Very few have."

"And . . . you're collecting the entire deck. I assume Reddick wants the deck as well, and Uni?"

Vilcroft nodded.

"Interesting." He straightened and rubbed at the small of his back. "So what's the big deal, George?"

A long pause followed the question, too long for Lincoln's peace of mind. Besides, he was getting hotter, and his eyes were having difficulty focusing in the dim light. But he waited until Vilcroft reached for the lampshade and turned it to light his face.

"I have them all but one, Lincoln. All but one.

The other suit," he added quickly to forestall interruption, "is in the vault. I don't dare take it out. And I'm missing one." His voice grew strained. "The King, Lincoln. I'm missing the King."

"Is it that important?"

"Lincoln, I don't lie to you very often. This time I'm not. It's very important indeed. Too important to let someone like Reddick get hold of. I must have it, for reasons I pray you'll never have to know. And now Reddick is loose. Damn the man!"

Lincoln pulled his hand away from the deck and wiped his palm on his grimy shirt. "I take it he's willing to go to extremes."

Vilcroft smiled without mirth. "You could say that."

"So what, old friend, does this have to do with me?"

"He thinks you're working for me."

"But I'm not!"

"He doesn't know that."

"Then you'll tell him, right?"

"No. As long as he thinks so, you might as well."

His eyes widened. "But George, he tried to kill me!"

"Yes. Yes, it seems he did."

"Seems has nothing to do with it."

"And he'll keep on, Lincoln. He'll keep on trying until you're dead and he has the King of Satan's Eyes." The hands placed the deck back in its box, the box back in the drawer, the key in the lock. "Lincoln, I hate to say this—but as sure as I'm sitting here, if you don't help me, you're going to die."

"No," Linc said.

Vilcroft shrugged.

"I'm supposed to take Carmel out tonight. She'll kill me, you know. Her father is a sonofabitch, too."

Vilcroft shrugged.

"Hell, tomorrow is the Fourth of July! Old Alice, Macon, and I were going to the fireworks at the high school."

The Tiffany lamp switched off, the chandelier glowed on.

Linc stalked back to his chair, around it, and held on to the back. Involvement was one thing, but he'd never been forced into doing anything in his life, and he was not about to start now.

"You'll have to find someone else, George."

"No, I won't."

"Really? Why not?"

"Honestly, Linc, you're making this difficult, and it's going to take hours to get back into my meditations, thank you very much. But"—and he took a deep weary breath—"but do you really think you'll be able to convince Reddick you're *not* working for me? Do you think he'll give you a chance to? Of course not, and you know it. What he'll do is torture you a little—do you recall the chamber in his basement, the one with the women with razors on their nails?—and then kill you just for the fun of it if you don't tell him what he wants to know. And as long as Uni-the-Toad is on your tail you'll never get rid of him. He's too stupid to believe you." His smile saddened. "Face it, Linc, you're stuck."

Linc thought as hard and as fast as his suddenly foggy mind would work, but nothing he came up with could deny Vilcroft's conclusions. He folded his arms across the chair back and rested a chin on his wrist.

"Assuming you're right, George, what do I get out of this?"

"The usual."

He shook his head. "Nope, not this time. This isn't usual, so I want a bit more."

Vilcroft stood. "We'll discuss it."

"Now, George!"

Vilcroft rang the silver bell and Clarise reappeared.

"Clarise, my dear, Mr. Blackthorne will be my guest for the evening. Please see him to a room and be sure he's comfortable."

She looked to Vilcroft, to Linc, and beckoned. "This way, Blackie, if you please."

"Oh Jesus, George," he said.

"My meditations," Vilcroft reminded him. "We'll discuss it in the morning."

There was no sense arguing, not when he couldn't keep his eyes from crossing. He sighed, and nodded, and took one step toward the silken-clad woman before he felt his knees begin to buckle. His hand grabbed for the chair, and his weight pulled it over; his head struck the floor, but it didn't hurt a bit. As he lay there, slow in realizing that the wine had been drugged, he looked up and saw Clarise standing over him. She was smiling, and in her right hand was a long silver dagger.

910785

FIVE

THE SUN was unconscionably bright, and Linc considered the necessity of killing himself for several minutes before opening his eyes. When he did, he relaxed, though the sense of something *wrong* wouldn't desert him.

He was in a vast bedroom far larger than the tailor shop, all dark Spanish pine, with flocked gold wallpaper, a walk-in stone fireplace, eastward-facing windows whose bronze velvet draperies had been drawn to admit the clear gold morning. He was lying on a crimson-canopied bed raised on a brown marble platform. The sheets were dark satin, the quilt red and white, and the pillow beneath his head stuffed with hand-plucked gosling down. He blinked once and rubbed his eyes, waiting for a nasty explosion to detonate in his head. When nothing happened he sat up and threw aside the covers, draped his legs over the edge of the mattress and stretched.

Directly in front of him was a rosewood standing tray, and breakfast obviously freshly made.

Beneath the ornate silver platter of whole wheat toast and fresh English marmalade was a thick parchment envelope. He stared at it, determined not to commit himself by opening it. Then he watched his hand pluck it up, watched his finger slide up the flap. Inside was a thick bundle of mint bills, none less than one hundred, and a piece of paper with a long note written on it.

"You're kidding," he said when he read his instructions.

"You're not kidding," he said when he counted the money.

He smiled, and ate without question, had just finished his second cup of Earl Grey when he remembered Clarise, and the long silver dagger. Immediately he checked his stomach, his arms, his chest, his neck, and realized he was naked. A raised eyebrow and a shrug and he glanced over his shoulder—the pillow next to his had the definite indentation of someone's smaller head.

He grinned ruefully, scratched his head vigorously, and padded over to a walnut valet where fresh clothes had been laid out. He yawned and tried them on, knowing Vilcroft would give him nothing if not a perfect fit for the season. When he was dressed he stood in front of a narrow, full-length mirror—the tennis shoes were pale orange, the trousers white cords, the shirt white linen with a bright yellow collar.

"Jesus Christ," he muttered. "I look like a duck."

Then the cathedral-paneled teak door began to open, and he tensed. Vilcroft may have been his friend, but friends don't administer drugs without prior consent, and he was ready for a fight when Clarise walked in. She wore the same tight dress she had had on the night before, and when he looked knowingly toward the bed she only crooked a ring-laden finger at him.

"Erotic amnesia," he said as he grabbed the envelope and tucked it into his hip pocket, followed her with a grin down a long carpeted hallway to a door at the end. She opened it, revealing an elevator that held at most two people. He stepped in and waited. She reached in and punched the last button, stepped back, and pulled the gilded cage shut. He waved as he sank down; she only nodded and walked away.

Two floors later the elevator stopped. He hesitated before letting himself out into the large foyer at the front of the house. There was no sound, no sign of movement, and after considering waking George and rejecting the idea, he touched at the envelope in his pocket and left in a hurry.

It was already afternoon, the sun lowering toward the hills, and he walked down the slope off the Knob as fast as he could, determined not to have any of his friends see him in these clothes. They might recognize him, but they wouldn't believe it, and he wasn't about to offer explanations.

But the center of town—the square and Creek Road—was deserted, ominously so until he remembered it was the Fourth of July. Picnics in the park, games at the fairground, and a shifting toward the high school for the evening's fireworks display.

He wasted no time. With one eye out for the cruising hearse he rushed for the tailor shop and let himself in, not bothering to be surprised that the door wasn't locked. A quick check of the front room to be sure nothing was disturbed, and he headed for the back, stopping suddenly when he realized the curtain that had been shredded the night before had been replaced with strings of large red and black glass beads. They clattered when he pushed through them, frowning, standing with hands on his hips as he surveyed the back room.

Someone had cleaned it.

The plaster was gone from the floor, the table and chairs set back on their feet, magazines restacked, posters straightened, the refrigerator cleaned—inside as well as out, he noticed when he checked.

He wasted no time trying to figure it out. He went immediately to a life-sized poster of Clint Eastwood in poncho and cheroot hanging from the righthand wall. He stabbed the gunbelt's bullets in programmed sequence, stood back and waited for the door to open. When it didn't, he kicked the baseboard and jumped aside as the hidden door almost clipped him.

"Brother," he muttered in weary disgust, and ran up the stairs to his apartment above.

The front room was casually furnished with anything he could find—couch, club chair, coffee table, television, no piece matching the other, none of it matching the brown-trimmed beige walls he'd never bothered to repaint. Behind it was a large kitchen easily thirty years old, and behind that a bedroom barely large enough for his double bed, a dresser, and low chest of drawers.

When he was satisfied no one had searched through the hidden apartment he returned to the front, dropped onto the Victorian couch and pulled the phone to his lap. He dialed four numbers, spoke quietly for one minute each call, then rang off and stripped, padded into the bathroom and took a long, hot shower without wasting energy thinking. By the time he was finished there was a knock at the door.

"You're going *where?*" Old Alice said, opting for the club chair, her shopping bag between her legs, her support hose folded down around her ankles. "You're crazy. Jesus, nobody goes there anymore."

Linc sat on the couch, bundled in a bathrobe, a towel around his neck. "I don't choose 'em, I just do 'em."

"Sure."

He opened a monogrammed, cork-lined copper box and pulled out a cigarette. He lighted it, leaned back, and stared at Old Alice. "Well?"

"Well, hell, sure I can do it. When do you have to leave?"

"Tonight."

She reached up to the skimmer and dusted the plastic fruit. "A little short notice, if you ask me. I ain't used to short notice anymore."

"Wasn't my idea."

"The old fart's gonna be mad. We were going to the fireworks tonight."

"The old fart has a job of his own."

She grinned, and clacked her false teeth. "I'll bet he just loves you, Blackie."

He smiled. "I'll need quite a lot, I imagine. Tips, air fare, hotels, bribes, things like that."

"Don't you got an expense account?"

His grin widened. "Why spend the real thing when I can save it for my old age?"

"He know about this?"

"Does he ever?"

"That's cheating."

"Think of him as the IRS."

She shrugged and rose, shuffled to the door and opened it, and turned as she took the first step down. "Hadda kick the damned wall again."

"I know."

"Oughta get Palmer to fix it for you."

"One of these days."

She turned again at the second step. "Twenty thousand okay?"

He nodded.

"Goddamned inflation," she muttered as the door swung shut behind her. "Ain't like the old days, Blackie. Ain't like 'em at all."

Macon sat primly on the couch while Linc buttoned his plaid shirt and stood at the window, looking across the street at Carmel's record shop.

"Excuse me, Blackie," he said, "but you're going *where?*"

"Macon, please."

"I'm sorry." The old man grinned. "But it's better than Thorny, isn't it?"

"Barely."

Macon sighed and fanned himself with his hat. "I don't suppose you'll consider using a *nom de plume* this time."

Linc shook his head, wondering if Carmel had stopped by last night and seen the wreckage downstairs.

"It announces you, Blackie."

"I don't mind."

"You stifle the creative urges."

"Macon, I don't have the time."

The old man shrugged as if it were no concern of his, reached into his red-striped jacket and pulled out a sheaf of papers, thumbed through them and dropped several packets on the coffee table. "How about a diamond merchant?"

"You're kidding."

"It's respectable."

"It's telling people I don't know that I'm carrying gems and lots of money."

"You are."

"Yeah, but they don't have to know that."

Macon grunted and poked a finger at a second batch beside the first as Linc sat on the sill. "A Hollywood producer?"

"Do I look like a Hollywood producer? Jesus, Macon."

"Do you look like a tailor?"

He said nothing.

Macon sniffed, pulled out a handkerchief and blew his nose. "Hay fever. Always happens on the Fourth. The nose knows, Blackie. The nose knows."

"A zoo scout."

Macon gaped. "A what? What's that?"

"I'm looking for animals for the San Diego zoo. Lots of potential money, an important place, and who'll give a damn when I traipse through the outlands."

Macon reached deep into his pocket and sifted through the remaining papers. "I haven't got one for that."

"Then make some."

"When do you need them?"

"I'm leaving tonight."

"That's marvelous, Blackie. Do you realize I

promised the old biddy I'd take her to the fireworks tonight? She says the rockets remind her of her first hushand. Or was it her first lover?"

"She's getting my traveler's checks, Macon."

"Ah."

"Can you do it?"

Macon rose and slapped on his hat, gathered his papers together and jammed them into his pockets. "I can."

Linc sighed. "Macon, I didn't mean to insult you. I've just had a bad day, that's all."

"Yes." He strode to the door, opened it, and looked down the stairwell. "I had to kick the wall again, you know."

"I know."

"It's very unsettling, a man of my age kicking a wall."

"I'll take care of it."

"Ten o'clock all right?"

"Ten is fine."

"Zoo scout?"

"Yep."

"Great," he said as the door closed behind him. "Frank Buck is alive and well and living in New Jersey."

Palmer Crowley handed him his gun and ammunition, an Apache throwing knife that fit snugly into a spring-sheath on his wrist and a blackjack designed to be kept unobtrusively in his hip pocket. When Linc asked him for something a little more modern, with a little more dash, the old man scowled and muttered for several minutes about the television generation and its singular lack of imagination and dependence upon flash and glitter in place of results. Linc apologized, and Palmer shut up, for so long Linc was afraid he'd fallen asleep. Then he shook himself suddenly, went to the door and started down. Halfway to the bottom he turned.

"I'll fix that door while you're gone."

"Appreciate it, Palmer."

"Damn near broke my damn foot."

"I'm sorry."

"Don't be sorry, just quit kicking the goddamned wall."

He stood at the window, looking down at the empty street, taking deep breaths as he watched for the prowling hearse. He hoped he could make a clean exit this time; otherwise the tunnel would be hell on his new jeans.

He also looked for signs that Carmel might come over, but there were no signs of life behind the curtained windows. He'd tried to call her once, after the shower, but no one had answered the phone across the street. He suspected she was furious at him for standing her up last night, and he didn't blame her a bit, though each time it had happened before she was on his doorstep at dawn, shrieking her rage at the top of her voice just to shame him into letting her inside. It worked every time. And every time without fail she showed him what he had missed by not helping her avoid another night with her family.

He sighed, but with a grin.

Carmel, he thought then, you are my millstone, I hope you know that. A pang of guilt, and he wondered if he should try again, before he left.

But before he could turn to the telephone a car

pulled up sharply to the curb. He paid little attention to it until a woman stepped out and peered at
the shopwindow. Her face was hidden by the maple's overhang, but when she moved to the sidewalk, Linc's eyes widened.

"Oh my god," he said, and sprinted for the door,
barely making it to the shop before the bell clanged
and the woman was inside. He stood at the back,
just behind the glass-bead curtain, and watched
her move thoughtfully down the aisle, dusting the
display cases with one finger, the other clasping a
simple thin purse to her waist.

She was tall, she was dark-haired, and she had
the kind of figure Linc knew beyond doubt was
going to get him in trouble.

When he stepped through the curtain she looked
up, and smiled, and pulled a gun from her purse.

SIX

"**M**Y NAME is Vanessa Lecharde," she said brightly, then looked down at the gun, blinked as if astonished to see it in her hand, and shoved it back in her purse. "Oh dear, I'm sorry, that's not what I wanted at all." She laughed self-consciously and shrugged. "Unfortunately, you never can tell about men these days."

Linc moved cautiously out of the shadows, switching on the overhead lights as he did. Her eyelids fluttered as her vision adjusted, and he took the few moments to decide that the outfit she was wearing—all white from summer-thin blouse to loose-pleated skirt—wasn't the sort she bought off the rack.

"I'm sorry too," he said, trying to shake the chill from his stomach, "but I'm afraid the shop is closed. It's the Fourth."

"Yes," she said, "but the door was open."

"My fault."

"You always work on holidays?"

He grinned. "I have work, I want to eat, I work on the Fourth."

She leaned over the display of ties, and he hurried behind the case, still smiling, though he couldn't help wondering about the gun, or about the long silver Mercedes parked at the curb.

"Are you Lincoln Blackthorne?"

His shoulders tightened, though his smile remained. "Yes."

"I see." Her finger traced a meaningless pattern on the glass before she looked up without raising her head. Her eyes were deep green, a startling and pleasant contrast to the ebony of her cut-short hair. "A dear, mutual, and concerned friend of ours suggested I talk with you before you leave on your impending vacation."

He lifted an eyebrow, but said nothing.

"You don't believe me, Mr. Blackthorne?" She seemed less hurt than surprised.

"I have lots of friends."

"This one believes, for the time being anyway, in intensive meditation."

He almost laughed, barely held himself in check. *I love you, George Vilcroft; but you're still not off my list.*

"What can I do for you, Miss Lecharde?"

She reached into the purse again, and he stepped back until he saw the envelope in her hand. "You can accept this as a token of my admiration."

He stared at it, stared at her, and took it, opened it, and saw the money, new bills, arranged inside, none less than a hundred. "I don't understand."

"It's not really from me," she said with a quick, bell-like laugh. "Our mutual friend thought perhaps you might be needing something more, for what he called possible unexpected expenses on your journey."

He considered for a moment, wondering what Vilcroft was up to. Then he pushed the envelope firmly across the case. "I have enough, thank you. The original will be sufficient. Too much, and I begin to be noticed. Not very good when you're on vacation to relax without a lot of attention." Then he smiled regretfully. "Really, I do have enough."

She leaned toward him slowly, her lips slightly parted. "Do you?"

"I always do." But it was getting awfully hot again.

She reached out before he could move and touched the hollow of his cheek. "Are you sure?" Her perfume carried a scent he could not place, but it was deep and rich, almost palatable, when she leaned still closer and the top button of her blouse parted to reveal an expressive, and expansive, contour of tan. "Are you really sure?"

"Miss Lecharde—"

"Vanessa."

He nodded. "Vanessa." And he wished she would back off a little; the perfume and the cleavage were much too pleasantly distracting. And her lips were close enough for him to kiss if he'd only lean just a little forward. "Vanessa," and he cleared his throat of the hoarseness suddenly lodged there. "Vanessa, why didn't our friend bring this himself?"

"He's meditating."

"I see."

"He doesn't like to be disturbed when he's meditating."

"You . . . you know him well?"

Closer—he could almost see his reflection in her eyes.

"We meditate."

"I see."

She smiled. "Mr. Blackthorne—"

He swallowed. "Linc, please."

"Linc. Short for Lincoln. That's nice."

"Thank you."

Her eyelids fluttered again. "Lincoln, there are a couple of things I'm supposed to tell you." She looked around the shop. "This is charming, but is there someplace we can go where we won't be . . . disturbed?"

The woman intrigued him, and since he had to wait for his money and papers anyway, he decided he might as well enjoy what was left of his time in Inverness. Calling Carmel would have to wait till he returned.

"There's always the back room, I suppose."

"Ah," she said.

"It isn't much," he apologized as he moved around the display case, "but this is just a tailor shop, you know."

She looked to the ceiling. "And who lives up there?"

"It's rented to someone named Timothy Forranato."

"Ah," she said knowingly. "A friend?"

His smile was one-sided. "Not very likely. He's a missionary, travels a lot, and doesn't exactly approve of people like me."

"But you're a tailor!" she exclaimed. "How can he not approve of a tailor?"

"Well, it's like this," he said, preparing to begin a story he'd perfected over the past decade, to give himself somewhat of a rakish veneer without being an outright reprobate. But he stopped when he saw a vehicle drift past the shopwindow. It was the black hearse. With an apologetic grimace that passed as a smile he brushed by her and sidled out to the street. The hearse was just into a slow circuit of the square, obviously intending to return. He spun around and nearly ran into Vanessa, standing behind him.

"Friends?"

He shook his head and slapped an angry hand on the Mercedes's front fender. Then he looked at it, looked back at the hearse caught behind a truck, and took the woman's arm.

"Can you drive me somewhere?"

"Well, sure."

He wasted no time. He raced to the shop door, closed and locked it, and was into the passenger seat almost before she had a chance to slip in behind the wheel. When she looked a question at him he only nodded for her to move—which she did, just as the hearse came down the street toward them.

"Not friends," she said.

"Nope."

And he barely had time to brace himself before she stomped her foot on the accelerator. The silver car shuddered and lunged forward, rear tires spinning blue-grey smoke as it bumped over the curb, swerved back into the street, and narrowly missed sideswiping the hearse and two trucks.

"Damn thing needs adjusting again," Vanessa complained with a scowl as she charged full speed into the square without bothering to check the traffic, or the traffic light that had just turned red.

Linc smiled gamely and looked back to see the hearse involved in an awkward mid-block turn. When he faced front again, they were taking the square's first corner on two wheels, the second the same, and gunning east on the road that led up to the Knob and out of town. An old woman with a shopping cart barely pulled out of the way, an elaborately painted van ducked out of the way into a one-way street into the back of a garbage truck, and Linc didn't bother to look when they passed the old cemetery and a funeral procession sedately left the gates.

"Do the dead have the right of way?" Vanessa asked, spinning the wheel to avoid the flower car and forcing the two-man police motorcycle escort to scatter into someone's front yard.

"Yes, we do," he said, checked the back again and saw Reddick's hearse trying to weave through the confusion they'd created. Then the police were back on the road, sirens blaring, one of the white-helmeted officers frantically yelling into his mike.

"Cops," she said. "Good heavens, they're fast." And stomped the accelerator hard a second time.

Inverness blurred out of focus as the Mercedes flew, fell behind as the street widened only slightly to become a county highway. Trees and shrubs along the verge melded into a green and brown wall, only occasionally falling back to expose small farms on the hillsides, pastures with grazing black Angus or a handful of horses. The houses were set well back from the shoulder, stone walls and rail fences marking those places where the land didn't rise sharply above the road.

The road that was anything but dragstrip straight.

It curved sharply and dropped, curved again and rose, more than once making Linc grab for his stomach and swallow. But when he looked to Vanessa, she was smiling as if she were doing thirty instead of ninety, every so often taking one hand from the wheel to readjust the rearview mirror.

"Pretty country," she said.

He grimaced and looked back.

The two policemen were still close behind, grimly determined, until they breached a low hill and confronted a sudden fork. Vanessa instantly chose the lefthand branch, which took her over a small wood-and-stone bridge spanning a shallow creek. She had made her choice at the last moment, causing the pursuit to split—one barely managed to stay with her, but the other failed to complete a sharp correcting turn just past the bridge and launched himself flailing over the low embankment and into the water.

Suddenly, Linc's eyes narrowed and he grabbed for the purse.

"Hey!" and she slapped at his hand, momentarily losing control of the car.

"Your gun," he snapped, pulled it out, and rolled down his window.

"That's a policeman!" she protested, torn between trying to take back the weapon and keeping the car tentatively on the road.

"Sure," he said, and turned until he was kneeling on the seat, his left hand out the window and aiming the gun. He fired once, and the police fired back. He fired again, and a third time, and he could see Basil Unicov grinning as one hand moved along the handlebar. A sudden burst of orange spat from the cycle's front fender, and the car was rocked by an explosion that tore up the road not far from its rear bumper.

"My heavens," Vanessa said as she crouched over the wheel.

Linc gritted his teeth and fired a fourth time, Unicov weaving around the crater he'd created, weaving away from the bullet that pinged off the road. He waved, and fired his fender again, this time the road's curve causing his missile to blast a hex-signed barn set right against the tarmac. Flaming boards showered the ground and the road ahead, smoke billowed, and the horns of a bull slapped against the windshield, clung to the wipers for a moment before slipping away.

"No tail," she said sadly, swung sharply into the opposite lane as they bounced over a low crest, just in time to avoid a slow-moving tractor grinding out of a pasture gate.

Unicov wasn't so lucky.

He flew over the hill, turned frantically, and ran off the road, through the gate behind the tractor and the angrily waving farmer, and into the pasture; when he tried to cut back the cycle's rear wheel slipped and he was down in a flurry of divots and patties.

Linc closed his eyes and rested his cheek on the seat back. After a moment he turned around and dropped the gun beside him. "God *damn*," he said with a shake of his head, not daring to look up to see how fast they were going. But the thump of the wheels over the rough blacktop was enough to prompt him to ask her if she wouldn't mind slowing down.

"But the police—"

"He wasn't a cop, and we're already in the next county. The interstate is just over the next hill."

"Oh, good," she said, grinning. "Now I can move!"

His mouth opened, closed, and he chanced a look over his shoulder.

"The hearse isn't there," she said calmly. "You won't see it again unless he knows where you're going."

"Yeah."

A mile passed in silence, and he was just about sure his lungs would work normally when she stamped on the brakes, sending the car into a long grinding skid that brought them to a halt at the interstate ramp.

"Hey, what . . . ?"

"East- or westbound, silly?" she said.

"East. Now if you don't mind—"

"I don't mind."

"I'm sure, but—"

The Mercedes coughed once and was running.

Ten minutes later, as they threaded between automobiles and huge tractor trailers, she fished for a cigarette in her purse, lighted it from the dashboard, and settled back to steer with one hand loosely draped over the wheel.

"Are you going to tell me where we're going?"

Linc continued to hunt for signs of the hearse.

"Lincoln?"

"Huh?"

"Where are we going?"

"*I* am going to the airport. *You* are going back to our friend and you're going to give him a piece of my mind."

"Oh no, Lincoln. I'm supposed to watch out for

you. Going back to George isn't watching out for you." She turned to him and smiled innocently. "It goes a lot faster."

The sweat had dried on his face, but his shirt was still coldly plastered to his back. "It does."

She nodded.

"Peru."

She almost rode into the back of a station wagon. "Peru? You mean like Incas and llamas and Indians with pointy hats?"

"Like that," he said.

"Good heavens," she said.

Linc kept his silence. It wasn't that he minded this beautiful woman's company, and he certainly owed her at least a portion of his life. But she troubled him. Her appearance was too coincidental, her gun not one usually associated with helpless females, and her ability with the car too expert to be accident. Which meant she was working for someone: George, or Reddick, or even Uni-the-Toad.

Unless, the thought occurred, unwanted and unfriendly, there was someone else in this mess he still didn't know.

SEVEN

THE MOMENT the airplane was off the ground Linc loosened his seat belt and eased back his seat. He crossed his legs as best he could, closed his eyes, and tried like hell to pray himself to sleep. He hated flying. He hated tall buildings. He hated anything that reminded him in any way of altitude. He used to joke with Macon, in the old days, that simply standing on an air mail stamp would give him a nosebleed. So he ignored Vanessa's vivid tour-guide descriptions of the land dropping lazily away below them, tried desperately to ignore the stewardess's clinical, mechanical instructions about finding the exits, reading the emergency card in the pocket, and using the yellow Mae West he was positive wouldn't fit him. He had heard the same routine on a dozen different airlines, virtually knew it by heart, and didn't believe a word of it. When the plane went down, the plane went down, and no one to date had ever given him a decent explanation about why, when traveling East Coast to West, they insisted on telling him what to do if they were forced to a water landing over Nebraska.

The only thing that pleased him was the way they'd fixed up the airport so that his previous pass through wasn't even noticed. In fact, he'd thought with a small pang of regret, even the sheep-dip had been washed clean from the walls —something he'd once thought marvelously ironic, though perhaps the symbolism was lost on the management.

Some hours later they landed in Miami for refueling, were airborne again just before midnight. The cabin was dimly lighted, quiet except for the engines' humming and the hiss of the air jets above the seats, and even the steward walked tiptoe up the aisle in search of someone to comfort or to rent a car to on their arrival in Lima. Vanessa sat with her hands folded in her lap, a magazine on her knees, and the clumsy stereo headphones plugged into her ears. She was smiling to herself, every few moments nodding as though in time to the music.

Linc stared at her for several minutes without her stirring, wondering just what she was doing in his life. Not that he didn't appreciate her further help—the money she brought more than made up for the money he'd been forced to leave behind, and when she returned from the ladies' room the passport she gave him, and the identification papers she held, were easily a match for what Macon would have done.

Only she had done it in less than twenty minutes.

He wondered, but he asked her no questions. For

some reason he felt safer with her close to hand instead of following him like Reddick.

He frowned and turned stiffly in his seat, again searching the sparsely occupied cabin for signs of Reddick or one of his men; or signs of Unicov, any signs at all. But the plane was considerably less than half full, and none of the others triggered any of his defenses.

"Lincoln?"

He turned back and smiled. "Hi."

"Did I sleep long?"

"I don't know. An hour, maybe a bit more."

She smiled back and stretched without moving her arms. "God, I hate sleeping on planes. It always gives me a headache."

"Yeah."

She smoothed the white blouse down over her chest, reached up, and switched off their overhead lights. The shadows were cool, so much so she shivered and rubbed at her arms. "Lincoln, why are we going to Peru?"

"George didn't tell you?"

"He said I was to take care of you, that's all." She hesitated. "And I'm supposed to let him know when you've found the King."

"Ah."

"He trusts you, you know. He really does. But—"

"You're his insurance."

She shrugged. "I guess."

"Just so I know."

"So why are we going to Peru?"

It took him several minutes to conclude a silent one-sided debate, several more before he decided she had a right to know. Some of it, not all, but a right nonetheless.

"Well, it seems, Vanessa, we're going to hell."

Vanessa sputtered but otherwise maintained a remarkable calm as she turned her head slowly to stare at him, her eyes wide and questioning. When he nodded, she nodded back and wriggled as deeply as she could into her seat. She blinked slowly several times, took a deep breath, and exhaled in a silent whistle.

"I think," she said, "you're going to tell me a story."

"Do you mind?"

"Does it have a happy ending?"

"If we get back in one piece it will."

She grimaced. "You're not very reassuring."

"You drive too fast."

She laughed quietly. "I don't think that follows."

"If it doesn't, you can tell George I'm not being totally honest with you."

"Tell him yourself; I'm going to reserve my own judgment."

"All right." He glanced yet again around the cabin, but most of the other passengers seemed to be asleep. There was only one light on, far to the back where he could see the rumpled top of a magazine poking over a seat. "All right. You asked for it."

"It's only fair, Lincoln."

"Yes," he admitted, "I suppose it is."

Four hundred years ago (he said quietly, leaning his head toward hers, his hands folded over his stomach and his legs stretched under the seat ahead), an explorer named Francisco Pizarro decided that Spain's manifest destiny wouldn't be complete unless she could lay claim to the South American continent (and it also occurred to him that it would really piss off the English). Part of his subsequent travels, then, took him to Peru, and to the sprawling empire of the Incas. Despite their handicaps they were a fairly advanced civilization, all things considered, and though they were much impressed by the prowess and seemingly magical technology of the Spanish, they were also doubtful of their real intentions.

They were right.

It didn't take long before full-scale war broke out, and those Incas who weren't slaughtered were scattered from the Pacific to the hinterlands of the Amazon. Before it all went to hell, however, Atahualpa, the Emperor (who had just beaten his brother in a vicious civil war), had taken a liking to something Pizarro's men had brought along for those boring nights when there wasn't any fighting—playing cards. Primitive by today's standards, but fascinating nevertheless. The Emperor ordered his goldsmiths and jewelsmiths to fashion him a deck that would prove his lineage, his direct connections to the gods. He figured this would keep Pizarro from cutting off his head.

It didn't, of course, and the cards were discovered by a man named Esteban Roderico de la Benevidez, a nobleman traveling with Pizarro for the hell of it, and the off chance there might be gold lying around for the taking. Benevidez barely made it back to Spain alive; he was torn with wounds received in the fighting, racked with a fever that would not quit, and by all accounts quite monomaniacal by the time he died. His daughter Dorotea refused any visitors, saying to her close friends that her father spent hours every day playing a mysterious game of cards with a phantom deck surely touched by the Devil.

Atahualpa's creations had been left behind, and it was Benevidez's single-minded intention to return to the sprawling and dangerous new empire and retrieve them. He died before that could happen, a horrible death that left him little more than a skeleton when he received the last rites.

His daughter grieved, and buried the man old before his time, and promptly forgot about the ill-fated voyage. Her husband, Hermano Villanueva de Cordoba, however, didn't. He was a gambler and a loser, and the descriptions he'd heard of the mysterious cards fascinated him to the point of distraction, finally gripped him even in his dreams.

Dorotea was not amused and threatened to have him locked away if he didn't wise up and remember his duties.

Hermano, fresh from a disastrous series of gambling losses, ignored her.

Late one winter he slipped out of the house with most of the jewels and, with a few proper bribes and a few inquiries among his friends, managed to get himself passage to the New World.

He returned two years later, a man of thirty-five who looked seventy.

He was as insane as his father-in-law had been.

But he had the deck with him, and he insisted to his wife that before the year was out they would be the new King and Queen of the Spanish Empire.

Oddly enough, from priests' and friends' accounts, the fortunes of the De Cordobas altered radically, and for the better. Suddenly, Hermano was being actively sought for his counsel on both domestic and foreign matters; he received tributes from Madrid and Cádiz; ambassadors from England and France stopped by his estate to pay their respects; and no one but his wife seemed to believe he had lost his mind.

In November Dorotea died. A fall from a cliff during a freak storm.

In December it was apparent to those who understood such things that De Cordoba could by the snap of his fingers dethrone Philip and his Queen.

Three or four days before the end of the year, however, a band of Basques from the northern mountains raided the province and sacked De Cordoba's mansion. Accounts differ here about the actual attack, but within hours the hacienda was burned to the ground, all the servants slaughtered, and De Cordoba himself strung up from an olive tree in the courtyard. He was flayed alive and, the way the Basques tell it, he couldn't possibly have been more than twenty-five years old.

Atahualpa's cards were missing.

The neighbors, the raiders, and a few slightly avaricious compatriots searched the hacienda and the grounds for days at a time over the next few months, in all sorts of weather, but the Incan cards were never found.

Not right away, at any rate, and it didn't take long before they were relegated to memory, vague, sometimes disquieting, until finally they were judged to have been nothing more than yet another disturbing figment of Hermano's rather active imagination.

By all rights, that should have been the end of it, but it wasn't.

Eventually, a young priestly scholar working

alone in Madrid unearthed mention of the curious legendary deck in one of Hermano's last letters. Another search was launched, but after three years it was concluded that the Basques had found them and taken them away.

The Basques, of course, denied it vehemently.

This time, however, the cards were not forgotten.

They turned up here and there, in rumors and stories, over the next four hundred years. Finally, their physical presence was made known, though never as a complete deck. It's said that Franco spent a fair percentage of the country's treasury trying to locate them, to bribe them away from their current owners.

Obviously, he failed.

Many of the newly rediscovered individual cards were sold at private auctions in Europe and Canada, and it didn't take long before dear old George became interested. It cost him a fortune to find out how many there were and to track them all down, but he did it. All but three—the King, Queen, and Knave of Satan's Eyes. The Queen he located in Buenos Aires, the Knave in Quito, and the King is now rumored to be held by an old man in a village outside Lima.

"They're incredibly beautiful," he said with a sigh. "And I suppose they're priceless. The King is the last, and it'll complete the collection."

"It's all true, then?"

"Most of it, I guess."

"You've seen George's collection?"

He glanced at her, looked away. "A few. Very lovely, as I said."

"My goodness."

"Yes."

A silence as the steward ghosted by, heading for the front cabin.

"So you're going all the way down there just for a card," Vanessa said warily.

He shrugged. "A card that probably would set me up for life if I sold it on the open market."

"And what about all the insanity? I mean, good heavens, all those people driven mad by these things."

He grinned and tapped her wrist with a finger. "Misers," he said, "are not exactly known for their firm and steady grips on reality. They are classic paranoids and, having seen the cards myself, I can almost understand how a man could kill to have them all."

"Would you?"

"Me?" The grin became a smile. "I'm not crazy, m'dear. I know my limitations."

"I'm impressed." She winked, stretched, then looked at him oddly. "May I ask you another question?"

"Ask. If I'm not bored, I'll answer."

She stared at the back of her hands, turned them over and flexed them. "You said you'd worked for George before. How'd you get started? I mean, you're a tailor, for crying out loud. And now you're going to Peru, for god's sake."

He considered not answering at all, and might not have had she not asked him again, softly.

"I've known George for a long time," he said. "From the time I got out of college. Eleven years ago I went on a vacation and promised to bring him back something. It was a statuette he said was easily obtainable from a friend of his in Arizona. Well, the friend wasn't a friend, and the statuette wasn't what it seemed to be. By the time I knew what was happening, I had had what you might call an adventure." He smiled at the memory. "I think I liked it. George knew I liked it, and one thing led to another and here we are."

"That's it?"

"No," he said. "But that's all you're going to get now. Otherwise, it's a long story."

"Ah."

"Yes. Ah."

"And I suppose it's yet another story how a college man ended up as a tailor in a town most maps forget about."

He squeezed her hand. "With insight like that, Vanessa, I predict you'll go far."

"Like to Peru, I suppose."

"Why not? Somebody has to."

She yawned, then, and slowly laid her head on his shoulder. He could smell her hair, and her perfume, and wasn't above taking inventory of her cleavage once more before his own eyelids grew weighted and he drifted off to sleep.

A sleep that was interrupted only by someone screaming, "My god, it's a bomb!"

EIGHT

IT TOOK several long seconds before Linc was able to drive the sleep from his eyes and the fog from his mind. When he did, he felt Vanessa's hand gripping his upper arm tightly. He looked to her, looked to the aisles, and decided that this wasn't quite the time to play at being hero.

All the cabin's lights were turned on full, the only sound the distant thrumming of the airliner's engines. At the head of the aisle nearest him stood a man, short and portly, his dark face grizzled and his charcoal-grey, three-piece business suit rumpled; he was stooped forward slightly as if his spine were mildly deformed. Around his chest was a worn leather bandolera filled with gleaming ammunition, and in his right hand was a long section of aluminum pipe from the sealed ends of which protruded an unpleasantly large number of colored wires, all terminating in a tiny box that hung around his neck from a length of braided rawhide.

At the head of the other aisle was a striking woman in a white linen business suit. Her hair was deep copper, her skin dusky and sheened with perspiration, and in her hands she held an M-79 grenade launcher.

After the outburst that had awakened him, Linc heard nothing from the rest of the passengers save a woman quietly weeping and a man in the back softly swearing. The stewardesses were not to be seen, and when he chanced a look around the seat ahead of him, Linc saw the one steward lying in the aisle of the first-class section, the back of his head matted with drying blood.

"You will say nothing," the man said needlessly. He looked over to the woman, who nodded once, sharply. "You will remain where you are until I say differently."

No one argued, no one protested.

The crying woman was silenced when someone slapped her.

"Very good."

"Who the hell are you?" Vanessa demanded suddenly, squirming in her seat to get a better view.

Linc smiled grimly as the terrorists swiveled their heads in his direction. "Shut up," he said without moving his lips.

"I will not," she said. "I want to know—"

"You will know soon enough, lady," the man snapped. "You will now please hold your tongue."

"Not—"

The man stepped forward menacingly, and the other passengers muffled their cries of alarm. Linc took the hand on his arm and pried it off, gripped the wrist and squeezed until Vanessa gasped into pouting silence. Then he smiled more broadly at the man until the tension finally eased, and the terrorist nodded his approval.

Once the cabin was silent again, the man's associate took her grenade launcher forward, out of sight, though Linc could hear her speaking softly and harshly to those in front. There was a voice raised in protest, and the wet sound of something thudding into flesh. A groan of pain, and moments later eight people staggered out of first class, two men awkwardly supporting a third between them, the third man's hands clasped hard to his face. Not hard enough, however, to staunch the intermittent flow of blood between his fingers.

She herded them into the center section and made them sit by twos, one pair behind the other. Then she walked straight to the back and gestured with her weapon until an elderly man rose from his seat and followed her. By the way he knelt in the aisle and took hold of the injured man's hands, Linc guessed he was a doctor.

"My friends," the terrorist said then, and waited until he had the cabin's full attention. "I do not wish to harm anyone. *We* do not wish to harm anyone. I can assure you on my honor that this magnificent airplane will land safely in Lima, and you will all be permitted to go about your business." He paused, smiled to reveal even white teeth, and cleared his throat. "On the other hand, we do have our purpose, our responsibility, and we do not take it lightly."

"For god's sake, man, get to the point," someone called out fearfully from the back.

The man's smile returned, and he pointed to the metal box hanging beneath his throat. "This," he said, "is a detonator."

A woman began crying.

"And this," he said, hefting the pipe high enough for all to see, "is a bomb."

The woman began wailing.

The woman in the white linen business suit jerked the grenade launcher around, and the wailer was cut off by the harsh sound of a stinging slap.

"I have no intention of blowing myself up if I achieve my purpose."

"And if you don't?" Vanessa said, with a scowl at Linc.

The man shrugged to indicate the extent of his helplessness should he fail.

"If you blow yourself up," Vanessa pointed out before Linc could stop her, "you'll blow us up too."

"No," the man said reasonably. "The plane will crash and you will die from that. I will be the only one to die from the bomb."

"You're splitting hairs."

The man came down the aisle and stopped just beyond the point where Linc could make a grab for his hand. "My dear lady," he said with almost unctuous courtesy, "when I'm dead I will not care."

"Well, you'll be dead before me, and I'm going to care a lot," Vanessa told him.

The man laughed unexpectedly and loudly. "But how wonderful! How beautiful!" He made an awkward bow from the waist, just barely remembering to hold on to the bomb. "Lady, I will introduce myself as Juan Alfredo Pizarro, direct descendant

of the famed conquistador who brought freedom
and self-determination to the peoples of South
America, and who broke the bonds of slavery which
entrapped the peasants of the imperialist Incan
Emperor."

"*Jeez*us Christ on a crutch!" the woman in the
white linen business suit muttered.

Pizarro ignored her. "Lady," he said to Vanessa,
"I like your spunk."

Vanessa smiled coldly.

"It would be a shame, then, if you should have
to die because you have a big mouth."

Vanessa's mouth opened in outrage, closed in
frustration, and she turned to Linc for support
against the deadly threat. He only shrugged, however, and pointed to the bomb.

Pizarro returned to his position at the head of
the aisle, scowling at his companion. As he did,
Linc sat up abruptly, paying no attention at all to
Vanessa's hissing admonitions to do something soon
before they all got killed. As he had seen from the
start, Pizarro's back was indeed oddly deformed,
and now he knew what it was—the terrorist who
was going to blow himself up was wearing a parachute. A small one, to be sure, but a parachute
nevertheless. He looked quickly across the cabin,
and stared at the woman. And nodded. She too
was wearing one, of the small, low-jump variety
developed for night commandos involved in anti-
terrorist campaigns.

"Now," Pizarro said, "we will begin." He nodded to the woman in the white linen business suit,
who moved directly to the first group of passengers on her side. She glared down at them. "My

friends," Pizarro said to them, "you will please tell my freedom-loving compatriot your names. And please, do not lie," he added quickly. "We can easily check the manifest for confirmation of your answers. In fact, we already have. We just like to attach the name to the face. It makes things much more pleasantly personal, I hope you will agree."

"Why don't you just ask for who you're looking for?" Linc suggested innocently. "You never know."

Pizarro swung around, his face contorted with disdain. "Do you think, fool, that our quarry will identify himself just because I ask it?"

Linc shrugged. "Might save you time, Señor Pizarro."

"Ah," Pizarro said, "you speak the language."

Linc waggled his hand: a little here, a little there, enough to get by on.

"Very well, I am only too happy to try." He looked to the woman, who rolled her eyes to the cabin ceiling while strangling the grenade launcher's stock. Pizarro snorted his disgust. "We are hoping to discover the immediate whereabouts of a man named Blackthorne," he said sternly. "Lincoln Blackthorne." He grinned humorlessly at Linc when there was no response but a frantic whispering from the other passengers. "Are you happy now, sir?"

"No, not really."

"Oh dear, and why not?"

"Because I'm Lincoln Blackthorne."

The first-class cabin, once emptied, now seemed immense. The young steward who had been ruthlessly clubbed was now sitting on the floor with his back to the galley entrance, groaning softly as he dabbed gingerly at his skull with a dampened towel. There was no guard at the cockpit door, but a large board had been jammed up against it and Linc assumed the stewardesses had been forced to crowd in there with the officers.

Pizarro led him to a plush red swivel chair in the cabin's center, took one opposite, and gestured him into place. Then he laid the wired pipe bomb carefully across his ample lap and smiled. In a circular insert in the armrest was a glass of amber liquid; the man emptied it with one swallow, wiped his mouth with his sleeve, and smiled again.

"Well, Mr. Blackthorne."

The woman in the white linen business suit muttered something to the doctor and held her grenade launcher at port arms to caution the others against foolish heroics.

"Well, Señor Pizarro."

Pizarro grinned and absently fingered the detonation cube dangling against his chest. "You are extremely puzzled, no?"

"Yes."

"You should like to know why someone as insignificant as myself is willing to risk his entire life simply to meet someone as well known as yourself."

"Yes."

Pizarro nodded, and touched the side of his broad nose with a manicured forefinger. "I think you know, Mr. Blackthorne. I think you know very well what my colleague and I are seeking in this imperialist night coach. And while we are engaged in this conversation, would it be asking too much if I were to get familiar and call you Blackie?"

"Yes."

"I see."

Linc shifted, lifted a hand toward his jacket pocket, and froze when Pizarro stiffened. He smiled, pulled back the lapel to expose the rack of pens he had in the inner pocket. "A cigarette, if you don't mind," he said.

"No tricks," Pizarro said.

"Wouldn't think of it."

"Then all right."

Linc forced himself to move slowly, to extract the cigarette with two fingers and light it with a match he fumbled from his trousers. When he had expelled the first puff in a slow upward stream, he relaxed somewhat and looked again at his adversary, wondering how in hell this one fit into the already crowded field. There was no answer in the man's dark eyes, in the tight set of his heavy lips, in the faint quivering of his jowls. He did notice a trace of Indian blood there, at the sharp angle of his nose and the crest of high cheekbones. And he was certainly no terrorist starving for the Cause— whatever Cause that might be, thirty-seven thousand feet above the Andes Mountains.

"You are on a quest, Mr. Blackthorne."

Linc sighed with a lift of his eyebrow.

"My associates in the United States would like to assist you, to keep you from the dangers that lurk in the Peruvian jungles and on the oppressor-held slopes of our lovely Andes."

"I appreciate the thought, señor, but I really don't—"

Pizarro's eyes narrowed. "I do not recall giving you a choice in the matter."

"One always has choices, my friend."

"One can always die, too."

"A choice, as I said."

Pizarro grinned. "You will tell me, now, where you intend to hunt for the King."

"No, I don't think so."

"My associates will be annoyed."

"Would you mind telling me who they are?"

"Yes, I would."

"I see."

The plane lurched slightly, rocking them in their seats as the pilot banked slowly to the west.

"We do not have much time left, Mr. Blackthorne," Pizarro said, all traces of humor gone from his voice. "You will tell me now, or I will blow us all up. I do not think you wish to have the deaths of all those innocent people on your conscience. Especially the spunky lady traveling with you."

"The spunky lady can take care of herself."

The man's eyes widened, blinked rapidly, widened further. "You can't mean you won't tell me."

"You speak the language well enough, señor, you tell me."

Pizarro sputtered, grabbed the bomb from his lap and thrust it toward Linc's face. "Do you see this? Do you know what it means?"

Linc crossed his legs at the knees and folded his hands loosely over his stomach. "I see what purports to be a deadly explosive device with which you are threatening me. What I don't see, señor, is your willingness to use it."

Before Pizarro had a chance to reply, the woman in the white business suit appeared at his side, snarling. "Well?"

"He doesn't believe we'll do it," the man said helplessly.

She closed her eyes in an effort to maintain her temper below the boiling point, opened them again to see Linc smiling gently at her. She snarled again, an effect somewhat spoiled by a quiver of a smile at the corner of her mouth. "You are not cooperating, Mr. Blackthorne," she said.

"My dear Estrella," he said, "what makes you think I'd ever cooperate with you?"

Pizarro's lips parted in silent amazement as the woman smiled regretfully and lowered the grenade launcher from its aim at Lincoln's chest. "What is this?" he demanded, his voice suddenly high-pitched. "How does this person know you?"

"We go back a long way, Juan," Linc said without taking his eyes from Estrella Cortez. Though he continued to smile, however, there was no mirth in his eyes. "Monte Carlo, I think, was the first time we met." He paused. "You were with Reddick at the time, I believe."

Estrella shook her head sadly. "I only wish it had been then, Lincoln. But you're wrong, as usual. It was one winter in Detroit. And I was working with Basil that year."

Lincoln's face twisted in self-disgust. "Stupid, that's what I am. How in hell could I ever forget that?"

"Estrella!" Pizarro said as the plane shuddered again, the engines whining to signal the beginning of its descent. The seat-belt signs flashed on, and the steward staggered to his feet, came down the aisle, and swayed with one hand held to the back of his skull.

"I have to get them ready," he said, pointing toward the back.

"Go then," Estrella ordered, shoving him hard between the shoulders.

And at the same time, Lincoln sprang from his seat.

NINE

THERE WAS no time at all for either of the terrorists to react properly: with a quick flex of trained biceps, Lincoln's wrist-sheath dagger was in his hand, Palmer's specially tempered and honed blade slicing easily through the braided rawhide that held the detonator, all before Pizarro realized Linc was even moving. Within the space of an eyeblink the deadly tiny box and the pipe had been scooped into Linc's free hand and dropped on the seat behind him. Before another eyeblink had passed, as Estrella was whirling around with her finger on the launcher trigger, her face dark with enraged betrayal, Linc had grabbed a handful of Pizarro's thick black hair and had pulled his head back, exposing his wattled neck to the dagger's gleaming point. The seat back was sandwiched between them.

"I wouldn't," he said to Estrella when he saw her finger tighten. "It could get messy."

She hesitated nonetheless.

Pizarro could only gurgle, and grip the armrests helplessly as his eyes tried a desperate pleading.

"Lincoln, this is foolish," she said, idly brushing back a thick strand of her flaming copper hair. "You know you can't get away with it. Not forever."

He smiled as if giving truth to her observation, then called Vanessa. Almost instantly she was in the forward cabin, shoving Estrella rudely to one side while snatching the grenade launcher from her hands. Then she hurried to stand behind Lincoln, the barrel of the weapon aimed over his shoulder.

"Are you all right?" she asked.

"Fair," he said, wishing the barrel weren't quite so close to his ear.

"Good."

He glanced out the nearest port and saw the outline of the Andes range sharpening as the sun rose over the highland jungles. "We don't have much time." He looked to Estrella. "Take it off, dear, you won't need it this time."

Estrella balked while Vanessa stared in confusion.

"Please," Lincoln said, and eased the dagger's point deeper into Pizarro's throat without breaking the skin.

Pizarro gurgled, and rolled his eyes.

"C'mon, Cortez, move it!" Vanessa snapped, jerking the launcher to one side and clipping Lincoln's ear.

"Please, Estrella," he said, wishing he had a third hand to rub his head. "For Detroit."

"What's Detroit?" Vanessa asked.

Estrella seemed ready to defy him despite the consequences, then sighed suddenly and began to

unbutton her white linen jacket. The blouse under-
neath was thin, and provocatively sheer, and the
rose lace of her well-filled brassiere was a pleasantly stark contrast to the dusky hue of her skin.
Linc, however, had had enough cleavage for one
trip; he was watching her loosen the parachute
straps from around her shoulders. When the packet
was in her hands he nodded toward the plane's
deck.

"Just leave it there," he said, "and back off."

Estrella dropped the chute and backed into the
main aisle, into a seat. She looked, and he nodded,
and she shrugged as she strapped herself in.

"Tell the steward to get them all strapped in,
and as tight as they can!" he told Vanessa. "And
for god's sake, hurry!"

Vanessa looked at the parachute, looked to the
forward hatch, looked to him and shook her head.
"Good heavens, Lincoln, surely you don't think I
intend to—"

"You want to stay? Stay. Just do as I say!"

She did, and was back within moments, just as
he had withdrawn the knife from Pizarro's throat
and turned the chair to its forward-facing position. He ordered the man to stand and take off his
jacket, remove the parachute and drop it. As soon
as he was obeyed he shoved him back into the
seat, disengaged the swivel and locked it, and when
the man's violently trembling fingers could not
adequately work the seat belt, he adjusted it himself. Hard. Making the terrorist gasp in pain as the
belt cut across his paunch.

"On," he told Vanessa, pointing to the chute
Estrella had left on the carpeted deck.

"Lincoln, I really must protest."

"Vanessa, damnit, do you have wings I don't know about?"

"My heavens—"

"On!"

Then he slipped the dagger back into its sheath, slipped the parachute straps over his shoulders, and snapped the safety belt around his abdomen. The mountains outside were clear now, green and brown and menacingly rugged. As the airliner dipped lower, the peaks rose out of sight and they were plunging through a broad verdant valley split in half by a stream that seemed filled with diamonds.

With a blown kiss and a regretful smile to Estrella, he pushed Vanessa ahead of him to the forward hatch, grabbing up the bomb as he did so.

"You could have been blown up," Vanessa said as he stared at the handle, and the warnings in red above it.

Lincoln gestured a dismissal.

"In fact, you could have blown us all up."

"Not a chance, m'dear." He lifted the pipe and shook it by her ear, grinning. "It's hollow."

"You mean it's a fake?"

"One has to take chances."

"You mean you didn't know it was a fake?"

"I do now."

"My *god*, Lincoln!"

He turned to her and laid a hand gently on her shoulder. "Are you ready? Do you know what to do?"

"I have a vague idea," she said, still looking doubtfully at the bomb.

"Then take a deep breath when I say so. I want us a little lower before we jump."

He watched the mountains slamming past them, heard the engines screaming as they shifted into reverse, felt the fuselage shudder when the flaps were lowered. He judged they were still at least thirty to fifty miles from Lima's farthest outskirts, and realized they would be too close to pursuit if he waited much longer. The trees below were clear in the dawn sunlight, a thread of river incredibly blue winding through them.

And suddenly he realized how high they were, how far he would have to fall before he reached the top of the nearest tree. His face broke out in a sweat, and a chill began a steady march up and down his spine. When he reached for the handle, he saw his fingers white and rigid, and it wasn't until Vanessa covered his hands with hers that he knew he would never be able to open the door on his own.

"It's all right," she whispered into his ear. "It's all right."

"Easy for you to say," he muttered.

And could say nothing more.

The handle turned, a red light began flashing, a warning buzzer split his eardrums just over his head. It took both of them to budge the stubborn thick door, and twice he nearly went down on his knees. Then the hatch, pinned by the wind streaming along the liner, finally opened wide enough to be slammed outward and back, its hinges shrieking their protest before giving way to the monstrous pressure that snapped them in half as if they were made of plastic. Suddenly the cabin was filled with a hurricane of sound, of wind, of temperatures that seemed to drop well below freezing.

He heard a woman screaming.

He heard Pizarro screaming.

He wasn't at all sure that he wasn't screaming himself.

Then Vanessa's hand was in the middle of his back, and he was out, and down, tumbling and rolling with his eyes tightly closed until he remembered to stretch out his arms and legs to steady himself.

And once done, there was a curious silence despite the air screaming past his frozen ears, a magnificently compelling silence that had his eyes open in spite of his terror.

My god, he thought; Peter Pan lives.

Vanessa was nearby, floating gracefully, turning, grinning when she saw him, waving cheerfully, then suddenly pointing frantically. He didn't know what she meant until he looked at his right hand and saw the bomb still in his grasp. He grinned, looked down the length of the spectacular valley, and saw the airliner skimming as close to the ground as it dared. He opened his fingers and the pipe and detonator hovered there for a few seconds, until he grabbed the red ring at his chest and pulled the ripcord.

A snapping jerk, and he was pulled up and away, the chute streaming yellow and red overhead, the thick forest below rocking as he rocked, blurring as wind-tears obscured his vision until he took one hand from the guide cord and wiped it across his face.

Oh hell, he thought then; I forgot to look for a clear place to land.

The bomb exploded when it struck the forest floor.

*   *   *

A miniature mushroom cloud of white and crimson, black and gold, billowed menacingly toward him out of the thick foliage. The concussion was deafening, but before the smoke and flame could reach him an abrupt updraft blasted into the belly of the chute and yanked him rapidly higher, rocked and nearly tumbled him before shoving him harshly southward toward the opposite wall of the valley. He looked frantically over his shoulder and saw that there were few trees there to impale him; instead, the south wall was littered with boulders that even from this height looked large enough to crush a mansion.

And they were moving toward him with incredible speed.

A quick search for Vanessa, and he saw her floating gently toward the ground, apparently unaware that he was about to get himself squashed.

He had no time for the luxury of thought; he pulled on the left cord to tip the chute's inverted bowl, spilling air and dropping him until he had reached the safe limit and had gone somewhat beyond. Then, oblivious to the wind, to the sights and sounds below, he maneuvered himself toward the bank of the river, allowing himself only one crooked and relieved smile when he saw that it was substantially wide enough to indicate a depth of more than a few inches in case his calculations were wrong and he was dumped there instead.

They were, and he was.

And Vanessa, unfortunately, was nowhere in sight.

Before he could compensate for the wind brawling along the valley floor, the water grew frighteningly near. Blue, clear, and as cold as the streams that fed it from the peaks hundreds of miles away, thousands of feet above him.

There wasn't even time for a halfway decent prayer.

He struck feet first, and the shock of the cold stunned him, the parachute instantly snapping downstream, sagging and growing waterlogged. It dragged him fiercely behind it. Water billowed and foamed over his head, filling his eyes and nostrils until he was gasping while he flailed for the release catches. Rocks beneath him slammed into his back. A dead branch caught by the current between two massive boulders struck his right shoulder and made him cry out. Instinctively he grabbed for it, and it held him for several precious seconds. But the pull of the current was too strong, the parachute too heavy, and his hands slipped from the slimy bark.

He thudded off a boulder, was spun around into clear water.

He went under just as the catches unsnapped, and he struggled with barely a breath left in his lungs to slip off the straps.

His chest burned, his arms ached, and when he broke through the surface again, he saw the rapids directly ahead.

He had no chance to swim for the embankment.

Seconds after he registered the danger, he was dragged under again and slammed into a submerged rock. Inadvertently, he gasped at the pain, and the river filled his mouth, and seconds later he was unconscious, and drifting.

TEN

HE WAS falling.

No question about it, he was falling, and there was nothing he could do to stop himself.

He was falling, and he was going to die.

He knew he never should have gotten into that airplane in the first place; it would have taken more time, but he should have taken the train, ridden down to wherever the trains ride down to in Texas, switched to Mexico City, switched from there to Guatemala and finally the Panama Canal. He could have ridden in style into Caracas or Bogotá, ridden in further style into Lima. Bandits didn't bother him, and neither did revolutions. Nobody wanted to harm a tailor except Reddick, and Reddick was riding around northwest New Jersey in a hearse with the license plates blacked out. Anything, he thought, anything would have been better than taking that stupid damned plane. Now he was bruised and cut and drenched to the skin, and he was falling and there was nothing anybody could do to stop him from smashing himself against the ground and grinding himself into a bloody pulp just like one of Old Alice's infamous cherry pies.

Not even the angels could help him now. All those angels swarming above him, smiling at him, talking to him, reaching out and touching him with their heavenly fingers stroking his cheeks and brushing the hair from his eyes, and that was all right but it would be a damn sight better if they stopped him from falling.

Good lord, they even knew his name!

Of course, he supposed angels knew everybody's name, and at least these angels didn't call him Blackie.

And he wasn't at all sure that angels really should have black hair and green eyes, or be wearing pleated white skirts and summer-thin white blouses that clung disturbingly to figures he was absolutely positive angels weren't supposed to have. The white part fit in, but not any of the rest.

Then he closed his eyes, and realized they'd been open.

He opened them again and saw Vanessa bending over him, her smile strained, her short hair gleaming in the twilight, her eyes intense with concern.

"Are you all right?"

"I'm alive?"

She nodded, the smile relaxing.

"Then I guess—" He attempted to sit up, and moaned as his dream shattered and the battering his shoulders and chest had taken exploded small bombs in his joints. Vanessa blurred, spun, came into focus, and he lay back again.

"We can't stay here."

"I know," he said, barely above a whisper. The taste of the river was still in his mouth, the taste of his fear metallic and bitter.

"Lincoln?"

"Yeah?"

"Where's here?"

"Peru, I hope."

Her lips moved, but he couldn't hear her. The early evening chill had suddenly vanished and was replaced with a heat that ran his face with perspiration, made his ears ring, made his vision suddenly pocked with swirling black gnats. His throat went dry and his lips felt as if they were going to split. He opened his mouth to ask for water; he tried to lift an arm to ask for help, sitting up so he could crawl down to the river and slake a thirst that had become suddenly unbearable, as if Uni-the-Toad had found a way to replace the inside of his mouth with a coating of filed sand.

But he could not move. Nothing worked: not his lips, not his limbs, and before he could cry out, not even his eyes.

It was comfortable in the dark, but it wasn't cool.

There were people in the dark, and they wanted to hurt him.

There was movement in the dark, bumping and swaying, rolling and falling, and several times he felt himself ready to vomit—but there was nothing in his stomach to void, in spite of the fact that he distinctly remembered chewing . . . something . . . sometime . . . and washing whatever it was down with cool water.

Vanessa, floating at his side while he drifted

through the thick rain forest, watching rainbows
of birds sweep through the shadows above him,
listening to monkeys chattering the news of his
arrival, listening to the nightscreams of jaguars
and leopards as they paced his gentle flying—like
sailing, he thought, sailing through the air less
than a foot above the ground.

Vanessa, holding his hand and forcing a cool
breeze into his lungs.

Vanessa, slowly covering his forehead with a
gratefully cool cloth that dripped heavenly cool
water down the sides of his face.

Vanessa, whose face suddenly narrowed, whose
eyes turned a flat and horrid black, whose chin
elongated and grew a cleft in which there was a
scar that formed a pallid, obscene cross. He held
his breath and tried to wish the face away, but it
wouldn't leave him, wouldn't become Vanessa again
until he said the name, and he didn't want to say
the name until Vanessa was back and he was lying
by the river, waiting to die.

"Reddick."

The face vanished.

He sat up abruptly, eyes wide as he scanned the
area around him.

"Reddick!"

A hand on his shoulder, and he whirled around,
grew dizzy with the exertion and nearly fell onto
his back. Vanessa smiled sadly at him and held
him until he steadied.

"I saw him," Linc gasped, putting a hand to his
forehead. "I saw him."

"It was a dream," she said.

"No. I saw him."

"A dream."

He wanted to argue with her, but he didn't have the strength. Instead, he took several deep breaths and looked around again. Astonished now, because the river was gone, or else the forest had decided to move closer to the banks. Then he looked up and realized he wasn't even outside. The rough boles he had seen were the walls of a tall hut with a conical roof thatched with broad leaves. When he stretched out a hand he could feel the ground around him, looked and saw he was sitting on a pallet of dried saplings mattressed with grass and leaves. There was a deep pit in the middle of the floor, and a small fire burned there, throwing his shadow on the walls, the smoke curling lazily toward a narrow hole in the roof.

"Lima's changed," he said.

Vanessa grinned her relief and sat beside him, giggling once when the pallet threatened to tip over. He noticed then she wasn't wearing the same clothes she'd had on when she leapt from the plane. Now she was in what looked like homespun cotton —shirt and slacks and high unpolished boots, a dark blue bandana tied loosely around her neck. He was dressed the same, and a surreptitious swift check showed him he was still wearing the wrist-sheath, and the dagger was still in it. There was no sense looking for the gun and the blackjack.

"You talk," he said wearily. "I'll listen."

"You can't swim."

"No kidding."

She shook her head in slow amazement. "I can't believe someone like you can't swim."

"I don't like to fly, either, and you saw what happened when I did." Then he looked closely at her. "Thanks, by the way. That's twice you've played cavalry."

"It would have been easier with the car."

She had pulled him from the river half-a-mile from where he landed, and realized at once he was too injured to travel. She also knew that as soon as Pizarro and Cortez arrived in Lima they'd waste no time avoiding the police—which she was sure they would do no matter what they had done— and find a way to mount an expedition to return to the mountains and hunt them both down. Quickly, then, she'd brought him into the forest and constructed a lean-to to protect him from the elements; anything else, and he'd have to fend for himself. Then she climbed the valley wall and discovered a small village halfway to the top of the encircling mountains. The Indians were astonished by her sudden appearance, but amenable enough to assist her when she explained what had happened—embellishing a bit by telling them they had been accused of being enemies of the state and had been thrown unarmed from the plane.

The village elder sent three men back down with her, bundled Lincoln into a makeshift stretcher, and brought him to the elder's home. He remained there for two days, unconscious and feverish, before word along the trail had it that a group of hunters from the coast were moving this way.

Vanessa didn't even have to ask.

The same three men scrounged more suitable clothes for them, packed knapsacks with provisions, and immediately started out for the interior.

They used rock-roads the Incas had built five hundred years ago and made superb time.

The hunters, according to the guide, Saca, were left far behind.

"How long ago did we leave?" he said.

"A week."

"Beautiful," he said, and promptly fell asleep.

He awoke the following morning ravenous, thirsty, and snarling at the discipline he needed to keep himself from eating and drinking too much. While he sat outside the hut—a way station built by long-forgotten travelers for those foolish enough to challenge the mountains on foot—he watched as Vanessa spoke with Saca, a tall, gangling Indian who seldom wore more than a sweat-stained pair of cut-off denims and thick sandals that gave him at least two more inches. The other two were in the hills, he was told, hunting for food.

The sun climbed, and he practiced walking, grimacing at the stiffness in his legs and arms, but gratified he no longer had to limp or groan.

No one stopped him, then, when he walked to the narrow road, crossed the worn grey blocks of stone set level with the ground, and stood on the other side. They were on the side of a mountain, a terrace choked with lush underbrush so brightly green it seemed artificial. On the opposite side of the gorge he estimated was four or five hundred feet deep, he could see more of the same, though the foliage there was covered with a fine mist that every so often broke out a brief rainbow when the light breeze shifted and the sun caught it just so.

He watched the light shift, watched the blue shade to cobalt, saw huge birds soaring far above him on the currents; they were black against the sky, but their wingspreads were impressive, and he wasn't really sure he'd like to see them in their nests.

Footsteps behind him.

He didn't turn. He slipped his hands into his pockets and waited until Vanessa joined him. Something pressed against his arm. He looked, and saw her pushing a small canvas packet at him. He raised his eyebrow, and she shrugged. He untied the leather thong binding the packet and checked inside—his gun, his papers, his blackjack, his ammunition.

"Damn," he said quietly, and tucked it under his arm.

"What, damn?"

He felt guilty, but he didn't dare say it. Twice she had saved his life, and after the first time he could only wonder what she was going to get out of it, how she was planning to steal the King when he found it. The second time, however, was different. She could have taken all his weapons, and his information, and she could have gone on alone. But she hadn't. She had struggled against formidable odds, nursed him, organized their escape, and was now proving her trust by returning all this.

"Damn," he said again.

"And I repeat: what, damn?"

He faced her, dropped the packet to the ground, and put his hands on her shoulders. She smiled. He pulled her closer. She smiled, and he leaned forward to place a tender kiss on her lips, warm lips and moist and filling him with a sudden wish that Saca and his men would get conveniently lost.

"That was nice," she whispered when they separated.

He shrugged.

"But I don't think we'd better stick around much

longer." She nodded south along the winding, precarious road, then beckoned Saca to them. The man shambled over, a machete tucked into his wide leather belt, his hair askew and his smile black-toothed.

"Where are we going?" she asked Linc.

When he hesitated, suddenly wary again, she poked his arm hard, but only partly in jest. "Linc, we wander off alone we'll end up in Brazil."

He looked at Saca, down to his boots, and nodded. "We need to find a place called Paccto Jico."

Saca's deep brown eyes widened.

"You know it?" Linc asked quickly.

The Indian shook his head just as quickly, then nodded when Linc scowled his disbelief. He spoke rapidly, in a dialect Linc couldn't follow; he had just about decided to throw up his hands in surrender when Vanessa interrupted the Indian with a few words of her own.

"I'll be damned," Linc said. "You know what he's saying?"

"Enough."

"Okay, what?"

"He says Paccto Jico is a village older than the mountains, that the people there are sons and daughters of Atahualpa, the last Incan Emperor. He says not even the Army from Lima goes there unless it absolutely has to."

"Fine," Lincoln said, "but will he take us?"

"I don't think so."

"Jesus, Vanessa, the man's wearing jeans!"

Vanessa sniffed, scratched at her arm, and spoke to Saca again, this time pointing to his thick-thewed legs.

He spoke, and Vanessa sighed. "Missionaries," she said.

"Then tell him we're on a mission from God."

"He won't believe it. He doesn't believe the missionaries, either. He just likes their clothes."

Frustrated, Lincoln slammed his hands on his hips. "Then tell him to point the goddamned way and we'll go alone. Pizarro isn't going to sit around waiting for us, you know."

At the question, Saca pointed north and dropped his arm.

"That's it?" Linc said.

"You asked him to point the way, Lincoln."

"Maybe," Linc said just short of sarcastically, "he might agree to be a little more specific."

Vanessa spoke with him again, and Saca, after plucking at his hair, dropped into a crouch and began drawing a map in the soft earth. Lincoln watched carefully as the Indian jabbed a finger at landmarks, grunting, shaking his head, finally looking up and pursing his lips.

There was a silence.

"What does he want now?"

"Money," Saca said. "I don't do this for nothing."

Lincoln would have hit him no matter what Vanessa said, but just at that moment one of Saca's men burst out of the forest waving his hands and yelling.

To Lincoln the word sounded very much like "Pizarro."

ELEVEN

"GOOD HEAVENS," Vanessa said angrily. "Just when we were getting comfortable."

It took them less than fifteen minutes to gather their belongings and erase as much of their presence as they could from the clearing. Then they moved swiftly along the ancient serpentine road, leaving the relative safety of the way station behind as they hurried deeper into the Andes. Lincoln gritted his teeth against the aching of his stiff muscles for the first few miles, wasting a great deal of energy cursing George Vilcroft and wishing he was back home with his antique Singer and his reliable Clark thread. And when that didn't conjure a simple escape from this mess, he pushed the throbbing into a distant, cushioned portion of his mind and concentrated on walking without breaking his neck.

The urgency he had felt at the initial warning faded as the hours passed. Saca's two men had no idea from the signals they'd received out of villages farther west, toward Lima, what sort of vehicles Cortez and Pizarro were using, but he knew it wouldn't be long before that transportation would have to be abandoned. The three-foot-square stone blocks had grown increasingly uneven, slippery from the clinging mist of hidden waterfalls in the gorge, overgrown here and there with thick beds of moss. Jeeps and trucks would be useless; Juan Pizarro would have to hoof it just like his namesake.

They came to a weed-choked, riverless valley and crossed it in an hour; they climbed almost to the tree line and descended again. Once, Lincoln asked if there weren't a more direct route, perhaps through the forest, and Saca took his arm and drew him off the road. They walked for less than ten feet before the Indian smiled and stepped to one side. And vanished. The underbrush was thick, the overhanging branches dipped almost to the ground. It was as if he'd been encased in a monstrous green bubble.

The point was effectively made, especially when he called out and no one bothered to answer.

He scowled, guessed at which direction the Indian had taken, and moved carefully, shuffling his feet along the forest floor until a thick, brown-green vine dangling from a branch snared his ankle. He struggled but couldn't kick it off, reached down to unwrap it with his hands, and fell on his face. The vine was still there, and he could swear it was getting tighter.

Jesus, he thought, a goddamn python!

Saca reappeared then with a broad grin on his face, sliced through the vine with one slash of the machete, and helped Linc to his feet. Linc nodded, and Saca's grin became a cautionary scowl before he took his arm and brought him back to the others.

They camped that night in a clearing barely wide enough for them to lie side by side.

On the second day they crossed a furiously whitewater river on a precarious rope bridge that swayed alarmingly with every step. Linc kept his eyes closed; Vanessa laughed and shook the vine handrail until he was ready to scream.

And there was the heat—in the forest that entunneled the roadway for miles on end it was suffocating, stifling, so humid there was no sense even beginning to mop his face, so penetrating he thought he even felt his hair baking; and in the open, on the high slopes where the trees thinned out for lack of sufficient air, it was sullen and murderous despite the cool breezes that found their way from the peaks all too infrequently.

Insects droned, and *things* swept through the trees like murderous shadows fleeing the sun; on a distant hillside he saw a herd of llamas being tended by Indians sitting on flattened rocks and staring at the sky, smoking what looked to be long-stemmed pipes; they passed through a village of less than a half dozen stone huts, but there was no one in the windows, no one on the road, though he could hear voices whispering and, once, a woman's giggling. The only sign of life was a pair of scrawny yellow dogs that barked at them furiously from the safety of a doorway, and an old dun horse that ignored them while it ate.

Saca's two men brought no more news of pursuit. Seemingly indefatigable, they were more like ghosts than humans, vanishing ahead and behind

at the start of each day, returning silently at dusk
to report what they had seen: nothing. Mountains,
trees, monkeys, parrots, a jaguar on one occasion.

Nothing.

They ate very little of the meager provisions
Saca had brought from his village; his two men
hunted well and they had plenty of fresh meat,
though Vanessa cautioned Linc the first night not
to ask what was cooking. That was when he decided that Vilcroft was going to pay through the
nose for bringing the King back.

On the fourth day they reached a narrow valley
cut through by a stream barely deep enough for
the water. The few trees were all saplings, and the
grass was low. There was an odd scent in the air,
almost. like charcoal, and Linc knelt to check the
soil. It didn't take more than a pushing aside of
the sharp-edged grass to see that it was charred. A
hell of a fire, he decided; lightning during the dry
season—if there was such a thing.

Vanessa walked beside him. They were using
tall stout staffs Saca had cut and stripped himself
when it was apparent his charges weren't exactly
used to hiking. They pulled themselves along more
than using their legs, Linc with sour grunting,
Vanessa as if she had been born and raised in the
Alps. She was tanned, and sweaty, and her hair
had long since lost what luster it had, though her
stride had lost none of its exuberant bounce. Saca
was twenty yards ahead of them, aiming for the
valley's northern wall, staring at the treeless slope
where the road vanished through a narrow gap
midway to the summit.

"Do you know," she said, "that there are people
living in these mountains who have never seen the
twentieth century?"

He thought of the village they'd passed through, and he grunted.

"Do you suppose that ... that woman is still back there?"

He shrugged.

She looked down at a clutch of multicolored feathers she'd picked up from the ground. "I think these belong to parrots or macaws or something. Do you think I could make a belt from them? Or maybe a boa—though that might be too constricting."

She laughed gaily.

Linc scowled and watched his feet hitting the ground—he didn't feel a thing.

"That was a joke, Lincoln."

"Okay."

She looked at him, frowning. "Lincoln, are you all right?"

He sniffed, and wiped a damp sleeve over his face. "My legs are killing me, but I can't feel them anymore. I'm dying for a cigarette, but the air is so thin up here I'd probably pass out at the first puff. My nose is sunburned and itching, I'd kill for a toilet, I have more permanent bug bites on my body than any ten redheads have freckles, and last night I dreamt I had found a helicopter in the middle of the road and we didn't have to walk anymore. But as soon as I climbed in, it turned into one of Unicov's damned bikes. And Unicov was driving. Other than that, though, I'm doing just fine."

They walked another hundred yards before Vanessa said, "It wasn't a dream."

He blinked. "Huh?"

She stopped and faced him. "It wasn't a dream."

Gripping the staff with both hands, he leaned on it heavily, feeling like a shepherd who didn't give a sweet damn about the state of his sheep. "What wasn't a dream?"

"The helicopter."

"But there wasn't any helicopter in the middle of the road, Vanessa. I said it was a dream. I think the altitude is getting to you. You may have noticed we're still walking."

"The helicopter flew over just after dawn. You were still asleep, as usual."

"What do you mean, as usual?"

She sighed impatience. "Saca insists we start moving every day at dawn. You, however, would rather sleep until noon."

"I, my dear, would rather sleep until next Thursday."

"You were probably just waking up," she said reasonably, "and the copter's noise got into a dream you were already having. It's not unusual."

He looked up suddenly, at the peaks and the forest and the brilliant white of cloud wisps coasting over the valley.

"It's gone," she said.

"Damn! Pizarro, I'll bet. The sonof—"

"No," she said. "Saca says it was Army. He saw it. He says they fly over now and then to check for rebels. Once in a while they rocket the hillsides for practice, or for the hell of it."

"For the hell of it?"

She shrugged. "What else can you do in Peru? Hunt wild llamas? C'mon, Lincoln, take it easy. We're almost there. I think."

They forded the shallow stream just past midday, picking up the road as it began the gentle climb toward the divided mountain ahead. Saca, though he refused to speak another word of English, told Vanessa that Paccto Jico was just on the other side. They had to be cautious, however, because the Indians living there had an instinctive distrust of anyone who wasn't born there. Linc recalled his earlier warning and so wasn't surprised; what did surprise him was the sudden change in the man's attitude. Cocky and self-assured before, now he was growing visibly nervous. His hands constantly shifted the machete from grip to grip, and every ten paces he checked over his shoulder, causing Linc to look over his and see nothing but the valley shrinking below them, the road barely discernible, the stream invisible as the grass on its banks closed slowly over it.

It was beginning to bother him. He told himself it was only his instincts fine-tuning themselves for the final push toward his goal, but the last time he'd felt this way was the afternoon five years before when Reddick sprang a trap that had, for a change, worked.

And he'd just as soon forget what had happened that night.

A huge bird glided across the valley, its shadow making the Indian jump wildly off the path.

"Condor," Linc said quietly, shading his eyes and watching the magnificent creature riding the currents it needed to move from peak to peak.

"I thought they were in California," Vanessa said, following the graceful flight openmouthed.

"A few," he said as the bird disappeared. "The rest of them don't speak English."

She scowled at him, but he didn't care; he was too tired to be serious, too out of breath to be erudite.

A dumpy brown rodent darted out of the grass and across his toe. He stamped at it, missed it, and looked to Saca, who wasn't smiling.

By evening he was jumping so much at shadows that he asked if anyone would mind if they camped here for the night and saved the cut and the village for the following morning. Saca was too relieved for comfort, and Vanessa only shook her head in obvious disillusionment.

The landscape was less barren than it had seemed from below. There were trees, but small and straggly; there was brush, but it held very little green. The ground was dark and rocky, and dozens of glacier-driven boulders loomed out of the earth as if they were trying to break free. It made the cool night air seem almost cold, and the first thing the Indian did was find a place between four man-high rocks and dig a fire pit for their dinner. It wasn't until the fire was going and they were huddled around it for warmth that they realized the others hadn't yet joined them.

One had gone hunting to replenish their food.

The other had gone ahead, to scout the cut and the valley beyond.

Just before full dark Saca silently stripped a thick branch and fashioned himself a torch, lit it from the fire, and headed back down the slope to search for his friend. He said nothing, only grunted and gestured that the fire should not be allowed to burn out before dawn. They watched until there was nothing to see but a single, bobbing flame that looked too uncomfortably like a spark ready to fade.

Linc took his shrinking knapsack and set it against the meeting of boulder and ground, used it for a pillow as he stretched his legs toward the pit. Vanessa stayed at the fire, staring at the flames.

Somewhere in the dark a jaguar screamed.

The scream echoed.

"I'd like to meet that beast face to face," he muttered as he cupped his hands behind his head. "I know a teacher who'd love to have him for a coat."

Vanessa didn't turn around. "Your girl friend?"

He smiled. "A friend."

"Like George?"

"George," he said sourly, "isn't a friend. He's someone who likes to butt into my life now and then and try to make me rich."

"You do what he tells you."

"I do what he pays me to do if I feel like taking his money to do it." He frowned. "Or something like that."

She shifted, putting her face in shimmering profile. "He must want this King very much, to put you through all this."

"It's a living."

She shifted again, and the fire was between them, putting shadows on her face he didn't much like to see. "That story you told me, it was true?"

"Which one?"

"About the cards."

"As much as any story is when it's been filtered through a few hundred years and a few greedy hands, yes."

"But . . ." She took a twig and poked at the fire. "But that one man, De Cordoba, you said he was twenty-five when he died. That means he was younger than he was when he found the cards."

"I said he *looked* twenty-five," Linc corrected.

"He obviously aged a lot better than his father-in-law."

"Do you think—"

"The cards had anything to do with it?" He laughed quietly and sat up. "Only if he used them for gambling and won. Honey, I don't even know what games they played in those days. I'll tell you this, though, I don't think those are playing cards. They're much too rich."

She shook her head. "I never saw them."

"George can be very touchy about his possessions."

"Like Clarise."

He raised an eyebrow. "You know Clarise?"

The jaguar screamed again.

And echoed.

Closer.

Vanessa scrambled around the fire and dropped down beside him, not protesting when he put a protective arm around her shoulders and patted her knee. From the crook of his elbow she looked up and smiled. He smiled back, tenderly, and was about to kiss her when the scream came a third time.

A second later he realized it wasn't the jungle cat at all.

TWELVE

LINCOLN PAID no attention to Vanessa's startled yelp when he shoved her roughly aside, spun around, and fumbled his revolver out of the knapsack. A quick check to be sure it was loaded, and he ducked behind the downslope boulder, his shoulders pressed to the stone as he sidled toward its edge, his free hand waving Vanessa to his side. She didn't move. Instead, she made for her own sack and began rummaging through it. He glared helplessly, then eased around the boulder into the open toward the road, out of the reach of the flames' twisting light.

The moon was high, the nightsky clear, but the silver-grey illumination only created more shadows than it dispelled. Linc scanned the valley, cursing softly when he could find no sign of the burning torch; he listened, but there was only the distant whispering of the trees, the brush of the light wind past his ear, and Vanessa swearing as she dumped the contents of the knapsack onto the ground.

Carefully, testing the rock-chipped ground ahead of him before each step, he moved in a low crouch across the road and into the shadows on the other side. The four boulders across the way effectively blocked most of the firelight, but their inner sides still glowed redly, and some of the light spilled out along the ground. He could see Vanessa's shadow tossing small objects from side to side.

A sound, then.

Stealthy, and soft, and moving unerringly toward him.

A hand shoved a lock of hair away from his eyes; his left palm covered the revolver while his right thumb cocked the hammer; his gaze shifted away from the valley to the terrain closer to hand.

There was a boulder directly behind him, nothing but smaller rocks and spiny shrubs covering the rest of the slope. A twig snapped softly. Something scratched against a stone. He crouched lower, hoping to find a shadow silhouetted against the star-laden sky. An insect buzzed in front of his eyes and he slapped at it angrily.

The fire vanished in abrupt stages as Vanessa scooped soil and stone over it with boots and hands.

The initial stabbings of a cramp tensed his left leg, and he rubbed his thigh as quietly as he could, as hard as he could until the pain eased; something fluttered to his nape, and he ignored the light touch of its legs as it crawled over his skin to his hair, into it, out again, and flew away; a droplet of perspiration rolled from his sideburns along his beard-mottled jaw.

The sound stopped.

Another cramp along the back of his shoulders, and he rolled them to relieve the sharp throbbing, stopping suddenly when he realized what he was doing. But it was too late. The knife in its wrist-sheath snapped out, and his fingers were too late closing around it. It clattered onto the ground, gunshot loud, and he winced as he stared helplessly at the blade catching the moonlight and turning it into winking stars. It had slid too far away for him to reach it without moving, and he bit hard on his lower lip to keep himself from swearing.

He listened, his head close to aching from the strain, and thought he heard Vanessa shifting her position across the road. He wanted to tell her to stay inside the natural protection of the boulders, but he knew she wouldn't do it. Somehow he'd managed to give her the impression he was clumsy in a crisis, and he had no doubts at all that she would try to save him again now, for a third time.

Something small and dark flew rapidly overhead. Nightbirds down in the forest called timidly to each other and fell silent.

And the noise began again, curiously muffled, until he realized with a panicked start that it was coming from the other side of the boulder behind him.

He turned slowly, wincing at every slight sound magnified by the tension that renewed the sweat on his brow and made his grip on the revolver slick and uncertain. He looked up slowly and wasn't at all surprised when he saw it looking down.

It was perched on the rock's wind-scoured, flat-tened top, half seated, its slitted green eyes meeting his gaze without blinking at all. It was large, sleek, its lips pulled back in a silent and white-fanged snarl; and in the dim moonlight he could see that it was almost totally black.

Jaguar; and it growled, softly, cocking its head as it glared into his eyes.

A noise, then—something metallic striking against stone, and he glanced once to his right, his breath cold in his lungs, as he waited for Vanessa to call out, or walk over, to expose herself to a danger she didn't know. The jaguar had heard it as well, and its great head swung ponderously around. It blinked once. It shifted silently until it was poised in a crouch that could launch it in either direction once it had made up its mind.

A stone rattled across the ground in the dark, and the big cat leaned slightly back, ready to leap, its muscles coiled, its haunches quivering with the strain of impatient release.

It growled once, low like distant thunder.

One of its fangs glinted, and its claws scratched lightly on the boulder as it readied.

Without thinking, without knowing if it would work, Linc shouted wordlessly at the top of his voice and fired the revolver twice into the air. The jaguar screamed, and Linc fired again, this time deliberately low, the bullet ricocheting off the boulder just in front of the confused and enraged cat in a startling explosion of dust and sparks.

The jaguar screamed again as Linc emptied the rest of the gun's chambers, and by the time the shots' echoes had faded the cat was gone and Linc was racing across the road just as Vanessa appeared around the side of the boulder wall. They collided with a grunt, her eyes wide as she stared at him fearfully, stared over his shoulder at the sound of the beast plunging headlong through the underbrush down into the valley. Her mouth opened to ask a question, but Linc shook his head. He was trembling, and he didn't trust his tongue to form the proper words. Instead, he led her to the square where he relit the fire as rapidly as he could.

"I couldn't find my gun," she said softly, kneeling beside him, tossing small twigs into the low and warm flames.

"It's okay."

"I couldn't find my gun."

"It's okay," he repeated, taking her arm momentarily and squeezing it.

"We could have been killed."

He shrugged and stretched his hands over the pit—they felt as if they'd been gloved in ice.

She left him for a moment, returned with larger branches that soon began to crackle as the flames took them over. "Why didn't you shoot it?"

"It's an endangered species," he said without turning his head.

A moment passed.

"You don't like to kill, do you?" she said, almost in amazement, looking at him only sideways but as if she were seeing him without a disguise.

He watched a branch slowly split in half, watched the white-hot center flare to pulsing red.

She rubbed her palms briskly over her thighs and took a deep breath she held for half a minute. "Lincoln, have ... I mean, have you ever killed anyone?"

"That's a hell of a question."

Another moment passed, this one somewhat warmer. Then he grunted and rose, checked his revolver, and replaced the spent shells. He looked down at her by the fire and gave her the smile she seemed to require. When she finally smiled back, he tucked the weapon into his belt and left again, this time sticking to the road as he made his way back down the slope. There was sufficient moonlight to keep him from falling, scarcely enough for him to see more than a few yards either side of the trail. Yet he walked as if the sun were high in the sky and he was out for a stroll, nothing more. He wasn't worried any longer about the hungry cat returning; the noise and the shot had frightened it halfway to the coast, and he knew full well he was more than a little lucky in getting away with the maneuver. What bothered him was Saca's absence, and the fact that the torch had vanished just before they'd heard the man scream.

An hour later he reached the stream, sparking reflections from the moon, moving silently along its extraordinarily shallow bed. As best he could he retraced the day's march, sweat once again sticking his clothes to his frame in spite of the cool air that made his lips taut and his skin pull tight over his shoulders. The insects returned, and the soft calls of the night birds; a trio of what he thought were bats swung out of the trees and swooped and dove through the air over the meadow, hunting and feeding, suddenly unnerving him with a memory that somewhere on this continent those things actually were vampires, actually drank blood. He hoped to hell they were in Argentina, not Peru.

He stopped and looked back. The mountain was black against the fainter black of the sky, and midway to the place where the peak split in half he saw a flickering orange glow, and it saddened him somewhat not to feel more comfortable knowing Vanessa was there, waiting.

Curious woman, he thought with a slight frown, though the thought was not without a certain admiration. He still wasn't sure she was really working for George, especially when he recalled that she hadn't bothered to waken him the moment she heard the helicopter passing over. She had let him sleep. She hadn't said anything until he'd mentioned his dream.

It was either very considerate of her, very confident she was right and it was only an army patrol not looking for anything but a way to kill time, or very unpleasant.

And there was no way at all, now, to know the correct answer.

He shook himself as if shuddering and turned his attention back to the trail. Dew was beginning to form on the low grass, staining his trousers, darkening his boots. He moved less quickly, less casually, until he reached the place where he'd last seen Saca's torch burning. He lowered himself slowly into a crouch, squinting slightly, slowing his breathing until all distractions were gone. When he was ready he stared at the ground, one hand reaching out to brush over the area as if reading its shadows, the other holding his revolver at the edge of one knee.

He rose and moved again, knelt again, listened again.

Twenty minutes later he found the torch, thrust into the stream, its head half buried in the bed.

Five minutes after that his left foot kicked a branch to one side, and he leaned over to pluck Saca's boot from a shrub.

He filled his lungs, gnawed thoughtfully on his lower lip. Despite the darkness, he was confident there was no blood in the places he had searched; and if the jaguar had gotten the Indian guide blood would have been splattered all over the valley. And unless the animal had grabbed him instantly by the throat, there also would have been more than one scream.

Lincoln, he thought, this is getting a little nasty.

Another thirty minutes, and he kicked another branch to one side, knelt to peer into the shadows, shook his head, and rose again. He'd taken two steps back toward the campsite when something triggered recognition. He turned around and looked down.

The branch lay right behind him.

And it wasn't a branch—it was Saca's right arm, the machete still gripped in the right hand's bloodless fingers.

He closed his eyes and swallowed hard, opened his eyes and looked quickly around the valley. There was no sound, only the wind, and he decided there was no need to look for the rest of the guide's body. Even without examining the limb closely he could see that it wasn't torn from its socket, as it might have been had the jaguar gotten to him. It had been severed, and it hadn't been hacked—a clean, deliberate slice just below the shoulder.

He could taste the nausea before he could feel it, and he turned around quickly. His head shook once. His hands fisted and relaxed. Then he broke into a slow trot that took him back to the slope and halfway up before his legs gave out and he was forced to walk back to camp.

Vanessa looked up fearfully when she saw him, rose and took one arm when she saw the expression on his face.

"Saca?"

He nodded and dropped as close to the fire as he could get.

"The cat?"

He shook his head.

She wanted to say something else, but instead she pulled the knapsacks close to the rim of the pit and pushed him gently down, curled up beside him, and placed his arm firmly around her waist.

"It's cold," she whispered into his chest.

"Yes."

"Can I vote for going back?"

He said nothing. He only stared at the sky, at the moon and the stars, and listened to the sound of all that dying on the wind. And though he didn't say anything to her, he had the definite feeling that visiting this village of George's was not going to be as easy as Vilcroft had led him to believe.

The worst part about it was, the feeling had nothing at all to do with Saca's death.

It was a feeling he always had, when the easy part was over.

THIRTEEN

"**I**T'S COLD," Vanessa said.

"It's your imagination," he told her flatly, trying to keep his teeth from chattering and the hastily balanced backpack from slipping off his shoulders.

"If it's my imagination, why are you shivering?"

"You have a very strong imagination, my dear. You are able to influence others by a mere flick of your whim."

"That sounds like a horoscope, and you're not funny."

"Funny is as funny does."

"And beauty is in the eye of the beholder, I know, I know. But you're still not very funny, and I'm still cold."

"Grin and bear it, Miss Lecharde, and consider the points you're scoring for dear old George."

"Dear old George," she said, "can go suck a meditation."

They walked slowly, single file, two hours from

124

camp and nearing the division of the mountain's bleak summit. He had been too busy wrestling with his nerves and suspicions the day before to notice much about their destination; once they had awakened, however, and hastily repacked their provisions and had left the safety of the four boulders, he had taken a good look at the trail ahead and didn't at all like anything he saw.

The gap was there, just as Saca had told them, but from the valley floor it had seemed wide enough to permit an army through ten abreast with ample room for flanking tanks; now he realized they had only been able to see the topmost portion of it, the split of the ragged upright Y, which was indeed rather broad. The base was another matter entirely, an opening barely sufficient to admit them side by side.

It began as an ominous jumble of rocks and boulders overgrown with tenacious brown shrubs and bilious green moss several inches thick. Soon enough, however, it blended into the sides of the gap, closing in on them rapidly, rising several hundred feet above them without the grace of a single handhold or anything remotely resembling even the shadow of a ledge. The overcast sky shrank to a narrow band of grey; the wind funneled at them from the valley beyond, snapping at their faces and forcing them to shout whenever communication was needed; and more than once Linc's curiosity was taken by the gap's glass-smooth walls. It didn't seem natural to him, and as they walked on, climbing now over falls of small rocks and sundered boulders, he decided that either a long-dead river had cut through the peak as the mountains were born in volcanic eruption, or it had been deliberately and painstakingly created by the ancestors of those who lived on the other side—to limit an invader's choices. Go forward, or turn back. He did not want to think about the consequences of the former.

Vanessa looked up. "Y'know, if I were these people and I did not want company, I'd have a few men stationed up there," and she pointed toward the top of the walls, where they began to slant sharply back out of sight. "A couple of handfuls of rocks and they could bury an army down here without even breathing hard."

"Thanks," he said. "Who's your hero, George Patton?"

"Incredible."

"Yep."

He grunted his way over a spill of stone, slipping once and skinning his palms until he grimaced and cursed. If it hadn't been for that goddamned Pizarro and Cortez, he'd've been able to hire a private plane to take him here, not hike like a mountain goat burdened with arthritis. And the sour thought of the plane reminded him of the helicopter—and the fact that they hadn't seen it on its way back to its base.

He heard thunder.

"Y'know, Lincoln, I'll bet it's a couple of thousand feet or more all the way to the top," Vanessa said as she vaulted a rotted log, landed lightly on the other side, and placed her hands on her hips.

He looked up automatically, but the twin summits were too far left and right for him to see anything but the darkening clouds.

"And I think I know why there aren't any bones around here."

He paused and stared at her. "Huh?"

"Bones. You know, Linc—from the battles and things. There aren't any bones or weapons or any artifacts at all left that I've been able to see."

"Yes, I've noticed that myself. The carrion hunters are remarkably thorough."

She ignored the sarcasm. "It's the water, I think, that does it."

He heard the thunder again.

"Water?"

"Sure. It rains up top like crazy, you see, eventually comes down the slopes and turns this into one heck of a perfect sluice. Very narrow, very fast-moving—waterfalls all the way to the end. I wouldn't be surprised if a lot of Spaniards drowned standing up here."

He nodded, pushed past her, and moved on. The way ahead was blind, a gentle curve to the right preventing him from seeing the end and the rest. He thought of the envelope Vilcroft had given him, and the money inside, and he decided to double it as soon as he got back.

"Lincoln, I think we ought to move a little faster, if you don't mind."

"Oh, really? Why?"

"I heard thunder."

"So? So did I."

"Well, I don't know about New Jersey," she said in barely contained exasperation, "but where I come from, thunder generally means we're going to have rain." Then her hands moved in a grim pantomime of water spilling down the walls, trapping them, lifting them, and carrying them back the way they had come. "If we don't drown we'll be bashed," she concluded with a sharp nod and a smile that was proud of her deduction.

"I think," he said then, "I know why George likes you."

Before she could respond, he adjusted his backpack with an awkward snap of his hands and quickened his pace, taking more chances on turning an ankle or wrenching a knee, growing almost reckless when he reached the bend fifteen minutes later and scrambled over a loose rockfall more than seven feet high. Once on the other side, he waited for Vanessa, one eye watching her faltering progress down the rubble, the other on the clouds that had now turned morning almost to twilight.

"I think," she said when she fell gasping and grinning into his arms, "we're almost there."

"Good for you."

She frowned. "Are you in a bad mood, Lincoln?"

He smiled grimly and hurried away, his attention full on the widening gap directly ahead. What he needed now was a rest; the air was too thin and his muscles, despite their workout over the past grueling week, were protesting the pace he had set for himself. Nevertheless, he couldn't slacken; he needed to know what he was getting into and he wasn't going to be able to find out simply by looking ahead—whatever lay at the end of the gap was effectively hidden by a pale cloud of mist drifting out of the grey. It began to settle over him, foglike tendrils of spidery fingers curling around his neck, over his face, making him shiver until he wanted to break into a run. He compromised with slow trotting, ignoring Vanessa's protests when the light strengthened somewhat as the walls finally slipped aside.

Five minutes later he was in the open, his haste making him slip on loose gravel and sprawl cursing to his hands and knees. Vanessa came up behind him just as a stiff gust of wind blew the mist away.

"Jesus," he whispered, his eyes wide, his heart racing.

"Good heavens," she said, grabbing the straps of his pack and yanking him back toward her.

He had landed barely an inch away from the crumbling edge of a cliff that plummeted without relief more than five hundred feet straight down to the valley floor. The ledge they huddled on extended less than five yards left and right; the walls behind were sheer, and slick with slow-running water.

And below them, Paccto Jico.

As Linc stumbled to his feet and refused to think what would have happened if he hadn't tripped, he couldn't help feeling a slight pang of disappointment. He supposed he had been expecting some ancient Peruvian version of Ronald Colman's Shangri-la—a civilization vast and magnificent, grandiose and inspiring a gasp of reverent awe. A lost tribe of Incas, and their city of gold and diamonds. He knew it was fantasy, yet he had hoped it just the same.

What he saw was a treeless plain hemmed in by mountains much the same as this, and in its center a collection of what seemed to be thatched and circular wooden huts. Two or three dozen, he estimated, arranged in concentric circles around a plinth whose height he couldn't begin to guess. Running from the village toward the cliffs was a huge plaza of paving stones glinting in the dim light from embedded mica; and in the center of that was a massive round stone. He could see no temple, no ziggurat, no pyramid; neither could he see signs of any life. There were no people in the odd streets, no animals in the squared fields on the far side of the valley, no birds in the air above him.

Except for the wind there was no sound at all.

Vanessa sat beside him, hugging her knees to her chest and grinning as she looked over her shoulder. "Imagine," she said, rocking on her buttocks in excitement. "Raiders come barreling through the gap, following the road, and bam!, right over the edge." Before Linc could stop her she crawled to the lip and looked down. "Bet there are a lot of bones and old weapons down there." She looked back at him and smiled. "Beautiful."

"Oh, sure."

"But, Linc," she said, returning to his side, "you really do have to admire these people. It's a perfect place to defend. My heavens, five or six strong men could hold off the world here."

"Yes," he agreed reluctantly, "I suppose they could."

"Boy, if the rain didn't get them, and the rocks didn't get them, unless they knew how to fly . . ." She laughed and clapped her hands. "Beautiful, Lincoln; it's beautiful."

"Sure."

She frowned. "Now what's the matter?"

"Oh, nothing." And he pointed to the village. "But that's down there, in case you hadn't noticed, and we're up here and we don't know how to get down there, and I'm wondering how the hell anyone gets down there short of flying. Which we can't do."

"But that's impossible," she said. "Somebody had to have been down there to find the King, had to get back out for George to learn about it, right?"

"Right. And he probably had a helicopter, or a small plane, or Peter Pan."

The wind quickened, and she moved closer to him. "Lincoln, I'm cold."

He nodded.

"Lincoln, we have to get down there."

"Yes, we do."

She said nothing more, only stared at him until he groaned and stood, forcing himself to look away from the seductive drop as he kept his back to the wall and moved along the ledge to the left. When he reached the end he saw a small gap before the mountain extended past it; the gap was six feet wide and dropped straight to the valley floor. The wind nearly pitched him over, and he grabbed frantically for a handhold, found none, and scrambled back to Vanessa on his hands and knees, not giving a damn how foolish he looked. The wind died, and he moved to the right, seeing a gap just like the other. He was about to turn around when he noticed that here, unlike the other, the edge of the drop was worn smooth. There was very little water—what slipped down the walls quickly ran across the ledge and dropped over the cliff. He shuffled closer, not daring to lift his feet and risk a slip. At the second gap, with his palms pressed hard against the wall, his fingers feeling encased with ice as the frigid water trickled over them, he looked down.

And he smiled.

"You'll be happy to know," he said without turning his head, "that we don't have to fly."

The steps were laboriously carved into the cliff's face, a series of switchbacks completely hidden from eyes looking down from above. They were wide, broad, and, once into the odd chimney, fairly simple to negotiate. The only thing that bothered him was the open space on one side. He decidedly did not appreciate feeling so vulnerable, and his admiration for the isolated valley's inhabitants increased when a gust of wind howled through the staircase, and he dropped immediately to the step to avoid being sucked into the air. He suspected that any warrior who made it to the bottom alive was given a hero's welcome, simply for surviving.

He climbed most of the way with his eyes half closed, his face toward the inner wall.

He would not look around whenever Vanessa moved boldly to the edge and exclaimed at the view.

"How many steps are there, Linc?"

"I don't know, I'm not counting."

"Guess."

"Eleventy umptythousand."

"What?"

"You heard me."

"Well, how many is that, for heaven's sake?"

"I don't know, I got it from Brer Rabbit."

"Do we have much farther to go?"

"You're the one who's looking, you tell me."

"My legs are killing me."

"Mine died."

"God, it'll be years before I'll be able to wear heels again."

"It's the price you have to pay, m'love. Stalking a wild playing card isn't all fun and games, you know."

"I think I know what happened to Saca's man."

He imagined it vividly without her description; she gave it to him anyway, from the moment he reached the edge of the cliff .to the moment he reached the bottom.

"Just like the old days," she said reverently.

"Yes. The good old days."

The rock was cold, his legs were trembling, and though he thought he felt a definite warming to the air, he couldn't help wishing he'd stolen Pizarro's jacket.

"Lincoln, you can open your eyes now."

"No, thank you."

"Lincoln, please."

"I do not give a sweet damn how beautiful this place is. I do not care if a condor has decided to give us a lift. I—"

"Lincoln, goddamnit!, open your eyes!"

He did.

They were there.

FOURTEEN

THE GRASS was high and thick on both sides of the worn stone path that led from the steps to the open plaza; low brush littered the ground at their bases with brightly colored petals of flowers fallen from the branches; and the only sound Linc could hear was the rap of their bootheels. When he looked up the sky was unnaturally clear, strikingly blue, and he frowned just a moment when he remembered the clouds of distant thunder he'd noticed in the gap.

The silence was unnerving.

He wanted to whistle, wanted to hum, wished Vanessa would say something to shatter the peace, but she too seemed affected by the expanse that swept around them to the encircling slopes. There was a temptation to veer off the path and search for Saca's man, but he stifled it instantly—he had no desire to examine dead bodies just now.

The silence grew.

He wondered how George had known about this place, and about the old man he was supposed to see.

And when his eyes began to blur from staring at the plain too long, hunting for possible ambush, looking for any sign at all of human habitation other than the huts, he focused on the plaza.

"Incredible," he whispered.

"I don't believe it," she said.

It was one hundred yards square, the paving stones flush with the ground, multicolored and worn even, almost slippery. There were no remnants of seating arrangements, altars, or any other device that might have existed for comfort of populace or leader; there was only the sphere which, now that he approached it, was not quite perfectly round but, rather, flattened top and bottom and covered with faded designs.

Twenty feet tall at the center.

A circumference more than twice that.

With part of his attention on the back of the low huts on the plaza's far side, he walked up to the sphere and stopped. A moment later he nodded. Then he shrugged off his backpack and wiped a forearm over his face.

The designs he found there were all of a color, a dark shade not touched by god only knew how many centuries of sun; they were concentrated around the circumference, on a flattened band that extended three inches out from the stone's surface. He circled the monument once, nodding to himself in admiration, grunting, once in a while putting out a finger to touch the cold stone and pull back as if burned. When he was finished, he looked to the ground and saw shallow indentations ground into the paving stones, arranged around the monument one to a side. The bowllike depressions were of varying sizes and untouched by the dry weeds that struggled upward throughout the plaza, and when he knelt to examine one more closely he saw the dark rust stains streaked and running along the sides.

"Human or animal," Vanessa said quietly.

"What?"

"The blood," she said, pointing at a bowl.

"I don't know. I don't think I want to."

She had remained at a distance while he made his first inspection, now made an intense one of her own while he stared at the village. The huts were not thatched, as he'd thought from the cliff; the roofs were made of grooved dark stone that looked like thick slate. The walls were smoothed over by rock-hard dun mud, and not one had a window that overlooked the plaza.

"Those pictographs," she said, joining him again.

"Yep."

"Stags, Abbé, Hounds—they're the same as George's cards."

"Yep."

"The Satan's Eyes are missing, though."

"I noticed that."

"I wonder if it means anything."

"I would guess that this could be the village where they were first made. Or whoever made them stole these designs."

"You think?"

He shrugged.

She walked to the sphere again, brushed a finger over a stylized and elegant woman, turned and grinned. "Sure beats learning how to spell, doesn't it?"

"What?"

"I was a champion speller, you know. When I was a little girl I was in the national championships in Washington. My uncle came all the way over from France to see me."

He waited, hoping there was a point to all this.

A breeze touched his neck like a hand dipped in ice water.

"I came in thirty-first." She looked at the woman again. "I couldn't spell astrophysiological without giggling."

"Vanessa—" And he stopped, realizing she was blathering because she was nervous.

"I swear to you, Lincoln," she said, wiping her hands hard on her hips, "I haven't spelled a word wrong since. If I did, I'd be lying, you know what I mean?"

"Vanessa, let's go."

She sniffed. "It's getting cold."

He nodded, retrieved his backpack, and started toward the village. She hurried to keep up with him, though she said nothing, only keeping as close to him as she could without tripping over his feet.

They passed the first row of buildings quickly, the second more slowly. The doors and windows faced those of the hut ahead, and all were boarded up. Weeds grew at the bases, the light wind blew dustdevils and dead grass along the hard-packed ground. Large black birds perched on the roofpeaks and watched them, harsh calls soft in their throats. A wooden door creaked, a door slammed back and forth by a wind trapped inside.

Behind him, Linc could feel the presence of the sphere.

Vanessa pressed closer, and they walked into the square.

It was deserted, but when Linc checked the fronts of the huts facing the village center he knew they weren't alone. Here the windows weren't sealed and the doors were unsplintered. Low wooden benches were set near each threshold, and pottery of varying sizes and shapes was scattered around the bare earth.

He saved the obelisk for last.

It was not as tall as he'd estimated from the cliff ledge, less than fifteen feet and seemingly made of a single stone. It was grey, and in the side facing the gap was carved a thronelike seat in extended relief, on the back of which was a four-foot representation of the King of Satan's Eyes.

Well, well, he thought, gnawing on his lower lip and checking the huts again before returning to the stone spire.

The figure was that of a man facing outward, his scaled arms extended and clutching bolts of blood-red lightning in his massive fists; his narrow chest and muscular legs were bare, his waist girdled by a faded green and brown python that wove around him three times, vanished in back, and whose head reappeared between his thighs to raise up and over the head of whoever sat on the throne. The triple-forked tongue was black and tipped with red. The spiked tail looped over the figure's left shoulder.

The face could not be seen. It was hidden by a tall demon's mask sprouting fiery feathers from its pointed chin to pointed top, the mouth in a fierce grimace, the teeth like daggers.

But its eyes stopped Linc from looking away— they were oversized and staring, and even time hadn't been able to fade the dark and evil shade of a green that made him nervous. He had a feeling that if he looked in them too long he would see a reflection he'd just as soon not know.

There were three steps leading up to the throne, and after a moment's hesitation he climbed them slowly, turned at the top, and sat. He wasn't surprised—from this point he looked straight down one of the village streets to the sphere in the plaza.

Vanessa stood in front of him and looked up, grinning. "Very impressive."

"Whatever went on out there," he said, pointing, "the head man could see from here." Then he turned around, and looked directly into the python's lunging face. He stood quickly and stepped to one side.

"Nerves of steel," she said.

"Do you want to try it?"

"I'd rather find the old man and get out of here."

"I think you've finally—"

Then his right hand dropped instantly into his jacket pocket when the door of the hut he was facing opened slowly, and without a sound.

The man who shuffled into the square was old. His face was as creviced as the ancient cliffs overlooking his village, his drawn-tight skin a deep earthen brown, his hair long and dead white. He wore an elaborately designed serape over tattered trousers and a stained grey shirt, and on his feet were low hide boots bound with leather thongs. When he moved, a necklace of polished stones and bones rattled in a pattern that seemed almost musical.

Linc moved back down the steps cautiously, glad to leave the throne and the hypnotic serpent.

Vanessa joined him when he reached the ground, watching as the old man approached them in a sideways, crablike gait, his dark brown eyes hard on her face. He stopped only a few feet away and straightened himself as best he could. When he spoke, his voice was brittle and harsh, and Linc couldn't understand a single word he said.

"Oh dear," Vanessa whispered.

The Indian tilted his head and waited for an answer. When he received none, he spoke again, just as unintelligibly.

"Great. Just great." He looked to Vanessa. "You know what he said?"

She shook her head. "No, but he's awfully quaint, don't you think?"

He barely resisted the impulse to throttle her, instead walked up to the old man with the friendliest smile he could muster and held out his hand in greeting. The Indian stared at him, stared at the hand, and spat dryly into the dust, precisely between Lincoln's boots. Then he reached awkwardly under the serape, fumbled a bit, glared at the two of them as if daring them to move, and pulled out a small leather box.

It appeared to be as old as the man who carried it, fraying at the edges, held together by tarnished bands of brass studded with rusted iron. There was no lock that Linc could see; it was tied closed by hand-spun roping as thick as his thumb.

"Blackthorne?" he demanded, jabbing a crooked finger angrily at Lincoln's nose.

"Yes," he said, abruptly weak with relief.

"Blackthorne," the Indian repeated, his tone demanding yet another confirmation.

"Of course it's me," he said, "and that, I believe, is exactly what I've come for."

When he reached for the box, however, the old man scowled in disgust, yanked his hand back, and shook his head vigorously. "Blackthorne!" he said again, and jerked a thumb over his shoulder.

"He wants you to go in," said Vanessa.

"I don't think so." He smiled at the Indian and pointed to his chest. "Blackthorne," he said. He linked his thumbs and made birds' wings of his fingers, flapped them and made a swooping motion toward the sky. "Plane," he said. "George Vilcroft send me to you." He pointed to the gap. "We climb montaña, fight jaguar and . . . and . . . Jesus, this is stupid!" He thumped his chest, hard. "Blackthorne!"

"Jane," Vanessa muttered.

The old man shook his head again, vehemently. "Blackthorne there!" he insisted, and once again pointed to the hut.

"What are you, thick?"

"No, not really," a voice said from the darkened building.

"Oh hell," Vanessa said.

The old man whirled around, clutching the box to his chest as Anton Reddick strode into the square.

FIFTEEN

Linc's hand grabbed for the revolver in his pocket, but he stopped just shy of pulling it out when he heard Vanessa warn him with a sharp hiss. Reddick held his hands loosely at his sides, and they were empty; nor could Linc discern any bulges in the man's sweat-stained shirt or dust-covered trousers. He wore a large-brimmed hat that shaded his face, but the cross-shaped scar on his chin was lividly white. His smile was feral.

"Nice to see you, Lincoln," Reddick said flatly.

"Charmed," Linc said with as much bile as he could muster.

"Miss Lecharde, how are you?"

"Not too bad," she said brightly, "all things considered. I suppose this poor old man thinks you're Lincoln, right?"

Reddick's smile faded by degrees. "I wish it were that easy. It's not that I haven't tried, but he doesn't believe me, I'm afraid."

142

"Alas," Linc said.

"Why haven't you killed him, then?" Vanessa demanded bluntly.

Reddick swept a hand toward the old man's hut. "He stays in there all day, all night. If I didn't know better, I'd swear he had a television in there."

"Since when has a man's home stopped you before?" Linc said.

But further comment was stifled with a sigh when Krawn and Cashim, dressed in matching tailored bush outfits, came around the corner of the building. They too were unarmed, and he couldn't help feeling more than a little puzzled. This definitely wasn't like Reddick at all. My god, the houses were still standing and the men were still walking.

Cashim's bloodshot eyes widened when he saw him, and Krawn's massive hands bunched into fists. He growled but said nothing when Reddick turned with a weary shrug and gestured sharply at him to be silent.

"Reddick, I still want to know—"

He stopped, then, as the old man turned and shuffled toward the obelisk throne, still clutching the leather box in his arms. He climbed the low stairs laboriously, turned, and took his seat. The python was centered perfectly over the top of his head, and his hands on the armrests gripped the ends without strain.

A rustling, then, and the sound of feet on stone.

Reddick cursed, and Cashim whimpered.

Linc turned slowly in a tight circle as the roof-tops gave up their black bird occupants for Indian descendants of the Incas—nearly one hundred men dressed as the old man was, some wearing flapped

leather caps, a few in llama-hide vests, each wearing a large pouch at the waist and carrying a sling.
There were no guns, but Linc knew instinctively
none were needed—these men, at this distance,
could put a sharp-edged stone through a man's
skull with less effort than it takes to breathe.

Footsteps brought his attention back to the
square.

Reddick stood beside him, a full head taller, his
lean shadow rippling toward the old man's feet.
"It seems," he said out of the corner of his mouth,
"that our friend here has been unable to decide
which of us is which."

"I'll show him my driver's license."

Reddick grinned unpleasantly. "You don't change,
do you, Blackthorne."

"Bravado in the face of adversity is my motto."

"You should be dead."

"So should you."

"One of us will be come sunset."

The old man sneezed, and Vanessa jumped.

"You will explain that, won't you, Anton?"

Reddick snarled. "I must ask you again not to
call me that, Blackthorne. You know how I feel
about that."

Linc shrugged. "Whatever you say."

Reddick glared at him, and Krawn shifted impatiently, still growling. Cashim whimpered once and
quieted.

"He has decided," Reddick said with a nod
toward the throne, "to let us choose which will carry
the coveted King back to civilization."

Linc's mouth opened, closed, opened again to
emit a soft grunt. Then his eyes widened. "Oh, my
god," he said, "you've got to be kidding."

"What?" Vanessa asked fearfully.

"It's hardly fair, you know," he said. "Three against one."

"Oh no, my friend. One on one. You and I. Together again."

"Good lord, this is . . . it's . . . damn, it's medieval!"

"What," Vanessa said patiently, "is medieval?"

"Trial by combat," Lincoln answered without turning around.

"What?" She hurried to his side and grabbed his arm tightly. "What?"

Reddick managed an almost sympathetic smile. "I understand your astonishment, Miss Lecharde. It rather approaches my own feelings in this matter. However, you will note that this old fool has the advantage. Quite a considerable one, in fact, and I'm not going to jeopardize my intentions by testing him."

"Hell," Linc said with a scowl toward the old man, "we'll just refuse, okay?"

"I believe," said Reddick, "he's already thought of that."

Before Linc could move, four of the villagers were behind him, grabbing Vanessa roughly and dragging her protesting to the obelisk. There they produced a stout vine and tied her to the stone at the old man's side. As Linc lunged to stop them, the old man reached with a palsied hand into his serape and pulled out a machete fully three feet long. Without looking around, he lifted it—the point came perfectly to the underside of Vanessa's chin. He sneezed.

"I will fight because I want to kill you," Reddick said with maddening calm. "You will fight because you don't want to know what will happen to Miss Lecharde if you fail."

"Son," Lincoln said, "of a bitch."

They were escorted back to the plaza, the villagers leaping catlike to the ground as Reddick and Lincoln passed along the narrow street. There were no women visible, nor children, yet he suspected they were nearby, perhaps hiding in the fields until this matter was decided.

At the monument he was ordered to strip off his jacket and belt and was led to a vine-tied wooden ladder propped against the stone. He looked toward Vanessa and waved jauntily, looked at the men surrounding him, and grinned. Then he climbed quickly to the flat surface on top; Reddick was already there.

" 'Tis a far, far better thing that you do, Blackie," the cadaverous man said.

Linc put his hands on his hips and examined the fighting area. The leveled portion of the stone was only three feet wide, the monument itself sloping sharply downward to its extended stone girdle. A fall wouldn't kill him, but it would scrape him all to hell, and landing on the plaza stones would probably break an arm or an ankle, if he were lucky. The villagers stood on three sides, leaving the way to the obelisk clear. None were looking at him; all were watching the old man in the distance.

It occurred to him then that not one of them had uttered a sound since they'd appeared.

It also occurred to him that everyone, including Vanessa, was going through an awful lot of trouble for a playing card. Not for the first time did he suspect strongly that Meditating George hadn't told him everything; as usual.

"When do we start?" he asked.

"Patience, Mr. Blackthorne," Reddick said as he stripped off his shirt and coiled it into a tightly rolled garrote. "Patience."

Linc was about to comment on the starred patterns of scars across the man's chest when he saw again the bowls in the plaza. And suddenly, with a chill that made him shudder in spite of himself, he knew what they were for: there was one at the head of the monument, one on either side, an elongated depression behind him—the one on his left faced the Queen of Stags, the one on the right, the Queen of Hounds, and the last and largest, the Queen of Abbé.

Their configuration left him no room for doubt—when the battle was over, the arms and hands of the loser would be placed in the flanking bowls, the torso at the back . . . and the head in front—for the King of Satan's Eyes.

"Yes," Reddick said with a solemn nod. "I know."

"A bitch."

"It is indeed."

The wind came up.

Linc sniffed and rubbed his palms against his legs.

Reddick rewound his cloth garrote.

"I suppose you came in that helicopter we heard."

Reddick shook his head. "Would that I had, Blackthorne, but I was not able to afford such luxury. I drove."

Lincoln blinked. "You what?"

Reddick nodded to the south. "There's quite a good road just over that hill, you know. Peru is not precisely the backwater people seem to think. A little rough, perhaps, and not precisely my idea of cosmopolitan heaven, but nevertheless it does have roads into the interior."

"And . . . you drove."

"Oh yes. My goodness, Lincoln, did you think we would walk?"

Linc smiled painfully. "Of course not."

A murmuring distracted him, and he turned his attention to the crowd below. They were nudging each other, whispering, and when he looked into the village he saw the old man lifting a brilliant red plume.

"Uh-oh," he muttered.

The plume was lowered with a snap, and the villagers broke into a roar.

"Onward," Reddick said, and began slowly to advance.

There was no room to circle; Linc had thought he might be able to take advantage of the monument's slope to dart around the man, but one testing showed him what the gleaming was—someone had applied a substance to the stone that nearly made him lose his balance.

The flat surface, then, was the only arena.

The Indian crowd began shouting, their words unintelligible but their tone clearly impatient.

Reddick dropped into a slight crouch, grinning from under his hat all the while, a low noise in his throat that reminded Linc too much of the jaguar waiting to choose its victim. He curled his hands into loose fists and waited, content to let the man come to him. Suddenly, with a start that halted Reddick instantly, he grinned and straightened.

He had forgotten the knife he wore on his wrist.

With a short delighted laugh he flexed his shoulder and watched as the knife shot from its place, past his hand, and into the air. It landed between the feet of an astonished Indian, who jumped back as if stung, colliding with several others.

Palmer, he thought, is going to hear about this.

"Cheating is against the rules, Mr. Blackthorne," Reddick said without a flinch. Then he closed the gap between them swiftly, his arms cocked to snap the garrote over Linc's head, his hands crossed to close the vise. Linc took one step back, then another just as quickly forward, his left hand whipping out to slam against Reddick's forehead. The man gunted and staggered backward. Linc followed with a right to his cheek, a left to the side of his neck, missed with another swing that sliced the air where Reddick's jaw would have been if he hadn't dropped suddenly to his knees.

There was blood on his face, thin lines that snaked from the skin break on his brow.

Linc blew on his knuckles to ease the stinging.

Reddick released one end of the garrote and lashed out with it as if it were a whip, catching Linc on the throat. He gasped and spun around, swallowing, gagging, turning just in time to absorb a left hand on his upraised forearm. The makeshift whip lashed out again, flicking his ear and making him yelp, catching him just above his right eye and drawing blood with a gouge that had him bewildered. He wiped his face and missed an attempt to grab the shirt, missed a second, missed a third when Reddick aimed for his groin.

He thought he heard a faint rumbling in the distance.

The Indians shrieked.

Linc stole a second to look at them and nearly cried out when he saw Saca—alive and unharmed—standing at the back, his arms folded across his chest. He was laughing.

The shirt-whip caught the side of his neck, and he grabbed it, and saw the iron studs embedded in the stiff cloth. Reddick punched at him wildly, on the chest, the shoulder, twice on the cheek, but his blows were less than effective because Linc had yanked the shirt each time, throwing the man off balance.

Then he planted a fist square on Reddick's mouth and blinked when his own face was splattered with blood. Reddick groaned and went down on one knee. Linc yanked the shirt again, and Reddick whirled, snaking out a leg that thudded against his shin. He staggered and nearly lost his grip, quickly wound his end around his wrist as Reddick had done, and pulled the man to his feet.

They were less than two feet apart.

The rumbling grew louder, and a few of the Indians looked nervously over their shoulders.

"Two gladiators, Mr. Blackthorne?" Reddick said, panting and smiling.

"Thumbs down, Anton," he said, and kicked him in the groin.

Reddick screamed and fell, and slid off the platform. Only a sudden grab with his right hand saved him from slipping into the hands of the mob.

Linc, who had dropped his end of the shirt, stood over him, ready to grind his heel into the man's arm.

The Indians bellowed.

Reddick, blood and sweat mingling obscenely

on his face, looked up pleadingly. "They'll stone me to death," he gasped in a high-pitched voice as Lincoln lifted his foot.

"I think so," he answered.

"They'll do your job for you."

He paused, knowing what the man was trying to do, knowing too he wouldn't let it happen. That night, in Scotland, was not something he would give to these people.

"Are we about to make a temporary truce?"

Reddick, struggling to keep his grip on the platform's edge, reddened. "I'll kill you."

"Good," Linc said. "So long as I know."

He took the man's wrist and pulled him unceremoniously back to the top, waited until he was struggling to his knees before planting a boot in his side. Reddick smiled as he rolled over quickly and staggered to his feet.

"You had me worried," he said, and dropped immediately into a martial arts stance that Linc watched with caution. He'd been faced with this sort of fighting before, though usually from those who took aikido or karate for defense, and who lost their heads the first time they had to actually use it against a real human being in a real fighting situation.

Reddick, however, was not in class, nor, Linc suspected, did he ever use what he knew in pure self-defense.

"Good night," Reddick said, and his foot lashed out.

Linc took the blow on his shoulder and dropped to one knee, took another on his thigh and rolled onto his back. There was no pain—the first blow had stunned him into insensibility, but there was a dizziness that blurred his vision, that had him seeing double for too many precious seconds. He dodged a third strike and kicked out on his own, his heel slamming against Reddick's shin and driving him back.

Before he could regain his feet, however, Reddick was back with a boxer's blow to the side of his head, another to his chest as he fell onto his back.

The sky was blue above him, and the rumbling was so loud now he knew it wasn't thunder—but Reddick's face was dark. And he was still wearing his hat.

"Good night," he said, and Lincoln couldn't move.

SIXTEEN

THE BLOW never landed.

The rumbling bellowed into the full-throated guttural roar of a poorly muffled, racing engine, and Reddick spun around with an explosive curse on his lips, an expression of shocked disbelief and incredulous betrayal narrowing his eyes and baring his teeth. Linc could hear the Indians yelping now in angered surprise, and he wondered if the Peruvian Army had come to the rescue. He shook his head to clear it and struggled to sit up, gasping at the pain in his chest and abdomen, kneeling now and grunting, his eyes blinking rapidly as he saw Reddick snarling, his hands raised in helpless frustration.

Another grunt, and he was on his feet, swaying, taking in great gulps of air, while he watched . . . and grinned.

Out of the fields and onto the plaza roared a huge black motorcycle only barely slowed by a bullet-shaped sidecar that spewed to the right as the vehicle sped through the mob. The Indians leapt out of the way clumsily, spilling over each other, yelling contradictory instructions, while Saca tried frantically to get them back into some semblance of order.

Basil Unicov looked up at the monument and waved at Linc.

"You *bastard!*" Reddick screamed, searching wildly for a way to get safely to the ground.

Linc refused to give him a chance: he took one step and landed a stiff right hand on the side of the man's head. Reddick gasped and slumped slowly to his knees. Linc placed his foot on the man's side and pushed. Hard. Reddick realized too late what had happened; arms flailing, he toppled off the platform and slid without slowing down the monument's curve and out of sight over the edge.

Unicov circled the sphere once, twice, beckoning impatiently, until Linc took a deep breath, sat, and pushed himself off.

Had the timing been slightly off, he would have landed in front of the cycle, or in the arms of the enraged villagers. As it was, Unicov whirled his vehicle around expertly, just in time to catch him neatly in the sidecar. There was no time for either a look or a word—Unicov changed gears with a roar and charged straight for the village. A heavy stone slammed against the rear fender, another against the sidecar. Linc ducked away from a missile that just barely missed his skull, suddenly reached out without thinking, and plucked up his knife still protruding from the ground.

Saca anticipated them.

He was standing at the first house when they roared by into the narrow street. He leapt and landed grappling on Linc's back. The struggle was vicious, the Indian's weight pushing Linc half out of the car, his head close to the front wheel's blurred spokes. Punches were thrown without aiming, and twice Saca attempted to bite off his ear. The noise was deafening, and Linc only barely managed to get a grip on the man's throat and squeeze. Pushing. Staring into the wide, manic stare, absorbing the hysterical blows to his chest and shoulders until, with a twist and a snarl, he forced his knee between them and snapped out his leg. Saca screamed as he was launched out of the car, screamed again just before he was slammed against the wall of the last house and slid lifelessly to the ground.

The old man was standing by his throne, the machete waving impotently in front of him.

Vanessa was shouting as she struggled with her bonds.

Unicov, with a fearful glance over his shoulder, slowed and bumped the sidecar onto the obelisk steps, close enough for Linc to reach out with his knife hand and slice through the vine pinning the woman to the carved stone. A spin, a sharp turn that nearly threw him clear, and when they passed her again he grabbed her hand and pulled her into his lap.

Unicov cursed when a sharp stone landed in the middle of his back, ducked as the Indians, who had retaken their positions atop the houses, pelted them with deadly, sharpened rocks. Linc felt the back of his neck tear, his shoulders erupt with fire, saw blood on Vanessa's chest and didn't know whose it was.

Then the cyclist straightened the careening vehicle and drove straight out of the village, into the fields.

Vanessa was in Linc's lap, her lips pressed close to his ear. "This is the guy who tried to blow us up in New Jersey!" she shouted.

He nodded.

"Is he still trying to kill us?"

Linc couldn't do anything but nod. The rushing wind worked to steal the breath from the lungs, and the jouncing, sometimes flying motorcycle threatened to jar loose every bone in his body. Unicov was not trying to find the smoothest path through the green toward the far side of the valley; he was driving straight on, hunched over the handlebars as if the Indians were still in range to use their deadly slings. At one point Linc shouted a question and Unicov pointed at the heavily forested slope, grinning and nodding.

The fields were empty, no animals, no workers.

Paccto Jico receded swiftly behind them.

The sun finally reached the rim of peaks and began to slip between them, turning the sky a deep rose and indigo.

Just before the land began to climb, Unicov swerved onto a weed-grown, paving-stone road that took them into the trees. He slowed, finally, and the engine's roar subsided.

"Well, Lincoln," he said expansively.

Linc blew out a held breath.

Vanessa squirmed until she was able to squeeze beside him into the tiny seat. "You always wait until the last minute, don't you," she said with a scolding glare.

"I have trouble," he said blithely. "One has to tune even the best for high altitudes, you understand. One cannot mistreat one's steed."

Linc, who had been maneuvered to the sidecar's right, was puzzled. "You know him?" he said, nodding to Basil.

"Of course I know him," she said. "I work for George, I get to meet all sorts of uninteresting people."

Basil tsked at the slur and jolted the cycle over a low deadfall.

Linc felt a familiar and unpleasant prickling at the back of his neck. "I don't want to know, but did you know he was going to be here?"

"Oh, sure," she said without turning around. "I saw it in the stars."

He nodded, but he could not shake the feeling that Reddick, in this case, was only the frying pan. Then he saw the package nestled in her lap. It was the leather box. It was the King. He grabbed it up and stared at it, his mouth agape.

"Well," she said, "did you think I was just going to stand there while you two played carousel? He's only an old man, for heaven's sake. It wasn't that hard."

"But he had a machete, Vanessa!"

She smiled. "He sneezed."

An hour later they passed over a low rise and Unicov turned sharply through a screen of thorny brush. When it cleared, they were speeding along a tarmac highway toward Lima.

"I don't believe it," Linc said as he saw the road

twist and wind before him. "I don't damned believe it."

"Beats walking," she said. But when she reached for the package, Linc smiled politely and shook his head. "My god," she said, leaning back to stare. "My god, Lincoln Blackthorne—after all this time you don't trust me?"

"We're both working for George, m'dear," he said. "What does it matter?"

"Ah," Basil said then, "but I'm not."

"No, but you're driving. And if you stop I'll put you right back in the graveyard where I found you."

Unicov scowled. "I tripped."

Linc laughed, and fell silent, thinking about a chain of coincidence he did not believe was coincidence at all. His fingers brushed over the ancient leather box, and he barely noticed nightfall, only returned to the present when Unicov pulled off the road and killed the engine. When he looked a silent question, Unicov shrugged.

"My ass hurts," he said, "and that slime, Reddick, still has to walk. We will sleep. We will trust each other, and we will sleep."

"And suppose someone drives by?"

"In that unlikely event, we are tourists," he said simply, climbing off the cycle and walking several yards up the road. He examined the shoulder carefully, shivered, and began piling dead brush into a depression. Within minutes they were huddled beside a low, warm fire, and Linc was trying to ignore the aches that had taken root in virtually every muscle.

The package stayed in his lap.

Vanessa fell asleep first, and Linc watched Basil through the ribbonlike flames.

"Odd, isn't it?" he said. "You and I, here."

"Odd, yes," Unicov replied. "Odder still you haven't killed me."

"Basil, you know better than that."

There was a moment's silence. Then: "You don't know what it is, my friend, do you?"

"Of course I do."

Unicov shook his head sadly. "No, I think not. I think George didn't tell you everything you had to know. It's like him, don't you think? Keeping his cards close to his chest, so to speak."

"For instance."

Another silence while Unicov poked at the fire, added more brush, and ducked away from a brief shower of sparks. The jungle around them was noisy, the nightsky filled with more stars than he'd ever seen in his life. He wondered about Carmel then, and if Old Alice and the Crowleys had gone to see the fireworks without him. He thought about the suits he had to finish for the mayor, and about how he and George were going to have a very long, very private talk when he got back. It wasn't until Basil cleared his throat loudly that he realized the man had been speaking to him.

"My friend," he said, "you know that Vilcroft has many, many things in that house of his. Many things. He collects things the way Reddick collects souls—without caring for the cost to himself or to others. This deck of cards, it is not a deck of cards one sits down in the evening with and enjoys with one's friends.

"I suppose you remember Benevidez, the man who first brought it back to Spain? Yes. And you remember how he was when he died? Yes. He was a young man, Lincoln. A young man. He was a young man when he left, and a young man when he died."

"Ponce de Leon would kill for news like that," Lincoln said with a weary smile.

"Do not laugh, my friend. You are more right than you know."

"Bull, I say, shit, Uni."

"It is not the Fountain of Youth," Basil told him patiently, ignoring his skepticism, "and it is not a talisman for immortality either. What its believers maintain is that it will slow down the aging process, not by mere possession, but by the playing and winning of certain arcane games taught to the Spaniard by the Incan Emperor. It is a long ritual, and one not without its dangers, but the price for some was apparently worth it. What mattered was that the owner of the deck was able to manipulate his fate, and quite literally preserve himself for the future.

"Why else," Unicov wondered aloud, "would men travel to such godforsaken places as this for one lousy card? The jewels? The emeralds that make up the King's eyes are wondrous, and very likely would make someone wealthy beyond dreams. But," he argued, "Reddick has wealth of his own, and so does Vilcroft. They need another few millions like the ocean needs another drop of salt.

"No," he said, "they have been hunting the King for decades without letting anyone know about it. Reddick found most of the deck in Segovia, the Queen of Stags in Vienna, the Knave of Abbé in a small village in the Ukraine. Vilcroft had the rest, and over the years managed to steal all remaining cards from Reddick. Reddick, though enraged, didn't retaliate. The cards are useless without the King, and once that was found, then the real battle could begin."

Lincoln found himself shaking his head more than he was listening. He couldn't believe that George would fall for a fairy tale like this, and found it almost impossible to credit that Unicov was taken in as well.

"The old man," he said then, pointing vaguely back toward the valley. "If this thing works, why would he give it up, just like that? My god, if I were him, I'd have a fortress built just to hold that one lousy card."

"You saw how difficult it was to get in."

"I saw how easy it was to get out, and that doesn't answer my question. Why was he so willing to hand it over to me—once he convinced himself I am who I said I was?"

"Because George saved his life," Vanessa said softly.

"Back in the thirties," she told them without bothering to sit up, "Vilcroft was on an expedition in Uruguay when he heard about the missing King from some Indians he was living with; he refused to believe he was so close, and accidentally, but he took time off to make the trip over the mountains. The old man was having trouble at the time both with the government, and with an ambitious and thoroughly obnoxious archaeologist who was determined to make off with every artifact the village owned. George stepped in and drove the fool out. The old man promised to give George the piece when his time came.

"As Basil said, Lincoln, you don't grow young

again. You just don't age as rapidly. But you do age. As the old man did. He was born the year Washington was inaugurated."

"Sure, and I was born during the Wars of the Roses."

Vanessa rolled over and pillowed her arms under her head. Then, without looking up, she said, "In all the things you've done in your life, Lincoln, haven't you ever come across anything that refuses to obey the laws you think you know?"

He had, which was why he forced himself to remain as skeptical as he could. He had witnessed things, heard things, experienced things that any ordinary citizen would label more than fantasy—they would have been called delirium. But they were true. Yet none were as startling, and as potentially dangerous as this. Vanity, and fear of dying might well be the reasons why George was so desperate to get hold of the King; Reddick, on the other hand, would use its time-gift to consolidate and strengthen his bases of power. Once done, he could pretty much do what he liked, secure in the knowledge that if all else failed he would simply outlive his enemies.

Including Lincoln Blackthorne.

"You believe," Unicov said, staring at him through the lowering flames. "Good. Now I can sleep. You will not kill me in my slumber?"

Linc gestured disgustedly at him, ignored the smug smile, and stared at the fire until there was little left but embers. Then he stretched out on the ground and closed his eyes.

When he awoke, the sun was high, and the motorcycle, Unicov, and Vanessa Lecharde were gone.

He was lying on his back, head close to the road, feet aiming toward the forest. His hands and ankles were bound in vine, the roping slithering off the shoulder to a makeshift branch sling five feet away. He groaned at his own stupidity and started to rise, saw the Y-shaped branch tremble, and he froze.

In the crux of the Y he could see Vanessa's gun, the vine tied to the trigger, the hammer back.

If he so much as sneezed, he wouldn't be able to duck in time.

Then he looked over his shoulder and saw the jaguar sitting in the road.

SEVENTEEN

LINC IGNORED the sweat that began to run from his hair, that coated his chest and chilled him. Lying supine as he was, there was little else to do but wait to see how the big cat would react. It would have been a clever stunt, to maneuver the animal into the weapon's line of fire, jerk his legs, and shoot it; but the barrel was aimed quite a bit lower than his heart. Even if he were lucky enough to roll onto his side and catch the bullet in the upper thigh, it would probably take a long interior route before exiting somewhere in the proximity of his neck—and while a .45 shell doesn't make all that large a hole going in, a man could put his fist through the back door.

And if he didn't die instantly, the jaguar would return and finish him off without hesitation.

His eyes closed slowly, and he permitted himself the luxury of speculating heatedly on Unicov's ancestry and decidedly unorthodox self-sexual proclivities. Then he felt a muscle jump in his left leg and heard the sling rattle softly. He looked, realized that he couldn't even inch himself away—his legs were straight, and drawing them up just enough to give him leverage would be sufficient to pull the trigger.

The jaguar snuffled and padded across the road.

He took a deep breath and closed his eyes again, until he was just able to see, blurredly.

The animal snorted, loudly, directly by his ear, and shoved at him quizzically with its muzzle. A large black paw prodded at his hip. Then it moved down beside his leg and sniffed at the vine.

The branch-sling trembled.

He was about to shout, cry out, make any kind of noise at all to drive the creature away, when he realized that this might be an opportunity to literally kill two birds with one stone. If the jaguar moved between him and the gun, or if it could be lured into that space, all he had to do was pull up his legs and the cat would take the bullet while he rolled out of the way.

The jaguar sat.

"Jackass," Linc said.

The cat's head swiveled toward him, slanted eyes narrow, the side of its upper lip pulled away to reveal its teeth in an almost human sneer. It growled, deep and thunderously.

"Hey," Linc said, louder.

The animal slowly raised itself to its feet; Linc hoped it wouldn't decide to start nibbling right away, out of the line of fire.

"Hey!" he shouted, and clamped his eyes shut, neck muscles taut, jaw quivering.

A heavy paw rested on his calf, pulled away, returned and pushed lightly.

Stupid idea, he thought as he felt the weight shift and he had to tense the thigh to keep his leg from rolling over and pulling the vine; stupid idea.

Then, as he waited for the gun to fire, the paw vanished. He opened his eyes, half annoyed, half relieved, and saw that the jaguar had turned and was looking eastward along the highway. Its tail switched back and forth like an aimless whip, and it was growling again. Suddenly, it whirled and leapt, and Linc could not help yelling when it soared over his chest, landed silently on the slope beyond and disappeared into the trees. In less time than it took him to draw a breath, then, he heard the sound of an automobile engine. He turned his head just as a long silver limousine pulled to a smooth stop behind him. He looked up and saw a polarized window rolled down, saw Reddick upside down, his lips pulled aside in a mockery of a grin.

"Basil doesn't like you," he said.

"Basil is a—"

"Please," Reddick said, one finger up for silence. Then he turned to snap at a muttering that came from the front of the car. "I fear Cashim would like to see if that contraption works, my dear Blackthorne."

"I'll bet he would."

"And I imagine you would like to strike some sort of deal with me just about now. Something along the lines of: I get you free and you help me find Unicov and the woman and, I assume, the King."

Linc hadn't thought that at all but, even coming from the upside-down mouth of a cleft-chinned demon, it didn't sound half bad. Reddick, however, was shaking his head as if in sympathy for his naiveté.

"I suggest to you," the man said, "the idea is not the slightest bit intriguing."

"Didn't think so."

"I think, in fact, that I'll give this one to Basil and carry on in my own interests. I'm sure you can understand such thinking."

But he couldn't.

His neck was sore from the strain, so he relaxed, drawing his gaze back to the trees, and to the gun in the sling. He couldn't understand because Reddick had been struggling for years to get him into just such a position, and it wasn't like him at all to leave him as someone else's quarry. Especially Basil Unicov's. He thought he heard whimpering then as he listened to Reddick muttering something to Cashim and Krawn, widened his eyes when the automobile suddenly pulled away. He looked and saw Reddick watching him from the back window, smiling, and giving him a two-fingered salute.

Oh, he thought, hell.

He considered for a while that a miracle might happen, that it might rain and soften the vine, slacken it and allow him to slide out of the way; that the jaguar might return and take the bullet meant for him; that even with his hands trapped beneath him as they were he'd still be able to get the wrist-knife out of its sheath and cut through the ropes holding him. Then he'd be able to sit up without moving his legs, untie his ankles, and start walking.

There was also the chance that Unicov hadn't loaded the gun at all; he wasn't, Linc knew, the most violent of men even when his temper was as short as the lease on his brains, but though it made him grunt with the possibility, he couldn't bring himself to take the chance. Basil was still Basil, and dying, he finally decided, was no way to justify his faith in one loony man.

A dark bird coasted high overhead; there were noises in the forest he didn't want to hear.

It occurred to him then that perhaps this wasn't Basil's idea at all, that Vanessa had been suckering him along from the beginning and was using this to be sure he, and Vilcroft, never found out who had betrayed whom. Clever, unoriginal, and most effective; but though he suspected the woman's motives, he did not believe for more than the duration of the original thought that she would resort to killing him when a simple desertion would have done the trick just as well.

He stared at the mouth of the barrel.

He followed the vine from the trigger to the loop around his ankles.

He felt himself falling asleep in the warming sun and began to whistle to keep himself awake; what he did not need now was a nap during which he tried to roll over.

He heard the engine and thought Reddick had returned, felt the sudden blast of air snapping sharp twigs and stones into his face and realized that he'd been so intent on staying awake and considering the grim alternatives that he hadn't recognized the distinctive *whop-whop-whop* of a helicopter's rotary blades. By god, he thought, the Peruvian Army after all.

Ten minutes later he said, "I thought you were the Army, if you can believe it."

"I believe anything you care to tell me, my friend," said Juan Pizarro from the pilot's seat. "Just don't tell me again you do not have the King."

"I do not have the King," he said dutifully, turning to Estrella and shrugging.

"He says he doesn't," she told Pizarro.

"I don't believe him."

"Believe me," Linc said, "I'm not lying."

They were flying low over the jungle, the Andes' thin air preventing the large army chopper from rising much higher. He had not been all that surprised to see Estrella waving at him from the cargo hold of the Chinook, or the submachine gun in her other hand; in fact, he was relieved to be spared the agony of creating an explanation on the spot for someone official, someone who had the power to be sure he might never see the light of day again. He'd heard rumors about the prisons in Peru, second only to those already famed in Mexico and Argentina.

The two were dressed in custom fatigues, Pizarro's complete with epaulets and an admiral's cap, Estrella's complete with the cleavage Linc had admired on the airplane. She hadn't let him enjoy it for more than a few seconds, however; once inside, she'd ordered him to a seat behind Pizarro, sat on his right, and aimed the machine gun between them.

An hour later Pizarro was still trying to get him to change his story.

"I give up," Linc said in disgust. "For god's sake, Juan, how many times do I have to tell you I don't have the goddamned King? Jesus!" He glared out the window. "Six times," he said without looking forward. "The woman has searched me six times. Let her tell you."

"She has," Pizarro said. "I think, however, she has missed something."

"Not so I could tell," he muttered.

The helicopter descended suddenly, dropping into a broad meadowed valley criss-crossed with roads. Linc spotted several army vehicles parked beside low quonset huts, leaned over the seat beside him to look over Pizarro's shoulder—in the distance, just at the horizon, he could see the unmistakable signs of an airfield.

Estrella removed the machine gun from between them and slipped into the seat. A hand touched his arm. "Lincoln, this is insane."

"Yes," he agreed. "But—"

Her finger pressed lightly against his lips, and he resisted the temptation to kiss it. "We are working with Basil, you know. You know this, I'm sure. It stands to reason then, doesn't it, that Basil would not run off with the card when he knew we would be arriving momentarily to help him?"

"A double cross is not unknown in situations like this," he told her.

She moved closer, her hand at the back of his neck, one finger snaking through his hair and lightly scratching his skin. She looked down at her chest, looked up to see him watching, and she smiled and took a slow, deep breath.

"Lincoln, Basil does not have the King."

He watched the shadows moving beneath the fatigues. "You're making a mistake."

"No," she whispered, closer still until her chest was a hair's breadth away from his arm. "I think that Reddick has taken it, Lincoln, and you are covering up the fact. Not," she said quickly, "because you are working for him, I know that. Because you want to kill him, and this will give you the excuse you need."

"I don't need an excuse for that," he said coldly.

"But you do, *mon cher*," she said regretfully. "You always have, Lincoln. Despite your enviable record, you do not have the instinct to take a life. You always need a reason, and the King is the reason this time."

She kissed his cheek, kissed the side of his jaw, kissed the rim of his ear and blew softly, warmly. "Lincoln."

He bit down hard on the inside of his cheek, not daring to tell her the seduction tickled. When she kissed his lips he decided to return the favor, if only because he was squirming now as her right hand lay flat against his stomach and one finger had slipped under his shirt to stroke his flesh. And when she finally broke away and watched him carefully, he let his eyes close halfway, his lips part, his chest rise and fall in the manner of a bewitchment.

"Lincoln."

The Chinook swung sharply to the right, Pizarro squinting as he tried to find the proper pad for a landing.

"Lincoln."

He nodded at last. "I never could resist you, Estrella."

"I know."

"You do it to me every time."

"I know."

"Reddick has the King. He drove Basil off just before dawn, and I haven't the slightest idea where he's gone. Then he rigged that trap you saw and left me there to die."

"I know."

"I should have told you right away, but I want him for myself."

"I know."

He met her sympathetic gaze squarely, with respect. "You're a remarkable woman, Estrella."

She lowered her eyelids modestly. "I do what I must."

"You do it . . . well."

"Madre de Dios!" Pizarro snorted. "You are making me sick at the stomach."

"He's not very sensitive, is he?" Linc said. "He doesn't understand."

"I know," she said, pulled the machine gun back into her lap, and curled her finger around the trigger.

Then he looked through the windscreen and pointed. "He's also not a very good pilot. Unless I'm mistaken, we're going to crash."

Estrella's head snapped around in panic, and he snared the weapon from her grip, flipped it over, and pointed it square at her stomach.

"Oh, Lincoln," she said.

"Yeah, ain't it a bitch," he said, and pulled the trigger.

EIGHTEEN

"**R**EMARKABLE, ABSOLUTELY remarkable," Lincoln said in sincere, quiet admiration. "You two are the first terrorists I've ever met who don't arm their weapons. Remarkable, though I wonder if Che would approve of your methods."

Pizarro responded with little more than a dark-faced scowl and a clenching of his hands over the copter's controls; Estrella, though her eyes were eloquent in silent obscenity, was unable to say anything at all—she had been forced into the copilot's seat, Lincoln behind her with one hand holding her forehead and the other a blade against her long, exposed neck. Finally, Pizarro muttered, "You were taking a chance."

"Not much of one."

"The bomb was armed."

He shrugged, not wanting to admit he'd forgotten that detail until the moment before he pulled the machine gun's trigger, saw Cortez's eyes widen in pre-faint hysteria, and had his own weapon in hand before she could recover.

"Land, Juan," he ordered softly. "You may assume the usual instructions."

"Yes," the man said acidly. "No tricks, no funny stuff, no trying to escape the madman."

"You got it, Juan."

The pad he had chosen was far beyond the last of the visible barracks on the windswept plateau, but by the time they'd touched down the area was completely surrounded by a dozen armored jeeps and twice that many armed and puzzled troopers. As he waited for the rotors to cease their whirring, he watched a dress-uniformed captain swing himself limberly out of the lead vehicle and approach them, strutting, swagger stick under one arm and boots polished to a glare, scanning the area as if nothing were amiss. When he reached the port on the pilot's side, Pizarro pulled back the pane and grinned down at him.

"Easy," Lincoln cautioned through a smile, shifting his hand casually away from Estrella's head and the knife to her hidden side. Pizarro pointedly ignored the threat, clearing his throat loudly before starting to chat volubly with the frowning officer, laughing, gesturing to the others and then to the sky in an abrupt somber gesture. The officer's frown deepened as he too searched the sky, looked back.

Linc was unable to understand all of what was said, but from the officer's reactions and the few words he did catch he gathered Pizarro had spun some dark yarn about Reddick, American fugitives, the CIA and the FBI—perhaps even Interpol, though he wasn't quite sure—and the Peruvian secret police's interest in anything and everything that had to do with it all.

The officer blanched, swallowed, then laughed and snapped his fingers several times. When Pizarro muttered something else he twice scowled and launched into a tirade that darkened his face and had him slapping his swagger stick hard against the fuselage. When he was finished he gestured—an invitation for them all to step out of the Chinook.

"He is very unhappy," Pizarro said as he un-strapped himself and looked to Lincoln. "He says a man of Reddick's description passed through here not too long ago, ambushed a sleeping guard patrol, and stole a cargo plane made in the imperialist United States. They headed northwest, with the colonel in charge as hostage. He suspects they are heading for the idiots in that fool Venezuela."

"No one's chasing him?"

"No. The colonel is not loved, but he has many connections. No one would dare take the chance he might be killed by the madman."

Lincoln slipped back, allowing the pair to come between the seats and precede him to the door. "Basil? Vanessa?"

Pizarro shrugged. "Nothing. He knows nothing. He isn't very smart anyway. He comes from Cuzco, where the Incas started out. He thinks like they do, that the Spanish are idiots. That's why he's only a captain."

Linc wasn't surprised; Basil was resourceful, but he would never have had the nerve to steal an army plane from under the Army's nose. He probably went on to Lima and a commercial flight back to the States. Or, if Reddick had caught up with him and taken the King . . .

He tensed as the door slid noisily open and the captain was standing there, staring up and waiting with his swagger stick tapping rhythmically against his leg. Pizarro waved grandly and leapt to the tarmac, turned and reached up for Estrella's hand. She hesitated before accepting the assistance, and they both faced Lincoln. He knew it could be a trap, knew too Pizarro could be telling the truth. What he didn't know was how much the parade ground captain believed.

With the knife safely back in its sheath he jumped.

Immediately, a covered jeep sped up to the helicopter, braked harshly, and clouded the air with fine grey dust. "Say nothing," Pizarro warned as the captain gestured them all into their seats. Linc nodded, smiling broadly, wondering how he was going to get back on Reddick's trail.

"Nothing at all," Pizarro repeated with a finger to his lips as they were driven at top, spine-jarring speed to a long black Imperial parked at the end of the nearest runway. As soon as they stopped the driver was out and had opened the limo door, the captain was shaking everyone's hands warmly, and they were ushered inside. Air conditioned. Silent. And racing off the base, heading west, toward Lima.

Only when he was positive the car wasn't about to be blown off the road, or the driver wasn't going to release poison gas through hidden grill-work, or Pizarro wasn't going to pull a weapon on him did Lincoln shift until he was in the corner, one leg pulled up, his hands limp in his lap.

"I don't get it."

Estrella sat in the opposite corner, her expression sullen, her gaze on the lush yet increasingly urban scenery sweeping blurredly past them.

Pizarro sat in the middle, enjoying himself immensely.

"Juan, I said I don't get it."

"It is easy, Blackthorne," he answered with a broad, self-congratulatory grin. "The good captain—who is a fool, as I have previously explained—understands the necessity for cooperation between his service and the one I supposedly represent; he also realizes that it is of the highest diplomatic imperative that the governments of the overly wealthy United States and the struggling but proud Republic of Peru continue their fine mutual relations to everyone's advantage. He was, quite apparently, more than willing to supply us with the transportation we need to continue the pursuit of the villain who has openly and with no concern for anyone but himself stolen the national treasure."

Too good, Linc thought; too good to last, and I don't dare ask.

Pizarro waited.

Lincoln hated himself. "What national treasure? You can't mean the colonel?"

Pizarro chuckled indulgently and hooked his thumbs around his belt. "Mr. Blackthorne, in Peru, in South America, everything the government says is a national treasure is, in fact, a national treasure. Albino bat guano is a national treasure if it can be valued at something more than the national debt. All one must say are the magic words and you will have splendid armies fighting at your side to keep the bastard greedy gringos from stealing your heritage."

"I see."

"Yes," he said. "It is brilliant."

"Asshole," Estrella muttered.

"She is annoyed because she wanted to use her patriotically athletic and talented body to convince the young captain of the rightness of our journey," the man explained condescendingly. "The way she convinced you to tell us that Reddick has the King and Basil has pursued him to appropriate it for the proper figures."

"Not him," she muttered. "You. Reddick doesn't have the King. Basil does."

Pizarro blinked.

Lincoln sighed, folded his arms and closed his eyes. He estimated three hours, perhaps four if they didn't hit a llama along the way, until they reached the airport. Until then he needed sleep, and a chance to figure out where he was going next. He could always return to Inverness, to Vilcroft, and vent a few pounds of annoyance, or he could pick up Basil's trail and follow him following Reddick, or he could head straight for Reddick himself.

The last alternative, unfortunately, was the easiest, and the most deadly. Reddick being Reddick, there was only one place for him to go now. And Lincoln had been there more than once, the last time just before he almost died.

Dozing and thinking, however, were out of the question. Estrella would not keep her opinions of Pizarro's intelligence entirely to herself, and Pizarro constantly demanded to know at the top of his shrill voice why he was fated to forever waste his brilliance on liars and thieves and men of no honor. It was, he insisted as he pounded his thighs—and on one occasion, Lincoln's—incomprehensibly unfair, and worthy of only the worst possible retribution. He quieted only when Linc managed to let him know how long he would live if he didn't keep his voice down.

Following Lincoln's instructions once they reached the airport, the military limousine stopped at the opulent first-class entrance, the driver hustled out, opened the door, and waited for his passengers to disembark. Lincoln was the first out, turned around immediately and placed a palm against Pizarro's chest, pushing him back into his seat.

"I protest," Pizarro said warily, not at all sure why he was protesting.

"Estrella," Linc said, "will you explain to the man why you can't go with me?"

Pizarro whirled around, his face dark with anger. "Estrella, this is an outrage!"

"I will," she said. "I think then I will come after you and kill you myself, if I find out Reddick has not done the job for me."

"There are worse fates, *querida,*" he said, reached out and took her hand, kissed it, and smiled warmly. "Much worse fates indeed."

"If I do find you," she said with a gentle smile, "I think I will start by cutting off your *cojones.*"

"If you do find me," he said, releasing her hand quickly, "I'll introduce you to a teacher I know. I think you two will get along just fine."

"But this is so unjust!" Pizarro whined. "Do you not remember I have just saved your miserable life?"

"Is she pretty?"

Lincoln nodded and shrugged. "You know how it is, Estrella."

"Then I think I will begin with your—"

"I am vowed to revenge, you must understand this, Blackthorne, my friend!"

"Jesus, Juan," she sighed in disgust, and slapped Pizarro with her knuckles, instantly grimaced at his wailing, and cradled his head against her chest. Linc closed the door, shrugged to the driver, and walked into the terminal. It wasn't difficult to get a first-class seat on the next plane out, less so downing the free glass of champagne; the worst time he had was in convincing the efficient and bustling stewardess that he really did want to sleep all the way back to Miami.

He only hoped Juan would have some reasonable answer for the authorities when they asked him about his recovery of whatever national treasure he'd dreamed up out there on the airfield.

What was difficult was stopping the dream—of the high stone walls, the bleak landscape, the river arctic cold even in the middle of summer, and Anton Reddick standing in the middle of an endless road. Waiting for him. Patiently. And alone. With a smile on his face that made Lincoln's flesh turn brittle and crack.

When he awoke he felt as if he'd not rested at all.

When he stumbled to the first-class lounge desk and asked to have a wire sent, the lovely receptionist pulled out her pad and listened to the message dispassionately. Then she asked him where he wanted it sent.

"Mr. George Vilcroft, in Inverness," he said, rubbing his jaw and deciding he'd have to take the time for a shave and a haircut.

"Scotland?"

"New Jersey."

"Inverness is in New Jersey?"

"It is now," he said, standing, stretching, and looking for the barbershop.

"Well, I'll be darned."

"Yep. Some millionaire bought it. Shipped it over stone by stone. Like that fella who bought London Bridge."

"That's in New Jersey?"

"Arizona."

"What's in London?"

"The Queen."

"No kidding?"

He saw the sign at the end of a deep-carpeted blue corridor, turned and smiled at the woman. "No kidding."

"Stone by stone?"

He nodded and walked off, had only gone a half dozen steps before he heard her muttering, "Fucking millionaires think they own the goddamned world."

Another six steps and she called his name brightly. When he looked over his shoulder she was waving the message sheet like a lover's handkerchief. "Mr. Blackthorne, I'll have to call you for your flight. Where are you going?"

"Inverness," he said.

"New Jersey?"

"Scotland."

The smile froze, and he blew her a kiss, half tempted to tell her that more than likely he was also heading for his own postponed funeral.

NINETEEN

BY THE time Lincoln reached the British Isles he had no idea what time it was, little idea of the day, and less of the month. The transoceanic flight had been reasonably smooth save for a brief bout of turbulence encountered over the mid-Atlantic, and the only delay an endless, monotonous circling over Heathrow while the unions below decided which country it was they were embargoing that week; before the United States had been spared, the pilot had lost most of his patience and had been granted divergence to Gatwick. Not nearly as large, not nearly as prepared, but the annoyed and grumbling handful of passengers were rushed politely and apologetically through customs, their baggage fetched in near record time, and before he was ready Linc discovered himself outside the terminal just before sunset feeling the same as he had when he'd left Juan and Estrella behind to deal the military another joker-filled hand.

He wouldn't have been at all surprised if they tossed him in an ambulance for a shrieking ride to the morgue.

Luckily, he thought as he fished clumsily in his pockets for the money he'd changed inside, no one considered it odd that a man dressed like a poor relation of Clyde Beatty's should be standing in the middle of the civilized world in the middle of July looking as if he'd lost his faithful gun bearer and a record wildebeest both on the same day. In fact, a retired and portly colonel muttered in passing about the Empire and its demise, and saluted him until his wife dragged him away with an exasperated wink.

He didn't move an inch when a bright yellow BMW almost jumped the curb and put him back into the terminal.

Nor did he move when a burly German, his wife, and six children wasted several minutes demanding to know when he was going to fetch their luggage and why didn't he get his uniform cleaned.

When he'd finally had enough of staring blindly and mindlessly into the distance, he roused himself sufficiently to locate a cabby willing to take him out to Windsor and deposit him at the Watch Keep Arms, on High Street, in front of Windsor Castle. The driver clearly wanted to haggle a bit to prove he was competent, to prove he wasn't out to steal shekels from the tourists. Linc, however, only made him scowl in agreeing to the first price that came to hand. It wasn't, the cabby muttered as he slammed the door and pulled into the stream of traffic, like the old days at all, by god, when a good bit of bargaining was worth a damned fine tip at the end. Not like the old days at all.

The trip was uneventful, though Linc could not stop himself from checking the rear window every mile or so and frowning whenever he saw a disabled vehicle on lay-bys along the way. He ordered himself to stop feeling so paranoid, yet there was a comfort as well to the notion that half the people in the free world were out to stop him from getting to Scotland; it made matters a great deal simpler.

It wasn't until they were passing Runnymede and Englefield Green that he spotted the yellow BMW; he was sure he'd seen it before, but his mind was packed with loose cotton and he could not get hold of anything that resembled a coherent, lasting thought. Pressing into the seat's left-hand corner, he watched as the garish vehicle hung back several cars for nearly fifteen minutes, then suddenly and dangerously passed them on a curve, pulled in, and slowed down far below the speed limit. Lincoln tensed and waited for the gunshot, or the maneuver to drive them into a tree, a house, the front end of an approaching truck.

The sun was nearly down; vision was complicated by the strobic sweep of shadows slashing across the highway.

The cabby muttered a few choice oaths and leaned on his horn. The BMW slowed even more, and Linc tried to rouse himself into something that approximated a battle-ready condition. The best he could do, however, was sit up straight and peer over the driver's shoulder. The BMW began weaving from side to side, causing those in the oncoming lane to head for the verge and a possible dunking in the Thames.

Lincoln wondered if Basil was driving.

"Tourist," the driver spat in disgust.

"Really," Linc said. "How can you be sure?"

The driver pointed. "Idiot thinks he's drivin' on the wrong side of the road. Half of him is screamin' to get the hell back where he belongs, the other's tellin' him he's okay. You watch at the next sweep, he'll head out again."

Unsure but willing to wait another half mile before bailing out into the bordering woodland, Linc watched as the next curve approached, watched too with a relieved grin when the BMW swung too far to the right and nearly ended up on the opposite verge.

"See?" the driver said. "He oughta take a cab. Ain't no standards anymore, y'see. They'll give one of them things to any idiot what hands them money. Ain't like the old days, sir, I can tell you that."

"No," he said as he sagged again, "I don't suppose it is."

"It's all symptomatic, I say. Symbolic, you might say, of the way things are goin' to hell around here."

"You might say that."

"Right, sir, absolutely."

Once the curve leveled, the yellow car shot forward, braked, dove onto the verge where it idled, trembling. As the cab hooted past, Linc glanced into the front seat. It was the shadows, he was positive, but the driver certainly looked an awful lot like Uni-the-Toad.

Or Vanessa on a bad day.

Wishful thinking, he told himself; and realized with an unnerving start that Vanessa had been rather a lot on his mind over the past few days. It disturbed him, and he was grateful he was too exhausted to do more than note it, think it again, and file it for future consideration.

Just after sunset they passed into town, climbed the sloping High Street, and pulled over to the curb. He sniffed and stared at the castle wall opposite, at the gate to the right, at the Keep rising above the town and, hidden beyond it, the fields of Eton. Then the cabby half-turned to ask if he were going to camp out in the back seat, there were laws, y'know, and he had a wife waiting on his presence if it was all the same to him, no offense but a man has to make a livin'.

Linc nodded, overtipped, and once on the sidewalk stared at the hideous statue of Queen Victoria squatting at the castle's entrance. He had always been morbidly fascinated by the repugnance of that monument, and had noted not even the pigeons bothered to decorate it with their droppings; even in death the Queen was a formidable woman.

As the black cab disappeared down the street and he could detect no sign of the yellow BMW, he inhaled deeply and permitted himself the first smile he'd taken since he'd entered the country. The air here, despite the underlying reek of tourism and commerce, was fresh and different and touched with an age found only in Europe and the farthest outposts of Asia. The taverns and small hotels, the train station only a block or two away, the shops and overhead apartments gave him a sense of something not quite permanence—perhaps, he decided, it was a bit more valuable than that . . . continuance.

And perhaps, he thought further, you're so damned tired you can't think straight, boy.

With a shrug that startled a pair of nuns walking past him he turned around to the Watch Keep Arms on the corner directly behind him, entering the freshly painted Tudor building through an unmarked side entrance.

The large pub inside was crowded, mostly with summer-dress tourists demanding to know if Flags Up meant the Queen was in or out, and why not? In a second room tucked into the back and used primarily by the locals there was a dart game going on in the far corner, checkers and chess at several beaten and round oaken tables, a weathered old man playing softly at an upright propped against the outside wall. Smoke curled under the exposed oak beams, the talk and laughter mingled in a continuous throbbing roar that almost made the room seem silent.

He pushed his way through the milling, enthusiastic mob gingerly, murmuring what passed for apologies, until he stood at the corner of a short darkwood bar spiked from overhead by three racks of gleaming glasses. His muscles and aches had lost the numbing protection the airliner's seats had forced into them, and he was hoping he'd be able to stay on his feet until arrangements had been made.

In less than a minute one of the three barmaids was asking him curtly for his order, her full red cheeks flushed with the heat trapped inside the room despite the open windows, her synthetic Elizabethan peasant's blouse clinging to her chest and stomach in clammy ardor. When he didn't answer right away she repeated herself carefully, in three different languages, and was about to launch into a fourth when she finally took a good look at him and her black eyes widened.

"Kee-rist," she whispered.

"Someday, perhaps, with a little practice," he said with a weak smile. "A room, Meg, if you can, and some Guinness to speed me on my way to what passes for dreamland in this godforsaken place."

Meg Killestan blinked several times, her lips working to form his name and ask questions and fend off another customer in a simultaneous sputtering; finally she threw up her hands in surrender and screamed a name toward the next room, shoved two small bottles of mildly cool stout into his hands and screamed again. Before Linc had a chance to take a drink from the first bottle, a short middle-aged man in rumpled white and blue shirtsleeves, sandy hair combed sideways and hard down over his scalp, and a pince-nez dangling from a red ribbon around his neck, stomped over to her, grabbed her elbow and demanded at the top of his voice what the ell she meant talkin to im like that when there's people to be served ere been waitin half the damned night or didn't she have use of the eyes God in His charity had given her.

She shrugged off his grip, stuck out her tongue at a man determined to check the depth of her cleavage, and nodded briskly to Linc.

The sandy-haired man scowled, looked, looked away with a so-what shrug, looked back with thin red lips parted in a gasp.

"Kee-rist."

"Meg will explain," he said. "A room, Tommy, and some clothes, if you can manage it."

"You look like hell, if you don't mind me sayin' so."

"It's all in the breeding."

"You want a doctor?" Meg asked, slapping the hand of a young man in a red-checkered sports jacket.

"I don't think so."

"Can y'walk?" Tommy asked.

"You lead, I'll follow. Nothing that means I have to see Old Vicky in the morning, though, for god's sake."

Tommy Killestan laughed, slipped out from behind the bar and opened a narrow door in the back wall. A French couple—he in a three-piece pinstriped suit, she in basic black with pearls looped down to her waist—stepped in Linc's way just as he made for the staircase beyond, asking the proprietor why *this* gentleman was being given accommodations when they were to understand there were none to be had, even after they had written the proprietor several times over the past month to be sure they would not have to live in the streets while staying over here. Tommy rubbed at his chin for a moment, clearly embarrassed. Linc clapped his hand on his shoulder and looked squarely at the banker.

"When I was a boy I used to clean De Gaulle's bidet," he said with a stupid smile. "Shit gold every morning, pissed Bordeaux at night. Remarkable human being. A great loss to the world. Do you know if he ever played basketball?"

When the woman paled with a gasp and the banker imitated an affronted bantam, he turned away and dragged himself up the stairs, Tommy behind in a cloud of apologies clearly halfhearted.

"Y'shouldn't hae done it, lad," the man said with little regret, leading him around the banister on the first landing to a room at the end of the hall, in front. "His money's good."

"If his money's good, you would've given him a room when he asked for it, Tommy," he said, standing aside to let the man unlock a pale paneled walnut door and precede him over the threshold.

The room was small, barely large enough for a bed, a chair, a dresser, and secretary. Washstand by the bed, draperies on the window that overlooked the High Street. Killestan told him he'd have Meg bring him some decent food in a bit, would shepherd's pie be enough to hold him? Linc allowed as how it probably would, and hoped he'd be able to stay awake long enough to enjoy it. Though he'd slept on both legs of the flight from Lima, the uncomfortable position, the changing time zones, and his mind's refusal to forget his destination had drained him. He glanced in the dresser mirror and saw himself—hollow-cheeked, pouches under his eyes, his top lip slightly ticking. Boris Karloff in *The Raven*, he thought as he groaned while pulling off his shirt, sank onto the bed's thick, too-soft mattress and pulled off his boots; I look like hell.

Congratulating himself on the understatement, he lay back with hands cupped behind his head to await his dinner.

He wondered if the tourist in the BMW would ever get hold of his pride and hire someone to drive him; he wondered if he was really beginning to feel more than admiration for Vanessa that she should bother his thoughts so often, and so subtly; and he wondered if it would be rude to Tommy if he just closed his eyes for a moment, just until the supper came.

When his eyes opened again it was full dark outside, the small lamp on the washstand was glowing, and a woman was standing over him with a knife in her hand.

TWENTY

Linc's HAND snapped up, but much too slowly, and he was well into a rounded and panicked damning for his carelessness and his impending bloody departure when the woman deftly spun the knife in her hand and held it out to him, silvered handle first. He blinked, accepted it, and the last of the dozing peeled away from his vision.

He felt like a jackass and hoped she wouldn't ask any questions.

"I didn't have the heart to wake you," Meg said, the dim lamplight hiding the years that creased the corners of her eyes and the bow of her lips. "So I coughed."

He raised an eyebrow and lifted himself on one elbow, saw a wooden tray laden with steaming shepherd's pie, a steaming mug of strong tea, and a small blue pitcher of cream. No sugar, no lemon. The odors mingled well enough to make his mouth water, and he suppressed a groan as he eased along the mattress to his meal.

"You're traveling," she said after handing him the fork she held in her other hand. Below he could hear muffled singing.

"You know how it is," he said, hissing in at the hot meat and crisp crust burning his tongue. "I just can't seem to stay home these days. Wanderlust, I guess." He grinned around a mouthful of food, shrugged when she stuck out her tongue as proof of her disbelief. "Do me a favor, Meg. Take a look out the window. Tell me what you see."

She did as she was bidden without asking why. "The damned wall, the damned statue, a bunch of damned tourists, a guide with an umbrella—a fiver says she's lost her charges—and a bloody great bus filled with short slanty men with cameras."

He swallowed, took a drink of stout from the bottle he hadn't touched. "What does the guide look like?"

"My mother, if you have to know."

"Your mother's a wonderful woman."

"She's a shaggin' loudmouth."

"Shame on the language, Meg. Tommy'd be disappointed."

She turned with a grin and plucked at her costume. "Gotta play the part, Blackthorne. Bold and brassy, like the man says."

He laughed, ate, drank, wished he were feeling good enough to taste it all. "No yellow car? No hanging-about cabs?"

"No, and no, though I think the CIA is walking about the courtyard. Trench coats and passwords and all that, if you know what I mean. You done something against the CIA, Blackthorne?"

"Always, Meg. My very existence affronts them."

"Bullshit. They don't even know you're alive."

"Yes, I know. The curse of my profession not to have proper recognition."

She paused. "Will you be staying long?"

"Until I'm sure I'm not dead."

She looked pointedly at the bruises and fading latticework of scrapes and scratches on his chest. "We'd have to take a vote on that, I think."

"It'll be close, believe me."

"You want the National Health?"

"No. I'm okay, really."

"Try a mirror, Blackthorne, and tell me that again with a straight face."

"You know me too well, Meg. Now would you mind a bit of reverence here while I fill the rest of my stomach?"

A patient and silent waiting until he was finished before she gathered up tray and utensils and walked to the door. "Tommy isn't going with you, is he?" She said it without looking around.

Linc blew her an unseen kiss for her concern as he rolled himself back to lie on the pillow. "No, m'dear, he's not."

Her shoulders sagged. "He's not gettin any younger."

"He's not going."

"We've been married ten years."

"I'm on my own this time."

"He can still make a spring bounce, y'know, even for an old fart like myself."

"Jesus, Meg, are you deaf?"

She grinned at him over her shoulder. "Just need to be sure, y'know. Can't trust you worth a damn."

"Just don't wake me up until I wake up, if you please. I've a lot of catching up to do."

"I'll bet." She opened the door, braced herself against it with a hip. "Was she pretty?"

"Who?" he asked innocently.

A scowl darkened her cheeks. "Lincoln."

"All right, then. No. No prettier than you."

"Go on!"

He lay back, his head sinking into the feather pillow. "No prettier, Meg. I swear."

"You're a liar, Blackthorne."

He smiled. "Maybe. And Meg, there's a package."

"God help me," she said wearily. "Is it going to explode?"

"I hope not."

"When will it be here?"

"I don't know. Soon, I hope. I don't have much time."

"All right, then. It probably isn't flowers."

He said nothing, too exhausted to feel guilt for imposing on his friends, disappointed the package wasn't already there.

The door began to close, as did his eyes. The singing grew slightly louder, and someone was playing the piano with a vengeance. Then he heard her whisper: "Who am I to keep watch for?"

"Basil," he said.

"Weasel."

"And Reddick."

"Bastard."

"And a tall dark-haired woman calls herself Lecharde."

"Bitch."

"Hey, you don't even know her."

"You don't take care of yourself, Lincoln. Tommy says so as well. All your women are bitches. They don't know what they have and that's a fact."

"Is that a compliment of some sort?"

A shrug: *figure it out yourself.*

"Meg?" he said as she slowly disappeared into the hallway shadows.

"What now?"

"Maybe a couple of South Americans in fatigues."

"My god, Lincoln, how many eyes do you think I have?"

The door closed before he could respond and left him in the room's twilight, left him staring at the faint, recently plastered cracks webbed across the ceiling. By allowing his gaze to trace them for patterns, he hoped to drop off in seconds, instead found himself thinking about what he had seen in Peru, what Basil had told him about the King, and what in god's name he was going to do about it. There was no question of believing in its supposed powers; even if he didn't the others most certainly did, which made them no less deadly, no less sane.

Lord, he thought, for the simple life of a tailor.

An automobile backfired and he moaned silently for not jumping.

He felt a twinge along his spine, and he decided James Bond wasn't human.

He had contracted with Vilcroft for the card's recovery, and he had never broken such a pact before. But now that he knew what he was after, he couldn't help wondering what George was going to do with it once he had it. Even now, Reddick's men were probably besieging his friend back in the States, trying to locate the remainder of the deck; even now, Basil and Vanessa were probably already in England tooling their way north; and even now, Reddick was probably already in his own fortress, deep in the Highlands, waiting for them all.

Below him the singing grew more boisterous.

Outside he could hear a group of tourists arguing over the height and breadth of the castle wall.

An image of the yellow BMW flashed, and vanished.

And in the room he could hear little more than the sound of his breathing, hypnotically regular, slower and softer until he fell into a deep dreamless sleep from which he finally awoke in muddled stages.

He was still lying atop the coverlet, though his trousers and shoes were off, and a pot of fresh tea sat on the washstand. A glance at the window told him the sun was high, the temperature warm, and he'd just reached for a cup and the kettle when he drifted off again; a second time to moonlight; a third to sunlight that refused to be blocked by partially drawn draperies.

A moment to remember where he was, another to check the room without moving his head, without opening his eyes much more than a slit. And when he was satisfied he was alone, he stretched and groaned, pleased to feel his muscles responding without screaming, pleased to note his head felt less like a cotton-stuffed balloon. With a little more encouragement he might even feel human.

"Easy, boy," he muttered then. "Let's not go overboard."

He swung his legs over the side of the bed and sat up, saw a man's clothes draped over a nearby chair cleaned and pressed. He had no doubt they would fit him, though he wasn't so sure he cared for the dark green tartan trews and the matching green shirt. The oxblood brogans he could handle; it was the alligator belt that made him wince.

Tommy, he decided, would have to pay for this bit of doing.

Then he sniffed and wrinkled his nose, rubbed his hands over his chest and legs, and was wondering how he was going to clean himself up when he spotted a towel, terry-cloth robe, and soap at the foot of the mattress. On top of them was a stoneware shaving mug and an ivory-handled straight razor. Beside them was a small package wrapped in brown paper.

"My, my, Christmas in July," he said softly. There was a moment of concern, then, when it struck him he had to have been asleep for at least a full day. But he shrugged it off, pulled the package to him and opened it swiftly. Inside was a deep blue blackjack tipped with scuffed lead, a new springsheath for his new knife, and a revolver with two boxes of ammunition. How Palmer had managed to get all this through security devices at the airports was a question whose answer he didn't want to know; it was enough that his wire had been received, and that there wasn't a note from the old man scolding him for his losses.

He placed them all back in the box, put the box in the bottom drawer of the dresser and searched futilely for something he could use to cover it up. Then he slipped into the robe, grabbed soap and towel, razor and mug, and shuffled across the room. He opened the door with exaggerated caution. The narrow, low-ceilinged corridor was silent. He made his way down to the shower room, scratching his head and wondering how many days he'd wasted while he kept one ear cocked for noises behind each of the doors he passed. One started to open timidly, closed again abruptly when he smiled brightly at a young woman obviously not ready for the Queen. There was no one else, and by the time he was under the hot water, lathered and ready to sing, he could have easily convinced himself he was here only on a visit.

It was magnificent.

Even his butchering of "Chattanooga Choo-Choo" had a certain élan the Modernaires would have been proud of.

Then he toweled off the tiny mirror over the basin and examined his face critically as he reached for the shaving mug on the ledge. It wasn't until he had lathered his face that he realized the straight razor with the ivory handle was missing. He frowned, searched the basin and the tile flooring beneath it, and as he rose again someone turned on the shower.

He spun around, but the steam was already billowing over the top of the plastic curtain into the room.

And it wasn't until he looked at his reflection that he saw the man standing behind him in the corner. It was the French banker, and the missing straight razor was high over his head and descending swiftly toward the back of his neck.

TWENTY-ONE

THE ANGLED blade glinted blue-white in the shower room's warm, fogged air.

Immediately, Linc dropped to his knees as the razor sliced wildly behind his head. There was no time at all to speculate on the reasons for the banker's attack, and it was obvious from the man's manic expression that he wasn't inclined to explain. Linc pivoted as he dropped, paused just long enough to brace himself before he lunged when the assailant was pulled forward by the momentum of the blow. His shoulder landed just below the man's breastbone, punching the air from his lungs with a startled and painful gasp and driving him back against the wall. The razor flew from the man's hand and skidded along the damp floor. The thrumming of the shower muffled any cries as they grappled without either gaining proper purchase, neither able to land a decent punch until Linc broke away and realized the man's weapon was gone.

He whirled, saw it at the base of the shower stall, and dove for it, grunting when his knee collided with the slippery tiles, grunting again when a heavy weight slammed onto his back. He turned and drove his elbow back, solidly into the Frenchman's side, toppling him under the basin. When he tried to scramble to his feet, he cracked his head against the porcelain and yelped, cursed, and threw himself at Linc again.

Goddamnit, where the hell are you! Linc thought angrily as he crawled on his hands and knees over the floor, absorbing the barely effectual pummeling the Frenchman was applying to his back. Then he saw it in the corner, bucked like a horse to drop the man, and reached-dove for it.

The Frenchman, somehow managing to stay on his feet, got there first, snatched it up and brandished the blade slowly, back and forth in front of Linc's eyes.

The steam was fog-thick now, and breathing was rapidly getting to be a chore.

A misguided lunge, and Linc headed for the door; there was no sense trying to stay and fight when he had no weapon himself. The banker, dazed by the failure of his assault and the meeting with the sink, reached weakly for Linc's shoulder, slipped on the steam-moistened floor, and succeeded only in grabbing his towel.

The door stuck for a second, snapped open just as the banker found his balance again. Linc plunged into the hallway, his eyes no wider than the banker's wife's, who was standing in the middle of the worn carpeting, her hair in curlers, her figure swathed in a voluminous robe, and her right hand holding a snub-nosed .38. She gaped as he approached her at a dead run and stark naked, had her hand up and the ugly weapon aiming when he backhanded her sharply across the chin and knocked her into the wall. The gun fired deafeningly into the ceiling. A door opened farther down, and a young woman stepped out to see what the fuss was, saw Lincoln charging toward her, and screamed.

He nodded as he passed, was through his own door and kneeling at the dresser before her scream died and her door slammed shut.

The box was gone.

He opened the middle drawer, the top, and found nothing but white floral lining paper.

Footsteps launched him to the washstand, and he grabbed up the large porcelain bowl and was behind the door, ready to crack the skull of the first person who came into the room, when he heard the footsteps continue on around the corner and down the stairs. He waited a moment, then poked his head around the jamb. The corridor was empty; at the far end, steam drifted lazily out of the shower room.

There was no sign of the Frenchman or his murderous wife.

The woman was still shrieking behind her closed door.

Wonderful, he thought sourly and closed his own door, dressed quickly in the clothes Killestan had left him; just really and truly wonderful. He was ready to leave when someone knocked on the frame. He tensed, moved to the dresser, and told whoever it was to enter.

It was Meg, in a bulky green sweater and baggy slacks, her hair pinned back and her face without makeup. She looked at him and shook her head, walked to the bed and sat.

"You're not supposed to raise the devil, y'know," she said in mild reproof.

"It wasn't my idea," he told her, and pointed to the empty drawers. "My package, it's missing."

"Don't worry, we have it."

"We? Who we?"

The door opened again and the Frenchman spilled hard onto the floor, Tommy right behind him. In one hand he carried the .38, in the other the missing package, which he tossed to Linc. Then he grabbed the larger man by the shoulders, hauled him silently to his feet, and dumped him into the chair. The Frenchman squirmed but did not attempt an escape; instead, he chose to fuss with his three-piece suit, his tie, pulled up his socks, and tried to seem stern.

"I protest," he said.

"Belt up," Tommy said, and turned to Linc. "Bastard shot a hole in my ceiling."

"He nearly carved me up with that razor you left here."

"Yeah, but he shot a hole in my ceiling. You know what it's like, replasterin'?"

"The woman," Linc said to Meg.

"Fatter and faster. She was gone before we could stop her."

Linc stood in front of the Frenchman, hands on his hips, and ignored the sneering appraisal of his trews and tartan shirt. "I know who I am," he said. "Who the hell are you?"

The Frenchman's bloated cheeks puffed, and his lips tightened in refusal. Linc reached a hand out behind him, brought it back when Meg dropped the blackjack into his palm. "This," he said, tapping it lightly against his thigh, "will break your kneecap. I will help it if you don't stop playing games."

"Plasterin' is a bitch," Tommy murmured as he closed the door and stuck the revolver into his waistband. "A bitch."

"Lecharde," the man said sullenly.

Linc leaned forward. "What about her?"

"You know, you swine."

"Goodness," Meg said.

"What about her?"

The man clasped his hands at his stomach. "I am Yves Lecharde," he said primly. "You are acquainted with Vanessa?"

"Your daughter?"

"You have seen my wife? No, she is not my daughter, she is my niece."

"I see."

Lincoln stood back and stared at him until he began squirming again. The window was directly behind him, and it was difficult to see the man's expressions through the halo glare of the summer sun. He was puzzled, and wasn't surprised—little else had made sense during this affair, so why should this? The man was obviously not an assassin, yet he had done his best to fulfill the role; he claimed to be Vanessa's uncle, though there was no family resemblance that he could see, except for the propensity to use guns and blades.

"Lecharde."

"That is correct."

It occurred to him belatedly that if Reddick, or Basil, or both, knew he was here, then he had little time left. He also recalled Vanessa saying something about an uncle, but he couldn't recall if the man was supposed to be French or not. He stepped closer and leaned down, the blackjack lying on the man's trembling left knee.

"Why?"

Lecharde licked his lips, blew out a licorice-scented breath.

"Lecharde, please don't."

Meg began to hum; Tommy practiced aiming at the window just over the man's head.

Lecharde sagged. "There is a letter in my jacket."

Lincoln reached in, pulled out an envelope with only the man's name scrawled across the front.

"Messenger," Lecharde said to the unasked question. "I live in Calais. It is very near to here."

Linc opened it, carefully extracted a sheet of lavender paper folded in three. He turned slightly and stared at the writing. Great, he thought; just great.

"This," he said, "is in French."

"Of course."

He handed it back. "Read it."

"I most certainly will not." Lecharde seemed ready to bolt from the chair, but a touch of the blackjack forced him to second thoughts.

"Read it."

The man sputtered but snapped the letter open with a flick of his wrist, cleared his throat and gave Lincoln a glare that made him step back in spite of himself

Uncle,

There is a man staying at the Watch Keep Arms, in Windsor, in England. He goes by the name of Blackthorne, and he has done something terrible to me, so terrible I dare not repeat it. I cannot help myself for I am confined be-

*cause of what he has done, and I appeal to you,
my uncle, for justice. I am working for a man
named Vilcroft in the United States. He will
tell you that what I say is true. You have the
address; it will be in one of the other letters
from early this year. Uncle, please! For me, and
for the memory of Mama, take care of this man
for me since I am unable to take care of him
myself.*

Meg's eyes widened when he finished. Tommy
whistled, once and low.

"Are you satisfied?" Lecharde said, his voice
breaking with emotion, his cheeks flaring a deep,
angry red.

"You're positive this is from Vanessa?" he asked,
thinking that the man was a damned fine actor, or
a relative indeed bent upon avenging a woman's
reputation—and there was no need for an explanation of what awful thing she was referring to.

"She writes to her aunt and I every month. We
keep all her letters. I know her writing. What are
you going to do with me?"

Suddenly Lincoln smiled and slipped the blackjack into his hip pocket. He reached out and patted the man on the shoulder, turned and leaned
against the chest of drawers, his arms folded over
his chest.

"What we have here," he said, "is a failure to
communicate."

"Paul Newman," Meg said with a perplexed
laugh.

"Strother Martin," Lecharde corrected stiffly.

Lincoln nodded, impressed. "Indeed, Mr. Lecharde."

"You are still a swine, and your gang will not get away with this. I shall report you all to the embassy in London. Unless," he added bravely, "you intend to kill me."

"What you'll do is pay for the bloody plasterin'," Tommy snapped before Meg could grab his arm and yank him down on the bed beside her.

"Blackthorne," she said, "what *are* we going to do with him?"

"Let him go."

Tommy gaped, Meg frowned, and Lecharde looked uncomfortably skeptical.

"There's no time for any long explanations now," he said apologetically, "and no time to try to make Mr. Lecharde here believe me. You're just going to have to trust me when I tell you that the message was not meant for Lecharde, but for me. And it tells me what I needed to know about Vanessa."

"She is a victim!" Lecharde said angrily.

"Yes she is," he agreed, "but definitely not in the way you think. Tommy, I'm going to need a few minutes to get away. Do what you can to make the gentleman comfortable. Meg, if Palmer gets in touch tell him I'll be in the Highlands."

"The Highlands? Gawd, Blackthorne, that's uncivilized."

He grinned, crossed the room and kissed her cheek soundly. "You haven't a mean bone in your body, you know that?"

"Try marryin' her," Tommy muttered.

Linc made sure the sheath was on, the revolver in his pocket, and the cardigan Meg handed him buttoned to the center of his chest. Then he turned to the banker.

"Mr. Lecharde, I regret our having to meet this way. My best to your wife."

"I will kill you yet," Lecharde warned.

"I don't think so, but thanks for the thought."

Then he shook Tommy's hand and left, took the stairs two at a time, and exited the inn by the side door. The street sloped sharply down to his left, and the brown-red bulk of the train station displaced the businesses and homes several blocks along. With a glance to his right—at the castle and Queen Victoria—he broke into a leisurely trot until he was abreast of the station, then angled off the sidewalk.

It wasn't until he was halfway across the road that he heard the guttural sound of an automobile engine, turned, and saw the canary-yellow BMW bearing full speed down on him, less than five yards from where he stood.

TWENTY-TWO

SUNLIGHT GLINTED off the windshield, rendering the driver invisible. The engine raced again, and the tiny car jumped as it smoked rubber onto the road.

Linc had no time to leap to either side, and he knew the driver would be anticipating such a move. So he turned swiftly to face the oncoming grille, at the last moment throwing himself up and forward to land with a hollow thud on the hood. He rolled at an angle, slapping his arm against the windshield as he pitched off the automobile to land in a motionless heap in the gutter.

The car paused, then sped on down the hill.

After a few moments Linc groaned at the ache in his shoulder and arm, at the burning scrapes his hands and knees had taken. He blinked rapidly to clear his vision and sat up. A palm swiped the dust from his trews and sweater before he stood. There were no pedestrians on the pavement, no other motorists, and no one peeked through any of the nearby curtains as far as he could tell.

It's a bitch, he thought, when a man can't go to the police; and he made his way slowly into the station, purchased a ticket to Edinburgh, and found a place on a bench at the tracks. He had thirty minutes to wait, and he knew he was going to need all of it to wonder about Vanessa.

A train shrieked in and filled the air under the overhang with steam and loud voices; passengers scurried along the platform calling for children, for porters, for tour guides marching toward the exits with umbrellas held high so their charges would be able to mark them. A dustman pushed a cart of metal bins past the bench, mumbling about the days before Windsor had turned modern. A red-cheeked pair of schoolboys just barely ten stood gawking in front of Linc until their mother, with an apologetic smile and an odd look at his clothes, pulled them away. He rose and returned inside as the train pulled out, found a newsstand and bought himself two bars of chocolate, a copy of *Punch*, and a packet of Empires.

The bench was still empty when he returned. He ate one bar, lit a cigarette, and opened the magazine at random.

Vanessa. Not betrayal after all, if the message was to be believed. He did not understand French, written or spoken, but he knew enough to know she had deliberately misspelled George's name as a signal to him, and that mention of her confinement had nothing to do with a stay in hospital. Basil, or Reddick, had her fast, and it was probably George who had told her about his friends the Killestans. Unfortunately, his surmise that Reddick had sent one of his own "friends" to Vilcroft was probably correct or else they'd been following him from the airport. In light of the incident with the car, the latter was more likely; Vilcroft, if nothing else, was at least closemouthed when it came to giving up Lincoln's secrets.

A second train pulled in, less flamboyantly than the first, and he pulled the magazine higher, looking at the sparse crowds embarking and leaving the compartments. The shoulder throbbed. His knees protested whenever he shifted and the woolen slacks rubbed over the scrapes.

I am going to retire, he told himself in the middle of a wince; damnit, this is ridiculous.

Fifteen minutes later a third train shuddered into the station, and he rose slowly, tossed the magazine into the nearest trash bin, and headed for the first-class cars. When he reached the last one and with his fingers lightly on the handle he scanned the platform for a familiar face, scanned again for the suspicious he knew he wouldn't find, and climbed in. The compartment was empty, the racks above the seats without luggage. It was too much to hope that he'd be able to make the entire trip alone, but he knew he could insure an undisturbed one; he took the seat immediately beside the outer door, crossed his legs, and closed his eyes.

Five minutes passed before the train pulled out. No one joined him, though several walked the corridor and peered in through the unshaded panes.

The Orient Express, he thought as the car rocked gently, the wheels clacked against the rails; with my luck Michael Rennie will barge in with Orson Welles in hot pursuit. Or Peter Lorre will get

smarmy over my trews. Or Dirk Bogarde will de-
mand to know if I've ever heard of something
called the thirty-nine steps.

With my luck it'll be a liberated mother and
eighteen snotty brats.

He sighed, and shifted, felt slightly chilly and
folded his arms over his chest.

A whistle sounded as the train reached a crossing.

The conductor opened the corridor door and
asked for his ticket and would he be so kind as not
to spread himself over the seat if he were going to
take a nap. Just in case someone else wanted to
join him, you understand. Lincoln nodded politely
and assured him he was well versed in sleeping
sitting up. The conductor, fat-jowled and white-
haired, saluted him with two fingers and backed
out, moved on, bawling something Linc could not
understand.

There was green outside, a blur of trees, a blur
of houses in the distance. Low hills threatening to
grow higher, and a glimpse of a river before it
darted under a swaying trestle.

The car rocked, the rails talked, and it didn't
take him long to fall fast asleep.

And have a nightmare.

He was standing in an immense room, stone
walls unrelieved by windows or framed artwork.
No furniture. No rugs or carpets. The only exit a
tall narrow door in the opposite wall. The ceiling
was twenty feet overhead. Illumination was provided by a chandelier held to its place by a twisted
black chain secured on a winch next to the door.

He was wearing a tattered wool shirt that had
been white once, before it had been coated with

dried red mud; his jeans were filthy as well and torn at the knees and on his left hip; his boots were scuffed and one heel was loose; his hair was matted with perspiration, and there was an ominous bruise to the right side of his forehead. His hands trembled, and he found it almost impossible to stand without swaying.

He was dizzy.

He was hungry.

He was afraid that someone was going to come through that door.

When it happened he pressed back against the wall, his palms recoiling as the clammy stone pressed into his back. Sand seemed to lodge in his throat, his tongue turned to a rasp when he tried to lick his lips.

Time meant nothing to him as Reddick crossed the room, alone, carrying a long bullwhip in his left hand. Time had meant nothing to him for over a month, from the time he'd first been brought here, unconscious and trussed.

Reddick's thin lips were moving, but Lincoln heard nothing, saw only the sneer reflected in the man's arctic eyes. The lips moved again; he was asking a question. Despite himself, Linc shook his head defiantly and thought himself a jackass for not doing as he was told.

The whip uncoiled on the floor, anaconda quivering for the attack.

The whip snapped into motion and cracked the air where Linc's head would have been had he not ducked in time. Dust flaked from the wall and settled on his shoulders.

The whip again, slowly, so slowly Lincoln thought he'd be able to catch it and yank Reddick off balance. But his hand was just as slow, and his shirt tore at the left shoulder and the dried red mud became a moist, running pink.

The question; the refusal.

The whip lashed across his chest, and he cried out as he cringed against the wall, moving, always moving, and never able to escape the braided tip that pricked his elbow, breezed past his hair, knifed into his shoulder again and made him bite through his lower lip.

He heard thunder.

He heard footsteps outside the open door.

Reddick shredded the rest of his shirt without touching his flesh; Reddick tore gouts of cloth from his jeans without touching his legs. It was worse than pain; it was the anticipation of what that bullwhip would do when Reddick was tired of scaring him to death.

Thunder again, echoing in the huge room.

Shadows from the chandelier doubled and tripled, and Linc found it impossible to see properly, not knowing which Reddick was the one he should plead to.

The door slammed shut and locked just as he sidled to it.

Reddick laughed, and didn't make a sound.

The whip gouged the jamb and showered him with splinters.

There was no more time for playing; that much was obvious in the man's narrowed eyes. Whatever he wanted—and Lincoln could not hear him —he would have to discover it somewhere else.

The whip came straight for his throat, and Linc dropped to the floor, rolled and stood, his right hand out as an inadequate shield, his left up and back as if ready to deliver a blow to a shadow.

And his fingers closed around the handle of the winch.

Reddick saw his intent the moment Lincoln realized what he could do. The whip reached back, and Lincoln turned and grabbed the handle, yanked the linchpin and whirled to catch the lash across his back. The chain rattled, and echoed, and screamed as it fed itself through the iron loops in the wall; the chandelier rocked and trembled and plunged toward the center of the floor.

Reddick bellowed, as much in anger as in terror, and threw himself out of the way, but not far enough. An arm of the immense fixture slammed into his shoulder and hurtled him into the wall. Linc was running instantly, arm up to protect himself against the shards of flying glass, hissing as his flesh was torn and his blood stung.

Reddick was unconscious, sprawled against the base of the wall. Lincoln knelt beside him and fumbled through his pockets, found the large key and palmed it. Then he placed his hands around the man's throat and began to squeeze.

He squeezed until Reddick opened his eyes.

Then he screamed and ran, unlocked the door and bolted into a corridor unlighted and twisting.

He ran through the dark.

Not because he was afraid of what would catch him, or afraid that the whip would follow and shred him.

He ran because he hadn't killed Reddick, and knew that, because of it, Reddick would kill him.

It wasn't a threat; it was a nightmarish promise.

And when a hand reached out of the dark and

grabbed his shoulder he yelled and threw himself back against the wall.

Opened his eyes and saw an elderly man standing over him, green eyes dark with concern. He was wearing a worn brown sweater, worn corduroy trousers, and a Tyrolean hat pushed back over a naked pate. He had a full beard a rich gleaming brown.

"You all right, lad?"

Lincoln felt cold, felt the sweat already drying on his face.

"You all right? Shall I fetch some help?"

He managed to shake his head, at the same time clearing the last of the nightmare out of his mind.

"It was a bad'un," the old man said, taking his place across from Linc. He picked up a newspaper and snapped it open to his place. He smiled. "You're too young for dreams like that, m'boy, far too young."

An answering smile, stronger than he thought he was capable of. "I'm sorry I bothered you."

"No bother." He looked at his paper, looked up. "Would you like a page or two?"

Lincoln squirmed to make himself comfortable. "Sports, if it's all the same to you."

The man's smile faded. "My dear boy, this is *The Times.*"

"Oh."

He looked out the window, frowned at the unfamiliar view until he realized they were slowing down, approaching a small outland station. The bronze sun was near setting, and the landscape was already beginning to darken. Hills rose in the distance, and lights were already winking on in the houses of the town.

The compartment filled with shadows, and the old man switched on the overhead light.

Lincoln heard him sigh, looked, looked away, and looked back.

"Jesus," he said.

The old man put aside the newspaper, brushed a hand carefully down his sweater. "I think not."

"It is you, isn't it?" He wasn't sure. The lighting was dim, and he was still trying to shed the effects of the nightmare.

The man grinned and showed his teeth, full and white and perfectly straight.

Linc sagged and shook his head. "I don't believe it. I just don't goddamn believe it."

"We took a vote," said Macon Crowley. "I lost, and here I am. You need taking care of, Blackie."

"Please!"

"I'm too old to change my habits."

"How the hell did you find me?"

Macon's face creased as if insulted. "Well, you were not exactly unobtrusive, Blackie. Once I delivered Palmer's package to that hotel, or inn, or—"

"Delivered?"

"—whatever it is, I stood around outside. In disguise, of course."

Linc sighed loudly. "You wore a trench coat, I bet."

"Natty one, actually."

"Jesus." He looked outside again; they were crawling now through an unpleasant concentration of dirty brick houses whose backyards abutted the tracks and were filled with large and small piles of junk and dirty children.

The train stopped, their car abreast of a crossing.

Linc turned and smiled. "Good to see you, Macon."

Macon nodded. "The old bird sends her greetings."

"You're alone?"

"I most certainly am."

"Okay."

Macon sniffed. "George had a visitor a while ago."

"Oh?"

"That skinny one, with the funny white hair."

"Oh . . . hell."

"He has the rest of the deck, Blackie."

"Oh . . . hell."

"Yes."

He looked outside again, and blinked. The first car waiting behind the barrier was a canary-yellow BMW. A hand was out the passenger window, and for a moment Linc thought it was waving.

Then he saw the gun.

And the blue-white flare when it fired through the window and Macon pitched over to the floor.

TWENTY-THREE

"IT WAS a stone," Lincoln explained to the conductor, who had thrown open the outside door and was leaning out, peering up and down the tracks. "I'm afraid I was so angry I picked it up and chucked it back at the little bastards."

"Don't blame you, sir," the portly official said, pushing himself back inside and pulling the door to. Then he examined the fist-sized hole in the window by Macon's seat, shook his head, and told them he'd send a repairman around to stuff cardboard or something there, at least until they reached their destination. "It's all I can do for now, sir," he apologized. "Cutbacks, you understand. British Rail isn't in the best of straits these days."

"No need to explain," Macon said expansively. He was sitting as far from the window as he could get, pushed into the corner beside the green shade drawn over the corridor pane.

"Are you sure you're all right?" the conductor asked.

"Fine. Startled more than anything." A finger touched at a tiny cut high on his florid cheek. "Had worse in my time, believe me."

A few minutes more of fussing and mother-henning, another ten while a grizzled workman complained bitterly and loudly over the state of England's wayward youth as he cut out the old window and replaced it with a new, and a few more while passengers from other parts of the train managed to find excuses to drift by and stare. Finally, Macon pulled down the other two shades, sank back in his seat, and blew out an explosive sigh.

His eyes closed, opened, and Lincoln was staring at him. "I said I was all right, Blackie," he insisted almost angrily.

"I want you to go home."

"Out of the question."

Lincoln moved down the seat until he was opposite the older man. "This isn't a matter of taking care of me now, Macon. This is self-preservation. Mine. If anything happens to you, Old Alice will have me drawn and quartered."

Macon waved away the objection, straightened his clothes for the dozenth time, and reached for his newspaper, scattered on the floor and scuffed with footprints. Lincoln leaned over and caught his wrist.

"Macon, I'm not kidding."

"Neither am I," the man said just as steadily. "You can rest assured that I have no intention of facing that ass with you, but you have to get there first. I intend to see that you do."

The staring match continued for a full thirty seconds, until the train lurched into motion again and their contact broke. Then Linc glanced outside, at the road paralleling the tracks, half expecting to see the BMW pacing them. But the road was empty, night nearly complete.

"I don't think it was Reddick," he said at last.

Macon scratched his dyed beard. "That makes no sense."

"It makes all the sense in the world."

"Reddick wants you dead."

"Reddick wants to kill me himself. He has no interest in sending his hired hands out."

"Then—"

"Basil."

"That toad wouldn't kill a fly."

"The mark of Unicov is his incompetence. He's tried to run me down, shoot me down, and serve me as the entree to a rather uninterested jaguar. He hasn't made it yet, but it's not for lack of trying. Don't underestimate him, Macon. He's not as stupid as he'd like us to believe."

When Macon's eyebrow lifted skeptically, Lincoln began a comprehensive but abbreviated narration of all that had happened to him since he'd left the United States, paying no attention to the other's exclamations of outrage, admiration, and wistful nostalgia. By the time he was finished the conductor had been past twice, announcing Edinburgh as the last stop on the run. The two men rose stiffly, massaging their aching joints, grunting, standing at the outer door as the train pulled into the huge station.

"We will have to be careful," Macon suggested.

"Basil's foolhardy, but he's not an idiot. He won't try anything here."

They made their way quickly through the early

evening crowds, out to the taxi stand where they instructed the driver to a small hotel in the shadow of Edinburgh Castle, near the Firth of Forth. The proprietor greeted them solemnly, knowingly, and gave them adjoining rooms on the topmost floor.

Their dinners were brought to them separately.

They spoke only for a few minutes before retiring, waking just after dawn when the proprietor knocked discreetly on Macon's door and told him the hire-car was waiting for them outside. The bill was paid, a few pleasantries exchanged, and before the city's rush hour had begun they were driving north, with as much speed as Macon could coax out of an old, dented black Rover.

At midday they stopped for a brief lunch, a brief walk around the restaurant, and a refueling. Within an hour they were on the road again, this time leaving the main highway for secondary routes not much wider than the car they were using.

Macon complained that the altitude was beginning to affect his sinuses; Lincoln told him they weren't in the Highlands yet and he could always go back to Old Alice if he wanted, and send Palmer over to baby-sit. Macon declined the alternative by speeding up and nearly plowing through a hedgerow when the road took a sudden and sharp left turn.

"You'll be the death of me," Linc complained lightly.

"Better at the hands of dear friends than dear enemies."

"Is that a quotation?"

"Yeats, I believe."

"I don't believe it. And this is a dangerous place to be quoting the Irish."

Macon shrugged and slowed down, draped a wrist over the wheel and wished aloud for some brandy. Then he glanced at Linc and smiled. "Your family, I take it, is from this locale."

"Farther north," he said with a jut of his chin. "Up past Inverness."

"Ah, Inverness. Loch Ness. Pipes skirling in the dawn mist and lassies dancing their little hearts out."

"You like that sort of thing?"

"The lassie part, of course."

"Macon," Lincoln cautioned, "I'm telling you now you will not attempt to improve relations with the natives."

"I have no intention of jeopardizing your task, Blackie."

"I know. I just wanted to hear you say it."

"I am insulted."

"You are driving off the road."

Macon made the correction deftly, muttering, and Linc turned to watch the land roll into higher hills, into mountains in the distance. He knew that in spring there was no more beautiful place on earth than the Highlands in bloom, and knew too there were few who found that beauty again when the heather stopped flowering and the grasslands turned a dark rusted brown. It was in all senses of the word rugged, and easy to see, now, why the Highland Scots were a breed unlike their countrymen to the south. Not everyone could live untouched in the midst of such magnificent melancholy, not even with the pine forests blessing the land with the only green for miles.

When twilight threatened to rob Macon of his vision, Linc insisted they stop at an inn for the night, a small place off the road near an even smaller lake. Macon, as they walked to the door, began recounting stories he'd heard about just such places, where the maids were buxom and willing, the innkeeper more than willing to turn a blind eye, and the locals jolly in their acceptance of the weary traveler.

The barmaid was fifty-three, a broomstick complete with straw hair, and so reminiscent of Old Alice that Macon refused to say a word once he'd ordered himself a glass of whisky; the innkeeper, a young man who claimed graduation from the University in Edinburgh, asked for their passports and the night's fee in advance; otherwise, the place was empty.

"He'll go far," Macon whispered as they climbed a narrow staircase to the upstairs rooms. "Has the soul of Silas Marner."

Linc shrugged, shrugged again when he saw that the accommodations were considerably less than he generally expected, had no time to shrug a third time when he realized how tired he was, how many miles they had driven since dawn.

And by the following night they would be skirting the southern tip of Loch Ness, sweeping around to the north, away from Inverness. To Craig Dellaugh, Anton Reddick's retreat in the mountains.

"I feel it my obligation as an observer of our planet's continual attempts to stupefy its inhabitants."

Lincoln said nothing.

"It is an overwhelming passion with me, Blackie."

The road crawled along the contours of the lake, the water bright with lances of reflecting sun between the tall trees that lined its banks.

"Scientific curiosity should not be denied. You remember, of course, what happened to Galileo."

"No."

A pause. "Be that as it may, I cannot but register a strong and decisive protest against your single-mindedness."

They swept past a caravan of Romanian tourists setting up a barrage of cameras both still and motion between the boles of two hundred-foot Scotch pines; they slowed when they spotted a man in a rowboat dropping small packages into the clear, cold water, then scooping them out again hastily, examining them, and dropping them into a creel; a constable on bicycle waved them on politely when Macon stopped to watch a trio of lab-coated Japanese make fine-tuning adjustments to a battery of computer consoles while a colleague stood in a skiff a hundred yards from shore and waved a red flag over the rippling surface.

"They're having all the fun," Macon complained.

"They're using contemporary magic to conjure a decidedly noncontemporary critter," Lincoln said, and pointed sharply at the road ahead. "Drive. Nessie will wait for you, I'm sure."

"I promised Old Alice."

"I am not moved."

"You're not in a civilized mood, either."

Linc admitted as much with a one-shoulder shrug, but said nothing. He could only watch the spectacular scenery sweep past him around Loch Ness, but he could not appreciate it. All he saw beyond the mountains, beyond the forests, was his destination, even in the startling July sunlight cloaked and shimmering in defiant shadow.

He had got only a glimpse of it the last time he

was there, half a decade before, but it had been enough: a narrow valley between two mountains virtually denuded of woodland and ground cover, scoured by the harsh Highland winters, the vicious winds and snows that swept over the peaks from the North Sea; boulders the size of cottages littering the roadside in hues of brown and deadly grey; a solid wooden bridge over a swift-moving stream midway along the valley floor; and the place itself, no name needed since it was the only inhabited building within fifty miles.

It should have been a castle, he'd thought that first time; someone like Reddick should have a Bela Lugosi castle complete with bats in the turrets, odd spectral women in the corridors, and cobwebs so thick the air would be almost white.

But it wasn't.

It was a two-story stone building of indeterminate architecture set in the middle of a circular lawn that extended from the walls a hundred yards to the slope of the mountains; its windows were high, narrow, and arched, its entrance a pair of oaken doors unpaneled and unsculpted; four or five chimneys poked through the peaked slate roof, and gables abounded, their panes blind and nonreflecting. To one side a garage that may once have been a stable, to the other a large cottage he later learned housed Cashim and Krawn.

He had been nearly unconscious when they carried him from the truck, so the inside was a mystery. Except for the huge room with the crashing chandelier.

And where others might have thought it bland, or a confused mixture of this style and that, he had known from the first sighting that it truly belonged to Reddick—it was dark, and sly, promising nothing by way of comfort, promising all in the way of evil.

He shuddered, glanced at Macon to be sure the reaction hadn't been seen. It was foolish, all these nerves. Reddick was a man and nothing more than that. He could be beaten, and he had been beaten, and if Linc didn't beat him again the man would have the power to construct a base that would, in time (since he would have more time than anyone), turn as much of the world as he wanted into another Craig Dellaugh.

Loch Ness slipped behind them, and to the northeast they could see the first signs of Inverness—more roads, buildings, a section of railroad that followed the skirts of the hills. They shifted northwest, however, and left the city as they'd left the lake, and Macon fell curiously silent as noon passed and the afternoon lengthened with the shadows.

They drove past small crofts, Macon muttering at the shaggy Highland cattle he likened to yaks lost on an expedition; they ducked through several small villages, found themselves more frequently driving around lochs and over streams. There were stags on the slopes, pheasant and grouse. A flock of sheep slowed them to a walk as it crossed the road, the shepherd waving to them as he prodded his charges with a long hawthorn staff.

"I assume," Macon said at last, "you have not directed me through some maddened time dilation."

"No, Macon. This is all for real."

"It's not for real. It's positively bucolic."

"You don't exactly live in a metropolis, you know."

"I don't have to smell sheep when I go to bed, either."

He laughed, more than the comment would warrant under ordinary circumstances. He would never say it, Macon would call it bad form, but he was inordinately pleased for the company.

At three o'clock they reached an unmarked fork in the road.

Macon stopped, his hands massaging the steering wheel.

"Left," Lincoln said, pointing to little more than a dirt track that led toward a split in the range ahead.

"I think not," Macon said.

"Macon, for god's sake!"

"If we go left," Macon said patiently, "we will be shot. While you have ruminated on the course of whatever, I have been watching a gentleman in a Jeep riding the hills alongside. He has since maneuvered himself in front of us and is now, in fact, lying in wait in that stand of ungodly tall trees fifty feet or so up that so-called road. He has a rifle, Blackie, and I don't think he's going to bother with a warning."

"Drive!" Lincoln ordered.

Macon shrugged, and did.

And the man with the rifle fired through the windshield.

TWENTY-FOUR

THEY STOOD in front of the Rover, their hands clasped behind their heads. A chilled wind blew down from the hills, and Macon shivered while Lincoln waited for the man in the Jeep to step out of the trees. He'd shouted his orders, and they had complied, not wanting to measure the distance between the small hole in the windshield and themselves; not very far to either side and one of them would have been dead.

"Blackie, does this happen very often?"

"As a matter of fact, yes."

"I do not approve."

"You can't say I'm boring."

"In deference to the situation, I shall pass."

They waited, shifting in place, listening to the wind.

"I am somewhat heartened by this," Macon said when they heard the Jeep's engine roar into an untuned sputtering.

"Are you really."

"He could have put one between my eyes."

"Indeed."

"He did not, which shows some small measure of compassion on his part."

"He could also be a lousy shot."

The Jeep bucked and crashed its way through the underbrush and onto the dirt road, stalled and skidded sideways to a halt. The driver, in a bulky black leather coat that reached to his knees and an oversized green tam, slapped at the wheel angrily.

Lincoln put down his hands.

"Blackie, that is ill-advised."

"Follow me," he said, put his hands in his pockets and walked over to the disabled vehicle. Macon swore under his breath but did as he was bidden, scanning the verge for something large to throw in case it was needed.

When Linc was within ten feet of the Jeep he stopped and shook his head.

"You really ought to stick to motorcycles."

Basil Unicov glared at him, finally threw up his hands in disgust and climbed out of his seat. "This," he said with a disdainful gesture toward the Jeep, "is trash, Blackthorne." He looked to Macon, who had stepped up to Lincoln's side. "And who the hell is that? His beard has white roots."

"Your eyes are as toadish as ever," Macon said stiffly.

"Oh god, not you."

"I have my obligations."

"Lincoln," Basil said, "I never expected you to hide behind a geriatric army."

Macon reached for the man's coat, yanked him forward with one hand and gripped the back of his neck with the other. Unicov gasped, sputtered, his face flushing purple.

"That . . . hurts."

"I do not wish to hurt you, Toad, and I do apologize for that," Macon said. "Geriatric martial arts, however, is not yet an exact science."

When Basil was released he staggered back against the hood and rubbed his neck and chest gingerly.

"Where's the BMW?" Lincoln said.

"It broke down yesterday morning." He whistled then and looked to the sky. "Damn, but I am possessed of the poorest luck in this thing."

"Basil, I would gladly beat the shit out of you if it would make you feel any better, but I haven't the time. Please, for old time's sake, tell me where Vanessa is and what the hell is going on."

Basil pulled himself up, looked to Macon, who was examining his nails, and sagged again. "It has all gone wrong."

"I've noticed."

"You know, my friend, in the old days men in our business didn't have telephones and telegraphs and satellites and things. We could get where we wanted to get without notice if we were the fastest. There weren't armies of clumsy assassins dogging our every step."

Lincoln nodded. Macon walked away, into the trees.

"Vanessa and I, we left that miserable little llama hut of a country in fine style, you know. We landed in Bogotá ready for a connecting flight to London. Reddick . . . ah, that sonofabitch."

"An army jet, I know. He beat you there, got Vanessa away, and left you in some miserable alley to die. And you don't even speak Spanish. He also took the King."

Basil looked at him suspiciously. "How did you know that?"

"I saw the movie. C'mon, Basil, I'm getting impatient."

"I saved your life," he protested.

"You fed me to the fauna."

"You got away. I knew you would." He smiled. "It wasn't a serious threat."

Lincoln didn't smile back.

Basil looked over to Macon, who was kneeling by a low clump of brush, examining a clutch of tiny blue flowers.

"Unicov."

"He has the King, yes," Basil said, sighing in genuine disgust at himself. "That pig, Cashim, threw me out a window and didn't check to see if I was dead. I landed in garbage. I tell you, Blackthorne, Colombian garbage is nothing to land in even if it does save your life.

"It took me a while—about a half dozen tourists—to reobtain the necessary funds for the flight to England. I knew he was coming here, he always does, and I suspected that if . . . when you got away from the big cat you would be here too. I waited at the airport. I needed to know, you see, who I had to negotiate with for the card."

"There is no negotiation, Basil."

Unicov frowned briefly. "You need me to get in there."

"You can't do it alone, either."

"Perhaps."

Lincoln studied his face for several seconds, then called to Macon. The old man stood slowly, one hand around to grip the small of his back. Then he strode briskly over to the Rover without comment, opened the passenger door and slid in. Basil grabbed the rim of his tam and yanked it emphatically over his eyes, but Lincoln ignored him, turned instead, and headed for the automobile. He had just opened the door when he heard hurried footsteps behind him.

"All right," Basil said, pouting. "All right. But only if you drive."

Lincoln pointed silently to the back seat, and Unicov scrambled in, had barely positioned himself when the car started and jounced over the hard ground around the Jeep, swerved back onto the path, and covered itself in dry, grey dust as it barreled toward the mountain ahead.

A hard hour passed before Lincoln spoke again: "Are you armed?"

Macon patted the underside of his left arm, and Unicov only grumbled as he revealed an army-issue .45 tucked under his leather jacket.

"Why didn't you bring the rifle?" Macon asked.

"I stole it. It only had two bullets."

"My god," Lincoln said incredulously, "who do you take lessons from, Pizarro and Cortez?"

"I learned," Basil said huffily, "all that I know from the best experts in Georgia."

"Atlanta-type Georgia?" Macon said.

"Please," Basil said, pained. "U.S.S.R., of course."

"Stalin country," Lincoln muttered.

"A misunderstood human being."

"Thousands did, I gather."

Basil refused to answer, staring out the window as the car began to pitch with the sudden dislocation of the road into a canted trail that was more grass than earth. They were climbing, and cloud peaks began to fill the sky with towers of black cut through with stark white. The scent of rain filled the air, and the wind buffeted the Rover continuously, several times causing it to leave the trail before Linc could correct his steering.

Shortly before dusk the trail vanished at the base of a barbed-wire fence that angled down the approaching slope toward them into a broad-based V. No one suggested they attempt to drive around it. Linc pulled the car under the protection of a blue-needled fir, pocketed the keys, and patted the warm hood. Then he checked the sky again, saw the massing clouds sweep over them southward in several conflicting layers. It made him dizzy to watch the display, and he was grateful when Macon touched his arm.

The wind had died.

The moon was already beginning to rise, wan and translucent in what remained of daylight.

As they stepped out from under the fir's long-reaching lower boughs they heard a grating cry and looked up. A pair of golden eagles were riding the currents around the mountain peak, looping and spiraling about each other without once using their wings. The display continued until the light faded and there was nothing left but the faint echo of their calls.

Lincoln watched then as the clouds assembled themselves into an impenetrable cover, considered for several minutes before suggesting they wait until daybreak before attempting to get into the valley. Macon agreed readily, but Basil stamped his feet and proclaimed his unquenchable thirst for Reddick's blood with such vehemence that Linc almost changed his mind. But the land was unfamiliar, and he suspected more than natural pitfalls awaited them if they moved out now.

Basil argued further.

Macon went back to the car, found a lap robe in the trunk, and wrapped it around his shoulders. He listened for a minute to Unicov's ranting, then climbed into the back seat and was asleep within seconds.

Lincoln only stood in the dark, finally and wearily told the little man he could go on his own if he wanted, reconnoiter, and let them know if there was anything they should be wary of. Basil nodded once and sharply and had taken but a half dozen steps before Linc warned him about the wolves.

"Wolves," Basil said, his disembodied voice flat and somewhat high-pitched.

"This is Scotland, Basil. And this is the most remote section of a rather remote country. I wouldn't bet on it, but I have heard stories."

"Wolves."

"Suit yourself."

He climbed in behind the wheel, pushed the seat back as far as it would go, and rested his chin on his chest, hugged himself and blessed the Highland shepherd who'd made the wool for his sweater. Five minutes later Basil was sitting beside him, humming as he squirmed into the corner.

It was cold, and shortly before midnight it started to rain.

It was still dark when Lincoln woke, shivering, muttering to himself when he checked his watch and found it to be three hours before dawn. The shower was over, but droplets thundered on the car roof from the branches overhead. Macon was snoring quietly in back; Basil wasn't making a sound.

He reached out, and a hand closed over his forearm.

"Thought you were asleep."

"It is very noisy out here," Unicov said quietly. "I am not used to it."

"Vanessa."

"I was wondering when you would ask, my friend."

"How was she?"

"When she was with me, talking of you constantly. She was wrong about everything, of course, but you lie so well, my dear Blackthorne, that I could not dissuade her from believing all those glorious things about you."

He thought he was pleased, though he could not help remembering that she'd taken off with the cyclist and left him with the jaguar.

"Afterward, I can't say. Reddick isn't predictable, my friend. You know this more than most."

"She was well enough to get a message to me." He explained about her uncle, and Basil applauded her ingenuity, loud enough to make Macon stir in the back seat. Then he decided he might as well get it over with. "Has she always been working for you?"

Silence.

"Basil, wake up."

"I am, Blackthorne. I just thought you knew."

"Knew what?"

"She doesn't work for me. She doesn't work for you."

Jesus, he thought.

"Shame, Blackthorne," Unicov said. "Not for Reddick either."

"Then who?"

"Who else?"

"Damn," he muttered, "she was telling the truth from the start."

Basil's laugh was more a snort, and he slapped Linc's shoulder heartily before pushing himself deeper into the corner.

Lincoln stayed awake for another fifteen minutes, chastising himself for doubting her, telling himself he had every right to be cautious. He hadn't yet decided how much guilt to accept before his eyes closed, and the night shifted to the dead hours that brought on the sun.

And when his eyes fluttered open again he yawned, stretched, and blinked.

Arnold Krawn was standing by his window, and there was a double-barreled shotgun aimed directly at his throat.

TWENTY-FIVE

THE LIGHT was dim, the air filtered through faint gold; ground mist lay in skirts around the trunks of the pines, lay undulating in depressions as it reacted to the slow-climbing temperature. Birds marked their appetites and territories with song, and a slight breeze brought with it the vague tang of the sea. There were no hard edges to anything, not even the boulders on the slope leading to Craig Dellaugh.

Krawn gestured with the shotgun.

Linc nudged Basil before he opened the door and slid out, noting as he did that the back seat was empty. He glanced around quickly but saw no sign of Macon Crowley and prayed somberly that Reddick's henchman hadn't gotten to him somewhere back in the woods. Basil cursed in disgust as he came around the car at Krawn's mute direction and only a brief narrowing of his eyes told Linc he too had noted Macon's absence. And would remain silent.

"Turn," Krawn ordered then.

"Good morning," Linc said.

Krawn was wearing an undersized tweed jacket leathered at the elbows, matching trousers, a pin-striped open-throated shirt, and green wool sweater vest. A brown racing cap barely covered his massive scalp, and Linc nodded to himself—a man out for an early morning hunt, no question about it. And the man might have passed had no one bothered to look at his eyes, deep-set, and black, and totally lifeless. Chips of onyx set in poorly carved stone.

Basil took off his tam and scratched through his red hair. "What now, if I may ask?" he said.

Krawn held the shotgun at his hip, still aimed at Lincoln's throat. "You weren't expected until tonight." His voice was a monotone, as flat as the noncolor of his eyes.

"Sorry," Linc said, and wished the man would make up his mind whether to shoot or drag them off to the house.

Suddenly, the weapon was at Krawn's shoulder, and Basil crumpled his cap between his palms. "My god," he said.

"I have orders," Krawn told him.

Linc judged the distance between them and relaxed as much as he could—there was nothing he could do. Krawn was too far away. By the time Linc might push himself off the car, the first shot would have been fired and the next exploding directly in his face. He couldn't remember the last time he'd felt so helpless.

"No last requests?" he said when it was apparent the man was enjoying watching Basil quiver like a leaf in a thunderstorm.

"None."

"Then do it, damnit."

Krawn smiled, and Lincoln looked away. The lips parted and the teeth were exposed and there was not a whit of humor in any of it, only a deep self-satisfaction as grotesque as the expression it caused on his face.

Then he heard a *crack*, like the distant firing of a shot. Instead of turning, however, Krawn stood there, his jaw slowly lowering, his eyes slowly closing. When he began to pitch forward, Basil leapt to whip the shotgun from his hands and aim it at his head, ready to pull both triggers should the man move. When he looked up, every inch of his face was a question, and Linc answered by pointing to Macon, who was strolling toward them from the road, a rock in his left hand much like the one lying at Krawn's feet.

"Wanted to be a pitcher when I was a lad," the old man said, kicking Krawn's boots to be sure he was unconscious. "Used to hit the umpire more often than not."

"Not bad," Basil admitted grudgingly, and Macon acknowledged him with a curt nod.

Linc, meanwhile, had dropped to his knees and was pulling Krawn's jacket off, motioning for Basil to help with the slacks. When they were finished, Linc was in the tweed, surprised at the almost perfect fit and wondering what Krawn was doing with such ill-suited clothes. Reddick, he decided, bought his men's wardrobe wholesale.

Basil found a length of cord in the Rover and bound Krawn's wrists behind his back, pulled up his legs, and coupled them to his ankles. Then he pulled Krawn's nose, thumped him once in the ribs.

"Beautiful. Could be dead, god willing.".

Linc finished buttoning the jacket and adjusting the cap.

"You'll never pass," Macon told him.

"From a distance, maybe."

"From a distance to a blind man."

He shrugged and started for the fencing, opening and closing his fists to relieve the surge of tension that had abruptly stiffened every joint in his body. There was no problem avoiding the barbed wire, nor did they run into any opposition as they took the easy slope as rapidly as they dared without wearing themselves out.

An hour later they had reached the top of the trail and were crouched on a ledged boulder as broad as a house and nearly as high. The trail led straight down to the valley floor, widened to become a passable dirt road that crossed a narrow stream and angled to the right into a long stand of trees. It reappeared on the other side, directly in front of Craig Dellaugh.

The surrounding slopes were bare of anything but low brown shrubs and a few daring wild flowers that gave the valley its only dash of color.

Behind the mansion was a helicopter pad, the garage and cottage where they should be.

Behind them a four-acre pond.

The barbed-wire fence stretched around the entire valley, halfway up the slopes.

It was exactly as he remembered in his nightmares—the stone, the high windows, the massive doors, the chimney pots interspersed with antennae and a pair of twenty-foot satellite dishes.

And despite the proliferation of modern paraphernalia that broke the lines of the peaked roof, it should have been impressive and inspiring—a manse in the middle of nowhere, a romantic oasis in the midst of mountainous isolation.

What he felt, however, was a powerful sense of overwhelming desolation. There was no life here, and he glanced at the sky as if expecting the approach of a hellish thunderstorm.

"It doesn't change," Basil whispered with a slow shake of his head.

Macon only nodded; he'd never seen it before, and Linc could tell by the purse of his lips and the way he stroked his beard absently that they shared the same sensations.

Ten minutes later Linc broke the spell and slid back to the ground, sat with his back to the rock and draped his hands over his knees.

"Now what?" Basil said. "That thing down there" —and he pointed back to the barely visible car, and Krawn's body—"won't wait until we're done."

"Now that we've seen it, perhaps an evening excursion might be best," Macon suggested, pulling his revolver from inside his jacket and opening it to examine the chambers.

"No," Linc said. "We can't wait. The deck, Macon. He has the deck."

"He's bound to have the house secured, Blackie. Expecting you or not, he will not underestimate you."

"Yeah, I know. The curse of being Superman."

"We are wasting time," Basil snapped, pushed himself to his feet and rubbed the side of his nose. Then he brushed back his hair and replaced his tam, handed the shotgun to Linc, and checked his .45.

"What do you think you're doing?"

"I'm going for a visit," Unicov said, brushing the dust from his clothes.

"You can't."

"Reddick and I are enemies, Blackthorne, but neither of us is your friend. He won't kill me right away, and I'll be sure the front door is unlocked before he does." He grinned once, without mirth, stepped out onto the road and began walking. He neither looked back nor waved. Both Macon and Linc scrambled back up the rock and lay there, watching as he finally vanished into the trees.

The sun began to reach over the top of the eastern hill.

"Why didn't you stop him, Blackie?"

"Macon, before we die I'm going to choke that name out of your vocabulary."

"I apologize."

"I didn't stop him because I don't have a tank or a missile or a bazooka handy. It's as good a way as any to get into the door."

"He could double-cross us."

Linc pulled at an earlobe. "Oh, he will, no question about it. But he can't overpower them all on his own. He needs us."

"Are you sure about that?"

He wasn't, but he hoped his silence would tell the old man otherwise.

When Unicov finally appeared at the far side of the trees, he took off his cap and slapped it briskly against his thigh as if dusting it. Linc hesitated, took a deep breath, and said, "Okay, let's go."

When they moved they moved swiftly. Macon walked in front, hands in his pockets and his head glumly down; Linc stayed behind him with the shotgun crooked over his arm, trying to position the old man between him and the house. If anyone was at a window and watching them—even with binoculars—it would seem, with a little luck, that Krawn was hustling a captive Crowley down the trail. And every few feet Linc reached out to give him a shove between the shoulders.

"Verisimilitude," he said once when Macon complained.

"My ass," Macon said.

Once in the trees, however, Crowley had his revolver in hand and Linc checked to be sure he still had his knife, the cosh, and his own gun before cracking open the shotgun to be sure it was loaded. Then they left the road and made their way through the early morning darkness, the air damp here and the dew soaking their trousers almost to the knees. At the last possible moment they ducked behind a wall of holly bushes and watched.

The front door was open.

Basil was standing arrogantly on the threshold, apparently arguing with someone who would not step out, the jist of his gesticulations a refusal to raise his hands. Then he stepped back and put his hands firmly on his hips, his diminutive size dwarfed even further by the height of the solid, unadorned oaken doors. He shrugged. Linc squinted, hoping to catch sight of whoever was giving him trouble. Then Unicov stretched his arms out and Cashim closed on him, frisking him expertly and pulling the .45 out of its hip holster. Basil shrugged again and followed the man inside.

The door closed, so loudly Linc could hear the slam where he knelt.

They waited.

They listened.

The sun rose above the hills and the valley lost all its shadow.

"The man will have chewed through those ropes by now," Macon whispered.

Linc knew. The front door was fifty yards from where they waited, fifty that looked like one hundred and fifty miles. His palms were moist, his back aching, and there was a peculiar buzzing in his ears that he couldn't shake away. He closed his eyes once and saw the room, the chandelier, the cobralike rise of the whip poised to lash at his chest. He opened them quickly and saw Macon staring at him. A reassuring smile would have been useless.

A deep breath, and he was on his feet, hurrying along the length of the holly in search of an opening. When he found it he didn't hesitate—he burst through at a dead run, and almost to the house looked down in time to see his left foot about to land on something glinting in the morning sun.

Nuts, he thought.

It was a trip wire for a land mine.

TWENTY-SIX

HE TWISTED around so hard he felt muscles pulling out of shape in his thighs and hips, hopped on one foot for several seconds before stopping himself.

He had missed the mine's trigger, but he wasn't positive it was a good thing to still be alive.

He froze until he could regain his breath and blink away the sudden shower of perspiration that fell from his brow into his eyes. A swallow, another, and he lowered himself to the ground, turning as he did to face the front door. There were only twenty feet left, but he had no idea how many more of the mines there were, suspected Basil had known about them, which was why he'd stayed on the path—as Macon had done, veering in that direction the moment he left the safety of the trees. The old man was staring at him now in bewilderment until Linc pointed at the ground and made a spraying motion with his hands. Immediately, Macon raced for the stoop and pressed himself against the wall to the left of the door, out of sight of anyone peering through the windows. Then he held up one hand, its thin fingers crossed.

Nice, Linc thought as he nodded; a great help.

He looked to his left, to the nearest window, and saw it was covered with what looked like heavy draperies. Small favors, he decided, and leaned close to the ground, sighting, hoping to see another wire. There was none. The one he'd barely managed to avoid must have worked loose in the rain. His choice was simple, then—to sit here until someone spotted him and perhaps offer him a way out, or to make his way across what little ground remained on his hands and knees, testing the soft earth every inch of the way. The lawn, such as it was, consisted of unmown grass a dull, listless green. He would have to pass his hand over the path he would take and trust that his fingers were sensitive enough to feel the next wire before it was pushed too far to either side.

A burr seemed lodged in his throat.

Ice sprouted along the length of his back.

He was glad Vilcroft couldn't see him now, kneeling on Reddick's front yard in broad daylight; assuming he lived, George would never let him forget it.

With his left hand pressed to the ground for balance, he stretched out his right and parted the first clump of grass. Each blade resisted him, each shadow seemed suddenly metallic. He prodded lightly, gingerly, until he was sure he could move forward. When he did, he held his breath.

He raised his head, positive he had gone at least half the distance, saw he'd moved a foot at most, and resolved not to look again until he could feel the gravel walk under his palm.

A fly swooped down in front of his eyes.

Perspiration blinded him until he wiped his face with his sleeve.

Another foot.

When he was certain he'd cleared a large enough path he lay on his stomach, the better to see ahead, at close range.

A bee landed on the back of his hand, and he was about to brush it off when he saw the wire poke between his first two fingers as they parted the grass. It seemed fat and obscene from this angle, and the bee triple its actual size. He blew at it gently, but its wings only ruffled and it strolled along one distended vein toward his center knuckle.

If it stung him his hand would jerk.

If his hand jerked . . .

Something crawled across the back of his neck.

So slowly he wasn't sure it was moving, he lifted his hand, watching the bee, watching the wire until it vanished. He tilted his fingers as far back as they would go, raised his hand another inch, and snapped it up and to the right, gritting his teeth in expectation of the sting.

Nothing happened.

He looked back, and a breeze began gliding down the slope, rustling through the grass and hiding the wire. His teeth closed on his lower lip, and his hand returned to the hunt, found the trigger again and slowly pulled out the grass around it. When he was certain it couldn't be hidden, he inched forward.

Another foot.

He found a wire next to his right shoulder.

He found another beside his left hip.

He was panting after five minutes, gasping after ten, and wondering why in hell someone hadn't come to the window to search the grounds. Surely Reddick didn't trust Basil all that much, for god's sake.

It occurred to him too that Krawn was certainly taking his time getting out of his bonds; Basil, he knew, could barely tie his own shoelaces. Of course, the man might be dead, but his skull was too damned thick for such a stroke of luck.

A wire sprang from beneath a dead leaf, and he held his breath, waiting for the detonation.

It didn't come, and he licked his lips, tasted the heavy concentration of salt, and decided he'd had enough. Macon gasped when he rose, clamped a hand over his mouth when Linc did a few knee-bends to limber up his legs. There was a fair six or seven feet left to the walk, and he would be damned if he was going to crawl all that way on his belly, only to have himself divided into birdseed by a wire trigger he missed because his vision was blurring.

The only thing for it was to jump.

Macon eased himself away from the door and down the walk, checking the windows as he did, beckoning Linc impatiently once he realized what was going to happen. Linc nodded, took a deep breath, and began swinging his arms back and forth, bending his knees, waiting for the timing to be exactly right.

Breathing, swinging, bending.

He was sure he would make it.

Until he heard the deep-throated howling of at least a half dozen dogs on the run.

He jumped.

The instant he was in the air he knew he was going to fall short, but there was nothing he could do about it until he felt Macon grabbing hold of his arms and yanking him as hard as he could. They collided and fell, scrambled to their feet, and ran to the door.

The dogs were nearing the corner of the mansion.

Linc grabbed the faceted brass knob and turned it. The door gave, and they were inside with the door closed before the first animal rounded the turn into the yard.

Bless you, Toad, he thought, until he looked up and saw where he was.

The building had no center hall, only a long, dimly lighted corridor that ended midway to the back at a flight of equally narrow stairs. On the stone walls hung shields and armaments dating back to the seventeenth century, pennants in walnut frames, electric lights shaped like burning torches in black iron brackets. To their left and right were darkwood doors, and another pair to the right and left of the staircase.

Except for their breathing, there was no sound at all.

Wonderful, he thought; pick a door, the lady or the tiger.

Macon was standing now, revolver in hand, and Linc did the same before moving quietly to the left and placing his ear against the door. Nothing. He took hold of the knob and realized it slid to the left, pulled it and peered into a massive room filled with islands of furniture extending from a man-tall stone fireplace on the back wall. The draperies he'd noted from the outside were all closed, and he could see little else in the faint light of a single lamp burning in the middle of the nearest conversation setting.

The room opposite was the same.

He chafed. Time was no longer neutral, and they had to find Vanessa and the King and get out before they were spotted. At the steps, then, he waved Macon up and decided to take the lefthand door by the staircase. Macon did not argue; he was climbing before Linc could even wish him well or arrange a meeting place should neither of them locate his target.

Yet the old man was right in not asking; there would be no meeting place because failure would most likely be accompanied by capture, if not worse.

With a salute to Crowley's back, then, he opened the door and slipped through into another, much shorter corridor whose only exit lay at the back. He ran lightly, hearing nothing, reached the door and tested the knob. It was unlocked. A frown at Reddick's offhand self-assurance, and he pulled the door to.

It was a kitchen, starkly modern and jarringly out of place in a building obviously more than two centuries old. Leaving nothing to chance, however, he made a swift search of the large cupboards and the pantry, opened the rear door and looked out on the slope behind the mansion. The dogs were howling, distantly, as if they'd taken the path he and Macon had used to enter the valley.

He returned at a cautious run to the staircase and the righthand door. Another corridor, this one with its exit midway down the unadorned stone wall on the right. The knob turned. He tightened his grip on the revolver and pushed.

"Jesus," he said aloud.

The room he entered was forty by forty, completely bare save for a facing thronelike chair in the center of the stone floor. There were exits in the far wall, two of them, and he made for the left one instinctively, brushing his hand over the burnished wood chair as he passed it, pulling his fingers away when they felt as if they were stroking dry ice.

The next room was much smaller, a library with shelves built into the walls—false books when he checked, and he wasn't surprised—the fireplace to his right, the club chairs scattered over an intricate Persian carpet that, he thought, would be right at home in Vilcroft's underground sanctum.

But there was no one here either.

And no sign that anyone had been here for days, for months.

He was growing somewhat frustrated, anxiety making his motions choppy, swift, as he returned to the larger room and tried the door on the right.

Lady or the tiger.

He was weary of choices.

Either way, he wasn't sure he would win.

Another library, and he cursed Reddick for his apparent love of mazes, ran to the back wall and the single door there.

He opened it; it was yet another corridor, this one much colder, more damp than the rest of the house, and he ordered himself to rein in his nerves, slow his speed as he made his way along the dark hall to the door at the other end.

It opened at a touch of the knob, and his stomach shrank around a leaden butterfly as brilliant light flooded into the corridor, momentarily blinding him. And when his vision cleared he saw a staircase leading downward in a tight spiral, the walls marked every five feet by the same electric pseudo-torches that were in the front hall.

He heard voices, low and murmuring, so much like casual conversation that he almost ran down the narrow steps. He took them one at a time, however, pressing against the outer wall as much as he could for a clear view of the area below him. His shadow paced him, ahead, then behind. He counted the steps, stopping at forty when he realized the next turn would take him into the room below.

It wasn't the nightmare room, however; that much he knew, that much he remembered.

The revolver lightened, and he touched at his wrist to be sure the knife was still in its sheath.

A brush of his sleeve over his face, and he eased down again, his back to the wall, his gunhand down at his right.

His shadow stayed behind him.

And at the bottom step he paused.

The enclosed staircase apparently opened from a side wall, giving him a clear view of the room at the bottom. It was as large as the throne room he'd found on the first floor, this one, however, richly appointed: medieval hangings on the walls between impressive displays of artwork, some of which he recognized as missing from every museum from the Metropolitan in New York to the Kremlin in Moscow; a walk-in fireplace blazed directly across from him, and the same electric torches flared brightly from their brackets; the furniture was massive and ornate, spread around the room less for comfort and intimacy than for viewing the centerpiece—a twenty-foot refectory table set in front of the hearth. No cloth, no place setting, no chairs around it.

But it forced him to focus on the sound of the voices.

Reddick, standing beside the table with his back to the fire; Cashim at the foot, holding a brass-handled poker whose clawed tip seemed to be glowing white hot.

And Vanessa, draped in a white sheet and lying on the table itself, her head directly at Reddick's waist. She was conscious, and her face was contorted in a mélange of rage and terror.

As Linc watched, unable to move, Reddick accepted the poker from his henchman and gripped it by its brass hilt, raised it until his arms were almost straight over his head.

Then he looked up, straight into Lincoln's eyes.

"Ah, Blackthorne," he said. "I'm afraid you're too late."

And plunged the white-hot tip toward Vanessa's heart.

TWENTY-SEVEN

VANESSA'S SHRILL scream galvanized Lincoln off the step and into the room, his gun up and his finger at the trigger. Almost instantly, however, large powerful hands grabbed his arms roughly and spun him around. The revolver fired harmlessly into the air as it was jarred from his grip, and he wasn't at all surprised to see Arnold Krawn drawing back his hand for a blow to his chin.

A sickening *thud* then, and a terrified scream.

Krawn hesitated, and Linc whirled, to see Reddick grinning at him, the poker now firmly embedded in the table beside Vanessa's throat. But the second he wasted in gaping angrily was the second Krawn needed to ensnare him again, squeezing most of the air from his lungs as he was lifted bodily and carried over to the table. He did not bother to struggle; as it was, he was sure all but one of his ribs were now inconveniently and permanently separated from his spine.

"Enough," Reddick said, as if ordering two children to stop their horseplay in the house.

Krawn released him after a good-measure squeeze, causing him to stagger forward and grab the table's edge to prevent himself from falling.

Cashim, running a palsied hand through his dead white hair, whimpered. "He's supposed to be dead. He's . . . he's supposed to be dead."

"He isn't," Reddick said without taking his gaze from Linc.

"You want me to fix it?"

"No. We need him."

"Please?"

Reddick made a low noise in his throat, and Cashim backed away, smiling, bobbing his head, finally clasping his hands at his waist like a penitent in waiting.

Krawn growled, and Linc could feel him less than a hand's breadth away. He rolled his shoulders and straightened, looked to Vanessa and smiled when she realized who it was. He wasn't sure if she were naked under the sheet, but the way it lay about her figure was enough to make it difficult for him to look her in the eye.

"Are you okay?"

"Thought you'd never ask."

She was pale but appeared to be unharmed.

Linc glared over his shoulder at the henchman until Krawn squirmed and stepped back. Then he turned slowly to Reddick and waited. He wasn't sure what the game was now, but as long as Vanessa wasn't in any immediate danger, he thought he'd be able to give himself valuable time.

Vanessa tried to sit up then, one hand holding

the sheet to her chest, but Reddick stopped her with a hand to her shoulder.

"Blackthorne," he said, "you have come just in time."

"I suppose," he said, rubbing at his arms where Krawn had gripped them.

"The young lady here refuses to assist me. I have, of course, offered her many inducements but she has refused them all. I was, as you saw, getting a little desperate."

Linc was puzzled, but he tried not to show it. "I see."

Cashim scratched hard at a bruise on his left cheek. "Let me kill him, please? I can get the woman to talk. I really can. I know how to do it."

Reddick shrugged at Lincoln: *what can you do with help like this?* "Cashim, I've said no several times. I do not intend to say it again."

Cashim whimpered, and scratched at the bruise on his other cheek.

"I want to go home," Vanessa declared. When Reddick attempted again to prevent her from sitting up she slapped his hand away and pushed herself to a sitting position, worked to wrap the sheet snugly around her, and crossed her legs Indian-fashion. "He says I know where the King is."

"He . . . what?" Lincoln raised an eyebrow, looked behind him to drive Krawn back again, then looked at Reddick. "You've got it."

"I had it."

"You lost it?"

"I found it," Vanessa said smugly.

"She hid it," Reddick said, leaning forward to pry the poker loose from the table and hold it in both hands as if it were a swagger stick. "I confess to an underestimation, Blackthorne. I arrived here with King and woman in full security. Unfortunately, I tend to forget I cannot trust my own people at times."

Cashim whimpered; Krawn growled.

Vanessa, Reddick explained wearily, escaped the first night they were here—with some rather extensive damage to a sleeping Cashim—rifled his room and found the ancient card carelessly left unguarded. She could not find her way out of the mansion but managed to stay secreted until this afternoon. When Cashim located her in a kitchen cupboard the King was missing and she would not, under any circumstances, tell them where it was.

"It's a minor problem, of course," he said. "Now that you've arrived, she will tell us."

"The hell I will," she said, folding her arms over her chest and glaring.

"If you do not, my dear, then Mr. Blackthorne here will never see another sunrise."

Linc sniffed, scuffed a shoe against the carpeting, and looked to Vanessa.

"So?" she said.

Reddick's smile was humorless. "Your bravado is commendable and predictable, Miss Lecharde. It is also a waste of everyone's time. I know you will break once you see what we have in store for your lover, so I suggest—"

"Wrong!" she said. "He is not my lover."

The smile broadened. "Compatriot, then. Co-worker. Friend. Whatever." He lifted a hand, and Krawn took hold of Lincoln's shoulders, pressed down lightly as a warning; Linc took it and re-

mained still. "You see, Miss Lecharde, Mr. Blackthorne does not entreat you to hold your tongue,
to have no thought for him, to carry on bravely
without him, because he knows where he's going if
you do not speak now. He knows because he has
been there before, and he didn't like it the first
time. Nor, I imagine, will he like it any better
now. If he has told you about it, all well and good.
If not, then I leave it to your imagination to draw
you a picture."

Her defiance wavered visibly, but she said nothing.

Good girl, Linc thought sourly; keep up the tra-
dition and get me killed.

Reddick turned away and stepped onto the hearth,
appearing to contemplate the dance of the flames
reaching into the chimney. His hands were clasped
behind his back, the poker still in their grip. Cashim
sat casually on the edge of the table; Krawn neither slackened his grip nor increased the pressure.

The silence was broken only by the sparking of
the burning logs.

"Where's Basil?" Linc finally asked when it was
obvious Vanessa wasn't about to play heroine.

"Hanging around," Cashim answered with a dry,
simpering cackle.

Vanessa shifted uneasily in place, and when her
arms dropped for a moment, Linc realized she was
in fact naked under the sheet. He frowned briefly
and took a deep breath. God only knew what she
had been forced to endure since Reddick had ab-
ducted her; god only knew as well what she'd done
with the King. When he tried to get her attention
with a clearing of his throat, however, she would
not look around—she kept her stare on Reddick's
back.

"I met your uncle," he said at last.

She smiled and faced him. "A lovely man. Did you meet Aunt Terese too?"

"I certainly did."

"Clever of me, wasn't it."

"Did you know he would try to kill me?"

She shrugged, and the sheet slipped off one shoulder. "He's a passionate man."

"He's a madman."

"He loves me. I'm his only family, except for his children."

"How many cousins do you have?"

"Thirteen."

"Where's the King?" Reddick asked, turning around without leaving the hearth.

"Piss off," she said, and smiled at Linc again.

Reddick's eyes narrowed slightly. "He will be tortured, you know. For a long, long time."

"I would imagine so."

"He may—probably will not survive."

"It wouldn't be the first time he's had to face death."

"Vanessa, wait a minute," Lincoln said.

"It goes with the territory," she said, ignoring him. "You win some, you lose some."

Another silence while Reddick looked to Cashim, to Krawn, to the backs and palms of his hands. "I believe you are bluffing."

"She is," Linc said quickly.

"She's not," Vanessa snapped.

Shit, Lincoln thought.

The sheet shifted again, and the other shoulder was bared.

Reddick blew lightly on his palms, sighed loudly and walked around the table to a large hickory wardrobe on the far wall. He stood in front of it for several long seconds before reaching out and opening the doors. Linc couldn't see what was inside, and when he turned to Vanessa to give her a hurt, questioning look she pointedly ignored him, again.

"Blackthorne," Reddick said loudly, "do you remember the last time?"

"Yes," Lincoln said, amazed his voice didn't crack.

"Wonderful. Then we won't have to play games this time, will we?"

He turned around, and Lincoln couldn't help stepping away from the sight of the whip coiled around the man's left arm.

He was taken to the wall at the right of the fireplace, Krawn gripping him so tightly he could barely move his fingers, much less his legs. Cashim pulled a Chartres tapestry to one side and revealed a pair of shackles bolted to the stone. Linc was turned roughly, his arms lifted before he could begin to struggle, his wrists snared by the cold iron and his ears ringing from the snap of the lock. He was stretched so far upward his feet barely touched the floor. A good stiff breeze, he thought, and I can hire out as a flag.

Vanessa watched wide-eyed, turned, and slid off the table. The sheet dropped to the center of her chest and she snatched it back up again, trying to arrange it so her arms would be free.

"He isn't kidding, Lincoln," she said, amazed.

"Right," he said as Reddick crossed the room slowly, caressing the whip as if it were a pet snake.

"Good heavens."

"Right again."

Cashim stood on his left, Krawn on his right.

Reddick stood directly in front of him, smiled, and uncoiled the deadly bullwhip onto the floor. A snap of his wrist, and it stretched out toward Lincoln's boots, not quite reaching the toes. At its tip was a tiny spiked knob of gleaming silver.

"Miss Lecharde, how brave are you now?"

Without waiting for an answer his arm moved, and the whip cracked the air less than an inch from Lincoln's chin. He flinched, but he would not cease staring at the man, would not give him the satisfaction of seeing how terrified he was.

"Miss Lecharde?"

"Lincoln?"

"Do what you want," he said. "He's going to kill us anyway."

"He is?"

"I am."

"You can't!" she protested. But when she tried to stride indignantly toward him her feet tangled in the sheet and she stumbled, swearing as the wrap threatened to leave her completely.

"Marvelous," Reddick said, laughing, a hollow laugh that was every bit as horrid as Lincoln remembered. "She's marvelous, Mr. Blackthorne! Wherever did you find her?"

"Don't blame her on me, Anton," he said, working his wrists slowly in the shackles in hopes they might slip through. They were just wide enough so that he might possibly make it, if he had some decent lubrication. When he felt the first tear of his skin he bit at the inside of his cheek and tried to widen the cut. "She leeched herself to me back

in the States," he continued, his tone contemptu-
ous. "I haven't been able to get rid of her since."

"Lincoln!"

"A shame," Reddick said, and snapped the whip
again, taking a length of Lincoln's sweater with it,
just under his heart. Linc could feel his spine press
hard against the stone, could feel the flesh tighten
in anticipation of a shredding. "A shame. She's
rather lovely, you know."

"Hell, you're the one who's seen her naked,
Reddick, not me. All I know is, she's a pain in the
ass."

"Well, pardon me for breathing!" she said. "And
he did *not* see me naked."

"Sure," he said, barely short of a sneer. "He
turned his head when he told you to undress."

"Well, he did!"

"Yeah."

"Goddamnit, Lincoln."

The whip slithered across the carpet, back toward
Reddick, who ran the length of it between two
fingers before lowering it again. "We will know
now where the King is, Miss Lecharde, or Mr.
Blackthorne will now commence his bleeding."

"He can bleed all over your frigging carpet for
all I care."

"Oh, shut up, you stupid bitch," Lincoln said in
disgust.

Her eyes widened in shock, her arms dropped,
and when Cashim and Krawn turned to look at the
wonders exposed, Lincoln grabbed the shackles'
chains for leverage and swung sharply to his right,
catching Cashim on the side of his head with the
heel of his boot. The man was propelled along the
wall to stop headfirst at the protruding fireplace

stone; but by that time Linc had directed his swing in the other direction, catching Krawn on the side of the neck and sending him gagging to his knees.

The shackles dug painfully into his wrists, but as he'd hoped, the blood acted as an able lubricant, and his right arm dropped suddenly free.

But when he turned to pull on his left he saw Reddick, and the whip, and the deadly silver tip hovering right over his eye.

TWENTY-EIGHT

LINC JERKED his head to one side, but not far enough—the tiny spikes raked along his cheekbone and slammed into the wall, spitting stone dust and chips into the air. Reddick would have recoiled and struck again, but Vanessa, unmindful of her own nakedness, had raced around the table to grab the poker that had threatened her life. She threw it just as Reddick was ready to deliver another blow, and it struck his left arm. He yelped and dropped the whip, his legs gave way and he slumped to his knees.

Linc saw little of this, but enough. He worked his other hand free just in time to use its fist on Krawn's rising chin. The man blinked and fell back against the wall; Linc kicked at the back of his ankles and sent him to the floor. There was no need to check the other—Cashim was dead.

"Blackthorne!"

He whirled. Reddick, his arm hanging uselessly at his side, had recovered his weapon.

Linc glanced at Vanessa, who was working frantically to rewrap herself in the sheet, then dove for the table. The whip followed, and a corner of the wood flew into the fire. He grabbed Vanessa and dragged her behind him to the far end, turned as the whip cut a furrow in the polished surface by his hand.

"Lincoln, for god's sake," Vanessa complained, pulling free her arm to adjust the sheet.

"Whatever you say," he muttered, watching as Reddick made his way arrogantly across the floor, grinning, breathing hard, his lips drawn back in a fearful grimace of pain. The closer the man came, the more Lincoln shifted away from the table, toward the hearth. Vanessa followed, muttering about propriety, until she saw Reddick raise his arm again. Then she snatched up a smoldering piece of wood snapped off from the main log and flung it. Reddick ducked but too late—the red-glowing shard glanced off his temple and he yelled in agony as he made an abortive lunge with his weapon.

Linc didn't hesitate; he grabbed Vanessa's hand and ran for the staircase. She followed willingly, pausing only long enough to lay a solid kick to Reddick's shin while he tried to brush away the burning strands of his hair and wield the whip at the same time. He yelled again, and she laughed over her shoulder, shook her hand loose, and followed Linc up the curving staircase.

At the top they slammed through the door and raced down the corridor, Lincoln's boots loud in the enclosed passageway, Vanessa clumsy in her bare feet until she finally grabbed the lower end of the sheet and pulled it up to her knees, to free her legs for running.

In the first library they paused with their backs to the door, listening and unable to hear any sounds of immediate pursuit.

"You know your way out?" she asked.

He nodded.

She started to run again, but he stopped her with a word. She turned and stared. "My god, Lincoln, we've got to get out of here."

"The King," he said, catching his breath.

"Christ, is that all you can think about?"

"Don't ask. Do you know where it is?"

When she nodded with a shy smile, he pushed away from the door and took her arm as he passed her, demanding she tell him so they could fetch it and be gone.

When she told him, he stopped, not realizing she'd run past him.

"Lincoln!"

He swallowed a taste of bile. "Are you sure?"

"Do I drive a Mercedes?"

He wanted to say something, anything, to stop her but could only follow when she trotted off, turned in the first library to the door he hadn't chosen. She went through without looking back, but the moment he reached the threshold he stalled.

Lincoln! he chided himself, but his legs would not move.

Beyond was another staircase, straight, dark, leading down to a heavy, iron-banded door. Vanessa was pulling it open with one hand, supporting the sheet with the other. When she saw him in the doorway she beckoned, and the sheet slipped.

"Linc!" she said quietly, as if suddenly fearful they were not yet free of Reddick and his men.

"Yes," he said, and put a hand to the wall to guide him down. The cold was intense, and he wondered how she was able to stand it, why her flesh hadn't turned as blue as he felt his own to be.

The door opened, and there was light.

She entered quickly, plucking at his sweater to be sure he would follow.

When she cried out, he couldn't help but go in.

It was the same.

It was his nightmare.

The vast, empty stone room; the monstrous chandelier hanging from its serpentine chain; the stifling air and the temperature more suited to a centuries-old mausoleum.

The difference was in Reddick—he was standing idly against the opposite wall, the whip in his hand, a pained smile at his lips. An ugly welt had been raised on his temple and Linc could see where the hair and flesh had been scorched off above his ear.

Vanessa was standing against the wall by the door, shaking her head, wondering aloud, over and over, how he'd done it.

Linc had no answer, though he knew now what Cashim had meant about Basil Unicov—the cyclist was bound several times over in thick rope and hanging from the chandelier's center spike, Reddick's way of preventing him from escaping as he had the last time. An involuntary glance toward the winch, and he saw the man had even loosened the linchpin for him.

Reddick saw the look, and he laughed.

Basil, spinning slowly, sputtered behind a bright blue gag that was tied around his head.

"Christ, Basil," Linc said.

Unicov rolled his eyes.

A grinding sound filled the room suddenly, and Vanessa pressed closer to him, closer still when he put an arm around her waist to hold and capture some of her warmth. A panel in the wall beside Reddick swung inward, and Krawn stepped out, a machine gun in his beefy hands.

"You will keep an eye on the girl," Reddick ordered. "Mr. Blackthorne and I have unfinished business."

Lincoln knew it was true; there was no possible way he could leave without ending it at last.

"The King," he said, still watching the two men.

"I hid it," Vanessa said.

"Where?" He looked around without locating a single place where she could have possibly left it. Then he saw her upward gaze, followed it with his own—and in a shadowed niche in one of the ceiling's beams he saw it.

"How the hell . . . ?"

"I climbed up the chain," she explained.

"You climbed all the way up there?"

"I had to find someplace, for heaven's sake. The man was after me, Lincoln! God, do you know what it's like?"

"But way the hell up there?"

"*I'm* not chicken."

"I am not chicken, Vanessa. I have acrophobia, a legitimate psychological illness."

"Cluck," she said.

Reddick stepped to the middle of the floor, Krawn

sidling to the far corner. Vanessa hesitated, then reluctantly pulled out of Lincoln's grip and made her way to the corner opposite Krawn. By the way she hugged herself, Linc knew she was feeling the same sort of cold that had affected him from the start. It was small comfort, and at a nod from Reddick he closed the door behind him.

Basil kicked feebly, succeeding only in sending himself into another slow spin.

Reddick laughed.

With Unicov's shadow marking the center of their arena, they began a slow circling, Linc watching the turn of Reddick's wrist, the set of his shoulder, the dead stare of his eyes, anxious for any sign at all that he would send the whip and its spiked tip for his throat, or his heart.

There was no playing now; Reddick knew where the King was, and all he wanted was to kill Blackthorne and be done.

The whip lashed out and Linc threw himself aside, catching the tip on his upraised right arm. There was instant blood, and a knifing agony that momentarily paralyzed his hand. Vanessa gasped, but Krawn's grunt and a thrust from the machine gun kept her in place.

The whip, again, and Reddick laughed silently when Lincoln tripped as he dodged successfully out of the way.

Circling.

Feinting.

He debated closing the gap and attempting to duck under the next sweep and tackle the man into hand-to-hand fighting, but Reddick anticipated him—for every step nearer Reddick inched back, shaking his head in sympathy and snapping the whip along the floor. Linc jumped, and Reddick snapped it again. Another jump, and the man laughed, this time loudly, obscenely over the echoes of the whip's cracking voice.

Vanessa muffled a cry behind her hands.

Basil kicked and spun.

There was no other sound but the kiss of the black leather slithering along the floor, the shuffle of their soles as they continued in their circling.

The temperature in the room rose.

Turning; Krawn behind him, and he could hear his hands shifting on the machine gun; Vanessa behind him and he could hear her breathing almost like panting; the door behind him and the nearly overwhelming temptation to use it and run.

Turning, until he could see Vanessa over Reddick's shoulder, and he gave her a quick smile.

And Reddick lashed out, the whip snagging through Linc's trousers and bringing him sharply to his knees. Another attack, this time tearing open his left shoulder before he could scramble away.

Reddick, however, did not close. He waited until Linc had regained his feet and was back in the macabre dance.

"You won't live to use it," Lincoln said, dodging a crack of the weapon.

"My friend, I will live forever if I want to."

"Not the way I hear it."

Circling.

"I know what must be done, and I know more besides." His lips pulled back in a feral grin. "I know a great deal more."

Warmer, especially when the blood on his

wounded shoulder soaked through his sleeve, the blood from his leg seemed to fill his boot.

There was a burning, but he was determined to ignore it, and there was a ringing in his ears he dared not shake away for fear Reddick would assume he was weakening.

Then Reddick snapped his wrist, and the reach was too long—the whip bit around Lincoln's waist and he grabbed it, held it, while Reddick tried to pull it free.

"If I get close enough, I'll strangle you," he said.

Reddick began sweating.

And the door opened behind him.

"Let's go, Blackie. I have a gun on him."

Lincoln didn't know then whether to laugh, cry, or simply pass out. He stared, Reddick stared, and Krawn turned with his machine gun. Macon fired without seeming to aim, and Krawn was slammed back against the wall, the gun slipping from his hands as he fell face forward with a bullet in his brain. Vanessa raced over and picked up the weapon, holding it up triumphantly, the grin on her face fading slowly when Lincoln didn't join her.

"Lincoln?"

"Take her out of here, Macon."

"Macon, for heaven's sake, talk to him."

"I refuse to talk to a man who keeps pictures of Clint Eastwood on his parlor wall."

She sputtered, but Linc would not say a word. He only waited until Macon walked over and put a hand on her shoulder. Deflated, she let herself be led to the door. She turned as the old man started to urge her out.

"Lincoln?" she pleaded.

He shook his head.

Her face darkened. "Y'know, for a tailor you have lousy taste in clothes."

The door slammed behind her, and Lincoln spun out of the whip's grip.

"What about the other?" Reddick asked as he flicked the whip in Lincoln's wake.

He looked up at Basil. "He's not going anywhere."

"Quite right."

Basil kicked and spun.

The whip, and Lincoln dodged; again, and he began circling more rapidly, deliberately catching one blow on the arm, another on his left leg. The pain was climbing toward his chest. The whip opened the side of his neck, and he was too slow to grab it.

Reddick laughed.

Lincoln backed out of the self-imposed circle and glanced longingly at the door. He knew it was unlocked, and knew Macon would still be on the other side. The old man wouldn't kill Reddick if the fight were lost, but he didn't like thinking about the possibility that Reddick wouldn't reciprocate the kindness.

"You're really quite foolish," Reddick said as he walked, almost strolled, under the chandelier, ignoring Basil's attempts to kick the top of his head. "I suppose chivalry and all that is rather interesting, but it's not very healthy." He sighed when he finally stopped. "You shouldn't have come back, Lincoln. You really shouldn't have come back."

He drew back his arm and waited, measuring the distance between them, coldly, the whip coiling, straightening, writhing on the floor behind him.

Lincoln held out his right arm.

"Oh my god," Reddick said. "You can't mean that."

Lincoln shrugged.

"You really should practice, you know."

"I have," Lincoln said.

The whip-arm swung forward slowly, once, twice, and in the hesitation before the last attack, Lincoln bent his hand down and flexed the proper muscle.

Reddick gaped.

The knife left its sheath without a hiss, without a whisper, and buried itself in the man's chest, just below the sternum. He stared at it, stared at Lincoln, and crumpled to his knees, the whip falling useless at his feet.

"I could have won," he gasped when Linc walked up beside him. "I will still win, I swear it." He groaned, the scar on his chin flaring almost red. "Don't ... brag ... Blackthorne. Don't brag just yet."

Linc knelt and picked up the whip, tossed it across the room, and pulled the knife from Reddick's chest. Then he looked up, winked at Basil, and threw it to him. Unicov reacted without thinking, snapping his legs together and trapping the blade between his knees.

"Nice catch, Toad. See you around."

A light blow struck his leg. He stepped back, saw the blood pooling on the floor, saw Reddick trying desperately to knock him off his feet.

"Don't ... brag," the man said feebly, his face

as pale as his white shirt. "Don't brag. I shall return."

Linc sighed and walked to the door, feeling pleased he had broken out of his nightmare at last, yet puzzled over the feeling he had left something unsaid. He turned and looked at Basil trying to get the blade to the ropes, saw Reddick dying and crawling toward the secret passage. It was obvious he wouldn't make it, and suddenly he realized that even someone like Reddick deserved a last word.

"Anton," he said solemnly, "you really are an asshole."

TWENTY-NINE

"**I**T AIN'T fair, y'know," Old Alice complained hoarsely as she lit a gold cigarette with a wooden match struck against her chin. "It really ain't, the way I see it."

Palmer snored in his place in the center of the green bench.

Macon, smoothing his sweater down over his chest, crossed his legs at the ankles and watched a pair of college girls walk by the tailor shop. When one of them winked at him, he fluffed at his beard.

"I mean, how is it you always get to do the traveling and I have to stay here and save the world from Palmer?"

"You get airsick."

"I do not."

"You puke within ten miles of an airport."

"I have a condition," she insisted.

"Yes, I would imagine."

She adjusted her skimmer, adjusted her paisley

Gucci scarf, and squinted up at the twilight sky. "Hot for August, ain't it?"

"No hotter than usual. Though perhaps a bit more humid."

"Was it hot in Scotland?"

"Hot enough."

"Thought so. That's why they wear them silly skirts."

"You wear a skirt."

"I ain't a man."

Palmer snored.

Macon decided never to show her his kilt.

The shop door opened and Lincoln came out, a pair of trousers draped over one arm, cloth tape measure slung over his shoulder. A patch of gauze was taped to the side of his neck, and when he moved he moved stiffly. He leaned against the window frame and nodded to Macon.

"Ain't fair," said Old Alice to the maple tree.

"What isn't?" he asked.

"He gets to travel, I don't."

"It's your turn next time."

She looked at him suspiciously. "You promise?"

"I promise."

"Big deal," she scoffed. "You don't ever keep your promises. And I'm stuck with twenty grand worth of traveler's checks and you can't go nowhere because you got the mayor's suit to finish." She snorted her disgust and turned her back on them.

"She's a bit out of sorts," Macon explained wearily.

Lincoln nodded.

"I don't think she got laid last night."

Old Alice turned back suddenly and snarled. "My

love life ain't none of your damned business, you old fart."

A long black hearse turned into the street from the square, and they fell instantly silent, watching until it passed them, trailed by a half dozen automobiles all with their headlamps burning.

"Wonder who it is?" Old Alice said.

"It isn't us, so who cares?" Macon said.

The door opened, and Vanessa came out, dressed in a sheer white blouse, sheer white slacks, a wide-brimmed white hat set at a cant on her head. She stood beside Lincoln and watched the funeral procession drift by.

"Ah, memories," she said quietly.

Lincoln smiled. A moment, and he sighed. "I almost regret we dumped that thing in the lake. George is still ticked."

"George," she said, "can go suck an Inca."

Old Alice cackled. Macon blushed and mopped his face with a pure white, starched handkerchief.

"Of course, Nessie will live forever if she can play solitaire."

Vanessa grinned, leaned over and kissed his cheek. "Have to go."

Old Alice looked away.

Macon decided to study the bark of the maple.

Palmer sneezed in his sleep.

"You'll call," Lincoln said, reminding her of her promise.

"I'll call."

They faced each other then, after Lincoln handed the trousers to Macon. A few moments to study each other's face, and they embraced, kissed, pulled away and Lincoln took back the trousers.

"It's been nice," he said, painfully aware of how inadequate that was.

She understood, and showed him by touching the tip of his chin, running her finger along the thin scar that highlighted a small section of his cheek. Then she nodded to Old Alice and Macon, blew a kiss to Palmer, and walked toward the square. Her car, she'd told him, was parked on the other side; she didn't want to end up driving him to the airport again.

Macon shifted to watch her.

Old Alice watched Macon.

Lincoln wondered if Basil had gotten himself down.

He hadn't taken the time to check. As soon as he delivered his eulogy to Reddick, he'd sprinted to the door and called Macon and Vanessa from the landing at the top of the stairs. Vanessa had climbed the chain as she had the first time and fetched the King of Satan's Eyes; as soon as they found her clothing they had taken a car from Reddick's garage and driven off without looking back.

When they reached Loch Ness Lincoln told Macon to stop the car. At the bank he held the card in his hand and shook his head, reared back, and was about to throw when Vanessa stopped him.

"You're crazy."

"I'm not crazy enough to give this to George."

"You don't trust him?"

"I trust him. I just don't trust anyone who'll steal it from him."

"Who could?"

He grinned. "Who couldn't?"

She had frowned, considered it a while, then walked back to the car.

He had thrown the King and all its jewels into the loch as far as he could, did not stay to watch it land. For all he cared, it could be in the belly of a now very wealthy carp, and welcome to it for all the trouble it had caused.

He sighed.

"She's lovely, Blackie," Old Alice decided with a sharp approving nod.

"Quite," Macon agreed, and Old Alice looked sour. "Well, she is."

"Anything happen between you two?" she demanded.

"I am not at liberty to say. A lady's reputation, you understand."

Old Alice took a wax grape from her hatband and bounced it off his head.

Lincoln ignored them, intent on watching Vanessa for as long as she was in sight. And when she vanished into the shadows, he decided that as soon as he was done with his next appointment here at home he would soothe George's raging brow and ask for another job. He didn't think he wanted to stick around for very long, not in the same place where she had nursed him back to reasonable health and had shown him how to press Clint Eastwood's bullets without kicking the wall.

Ridiculous, he thought, but there was no getting away from it.

Then the shop door across the street opened with a gunshot slam.

Old Alice stood up and stretched. "Macon, I believe Ginny's is having Happy Hour about now."

Macon shook Palmer's shoulder and helped him to his feet.

The three passed him in swift dignity, disappeared into the tavern just as Carmel stormed across the street.

"Lincoln Bartholomew Blackthorne," she shouted, "you goddamned sonofabitch!"

Yep, Lincoln thought; most definitely another job.

About the Author

GEOFFREY MARSH served in the Black Watch during the latter years of World War II. After leaving the King's service, he studied at Trinity College (Cambridge), but family tragedy forced him to leave before completing his degree in religion and fulfilling his dream of becoming vicar in his home village. After emigrating to the United States, he taught literature at a private school in New Jersey, where he still lives with his wife of forty-one years. Of this, his first novel, Mr. Marsh says: "I would not claim that Lincoln Blackthorne is a real person; however, his exploits are close enough to the truth that I sometimes give myself the willies."

MORE BESTSELLERS FROM TOR